THE SEER

Clara Berge

Published by Seraph Creative

Dedication

To the One who always encourages
and calls me deeper into His mysteries.
You are my life.

And to my other half and beautiful children,
thank you. This book wouldn't have been
written without you.

To everyone who shared their kingdom encounters
with me and allowed me to borrow some of it
for this story, thank you.

I honour the sons of God who have
trail-blazed seeing His Kingdom and made
the process easier for us.

Thank you for persevering.

The Seer - Clara Berge
Third Print English Edition, 2019

ISBN: 978-0-6485847-4-2
eBook ISBN: 978-0-6485847-5-9

Cover designed by IWill Media Uk – Contact them at www.iwillmediauk.com

Typesetting and Layout by Feline www.felinegraphics.com

CONTENTS

Jeremiah 1:5a
Before I formed you in the womb, I knew you, before you were
born, I set you apart.

Psalm 139:16
Your eyes have seen my unformed substance; And in Your book
were all written; the days ordained for me, when as yet there
was not one of them.

Matthew 13:44
The kingdom of heaven is like a treasure hidden in the field,
which a man found and hid again; and from joy over it he goes
and sells all that he had and buys that field.

Matthew 16:25
For whosoever will save his life shall lose it: and whosoever
will lose his life for my sake shall find it.

CHAPTER 1

No, not again. This can't be happening! Kirsty Knight shut her eyes before slowly opening them again. The lizard-like creature still hung over the shoulder of the man striding along in front of her, his claws making dents on the man's black Iron Maiden hoodie where he perched as if real.

Her steps slowed, stomach churning as time slowed down. Despite her fear, she followed the line of the dark blue-grey lizard over the man's shoulder to where the head reappeared on the other side. The scales rippled as it moved its head, the tongue flicking in and out, its small black eyes darting back and forth.

She knew that the creature realised her awareness of him. He hissed and she ducked into the doorway of the nearest shop. Breathing in short, shallow bursts with her eyes tightly shut, she repeated to herself, "It's not real, take deep breaths, it's just a figment of your imagination." She heard the sentence in the voice of her childhood psychiatrist in her head. How many times had she told that to herself over the years? The cold seeping into her heart felt colder than the frozen air around her.

Entering the shop, she unseeingly picked out a scarf, biding her time before going out again into the minus fifty degrees Farhenheit of her home city. Kensington Market was lined with quaint boutiques like the one she hid in. Kirsty snuggled deeper into her soft down jacket and quickened her steps. Snowflakes started descending on her in another bout of snow. Their three-bed apartment wasn't too far from there. All she'd gone out for was fresh air and coffee.

Reaching their favourite coffee shop, she made her way back as fast as she could, carrying the two take-away cups. The passers-by drew her attention to search for more things that she knew shouldn't be there, but she kept her eyes averted. With relief, she closed the apartment door behind her. The heated interior instantly started to make her feel too warm.

"I'm home!" Kirsty placed the coffee down on a small side table, discarded her jacket and gloves and sat down on the chair next to the table to remove her Doc Martin's. She liked that about winter, going about in comfortable house slippers. Her boot-shaped sheepskin pair stood ready by the door. She slid her feet into the soft lambswool interior before walking over to the sofa to drop her package and handbag.

Fetching the coffee, she made her way down the stairs. The strains of Metallica's song 'Nothing Else Matters' floated up from the studio, where she knew Jean-Pierre would be. Balancing a cup in each hand, she pushed the door ajar with her woollen clad foot. Her eyes took in the room filled with several art pieces all in various stages of completion.

Her eyes stopped at the glass patio doors which opened onto a small courtyard they called their own. It was the reason they rented this place. They had spent many happy hours, smoking and lazing around in their little, private outside space. Right now, the doors were tightly shut, the courtyard deserted except for the snowflakes that were flurrying down more heavily than before.

Kirsty focused on the broad back of the man sitting in the middle of the room in front of a large easel. She stood next to him and handed him his flat white. Her brows pinched as she took in the incomplete picture of a woman lounging next to a swimming pool. The girl had red hair like the latest model Jean-Pierre and his art class were drawing.

"What took you so long?" Jean-Pierre's rich baritone sounded loud to her ears.

"I saw a nice boutique shop and browsed around a bit. Sorry, I won't get distracted next time."

Kirsty took a sip of her cappuccino and stared at the picture, wishing she could transport herself into it, lie in the sun and pretend life was less complicated. She was aware of Jean-Pierre's stocky body next to her smaller one; his breathing slow and regular. They had been together for almost seven years. *I wish I could tell him.* The thought burned through her and she clenched her fist, biting her lower lip.

Jean-Pierre pulled his dark eyebrows together and inclined his head. With his left hand, he swiped his curly black fringe out of his eyes and took another sip of his flat white, observing Kirsty sideways. *What's up with her?* He could see her fist clenched inside her pocket and her usually dark brown complexion had a pasty look to it.

In a flat voice he asked, "Any plans for the rest of the day?"

Kirsty shook her head negatively. "I thought I'd catch up on some work. Maybe we could watch a movie tonight?"

Jean-Pierre dipped his head, but as she walked out the door, he remembered the ranch.

"Kirsty?"

"Yeah?"

Jean-Pierre studied the taut lines around her mouth and replied, "Never mind, I'll ask you later."

The door closed and he finished the dregs of his coffee with one swig. He got up, threw the empty cup in a small trash can and went over to a cupboard against the wall. Rummaging around in the bottom shelf he came up with a sealed bottle of white wine. It came from his family's own vineyard, the Ugarte Garcia vinery - one of the best in the world.

His thoughts flew to the Basque Country, to the small group of ethnic people in Northern Spain he called his own. It was a homeland he missed more and more recently.

Jean-Pierre fingered the label on the bottle which he had been saving for a special occasion. Since that occasion went up in smoke three months ago, he might as well have it. He pulled out the cork by inserting one of his sharp art tools into it and filled a glass to the brim.

The white liquid swished around in his mouth, and he took a deep whiff of the fragrance. Exquisite. His thoughts went upstairs. *We used to share a bottle of wine, but she's gone all health conscious on me since...* He halted his train of thought abruptly.

After choosing another playlist, this one of Guns and Roses, he seated himself in front of his easel again, the glass of wine held in his left hand. Slowly, methodically he continued with his painting.

Kirsty walked up the stairs to the second floor, the closed door next to their bedroom as usual giving her pause. *I ought to go in there; it's been three months.*

Behind the door were pink curtains, a cot filled with teddies, and a comfortable nursing chair. Familiar, burning tears pricked behind her eyelids.

Resolutely she took two steps past the door but stopped in her tracks. *That's why the hallucinations started again!* Kirsty loosened her long, dark hair from its ponytail and shook it loose. *Why now, after such a long time? It could be my side business, combined with me not taking my prescription pills.*

Going past their bedroom door to the next smaller room which held her office, her thoughts churned. *I'd have to find another way to raise money for our next treatment. Not opening that Pandora's box again. I could take my pills again for a few months, but it takes a long time to get them out of my system.*

Kirsty sat down behind her desk that faced the door. A frown marred her forehead; for all that she knew, the antipsychotic drugs she'd taken for years had caused her to lose her babies.

Drawing on everything her psychiatrist had ever taught her, she mentally locked away the fear and worry gnawing at her insides. By the time her laptop was on she felt in control again.

Looking around the neat, almost bare room, a sigh escaped her, her face losing its tightness. This was her domain. Designing websites and multimedia for a living kept her busy and a few customers were waiting for her to finish their projects. With her favourite piano music playing in her ears, she was soon lost in her work.

Three months earlier, October 2015. Nomansland, England.

Thomas Quinn poured the tea into the four mugs on his grey kitchen counter. They all differed in size and colour and had made their way to his house in interesting ways. The two floral ones were given to him by an elderly neighbour, who wanted to get rid of her old mugs. The one printed with big red letters *'Keep calm and carry on,'* he had bought on a day trip to London. The fourth one was blue, one of the last remaining mugs of a Denby set he had bought ten years ago when he moved into the Rectory.

Tonight, he was having a meeting with the pastor-parish relations committee which consisted of three men. He knew each one personally, not only as friends but as longstanding members of Nomansland Methodist church. As he walked into the small sitting room, he sensed tonight was different from usual. His friends weren't making eye contact, and an uncomfortable silence filled the room.

Thomas sat his tall frame down, and took a careful sip of his hot tea, before saying in his soft Irish accent, "You might as well just spit it out. What's the matter?"

Jeff, the eldest of them all, swiped his hand over his bald head, before clearing his throat and saying, "Thomas, we've talked with the district superintendent, and he's met with the Bishop and the cabinet, and they've agreed that it is time for you to take a sabbatical."

Rory piped up in his high voice, "You know you're way overdue for one, sabbaticals are normally every seven years."

Stunned, Thomas looked from one man to the other, "Are you saying you want me to go away?"

Marcus spoke in his calm voice, "No, of course not, but this is why we are telling you this before the committee does. We suggested it to them, since as your friends, we see the need for you to have a break. You've slaved away for ten years in this parish and a change of scenery might be good."

Thomas furrowed his brows and focused his blue eyes on Marcus, who broke eye contact with him. "What aren't you telling me?"

Jeff gave a big sigh, "We've prayed long and hard about it

and felt that maybe this parish needs a younger couple, who can connect with the young families that've been joining recently."

Thomas felt his body tense up. His nostrils flared and he clenched his jaw trying to prevent himself from saying something he would regret. *What the heck?*

Rory piped up again, "We've recommended a year sabbatical, in thanks for all the work you've done here, starting on the first of January."

All Thomas could manage was a nod while his world disintegrated around him. He found it ironic that he had chosen the mug with the red lettering on, which he held in his hand. The words ran around in his head as if mocking him *'Keep calm and carry on.'*

Wasn't that what he always did? The right thing? There was a pounding in his ears and an edgy, twitchy feeling in his hands like he wanted to punch something.

Back to the present. 4:00 pm, GMT+1. 1 January 2016. Outside Paris, France.

A few thousand miles away from Toronto, Leo Molineux stared at the silent phone in his hand. He felt his lungs constrict making breathing hard. *Where was she?* Camille was supposed to ring him hours ago, but her mobile kept going to voicemail. The private detective that he had watching her wasn't responding either. His stomach churned and he licked his dry lips. It wasn't like his daughter to miss their daily phone call; especially on the first day of the New Year. He walked over to the large glass wall that comprised the side of his office and stared out towards the extensive grounds.

He forced himself to relax. Camille would soon phone him with a valid excuse such as going on an impromptu dinner with her friends. Not for the first time did he wonder how she had talked him into sending her to do her residency at the hospital in Glasgow. She could have gone to Paris, closer to their home. Ruefully he smiled at himself, she probably wanted a bit of space.

At twenty-eight, she was more than ready to leave the house.

A sigh escaped his lips. Y*ou would've enjoyed seeing her all grown up, Elise. I miss you. Our little girl is making her own way in the world.* He scrolled to the calendar on his phone and seeing nothing that couldn't be cancelled, he let his secretary know that he'd be out for the evening and asked her to cancel all his other engagements. Then he phoned an old friend and arranged to meet at his favourite restaurant.

On the same day in a small rented room in Kazakhstan.

The hacker's forefinger hovered over the return key. He studied his short, clean nail for a moment, reflecting on the astounding fact that one little appendix could cause so much havoc. *I'm ready, but this will change everything.*

For many years he had worked undercover to get to this moment in time. Now that it was here, slight apprehension flitted through him. His finger showed no sign of trembling as he lowered it down until it touched the black plastic key. His eyes sprang to a picture of his wife and daughter, stuck to the side of the screen and he closed his eyes.

It took less than a second to depress the key, but the consequences might last years, maybe decades. He sat back with his hands clasped behind his head, a slight smile on his face. Closing his eyes, he felt himself relax. *It's done, the others will be pleased.*

6:30 am, GMT-5. Sunday, 3 January. New York, JFK Airport.

Thomas Quinn stood still, feeling the bulk of the keys in his pocket. *I can't believe this beast will be mine for the next month.* He walked around the yellow and black Mustang, his eyes drinking in his dream car. It was the GT Special Edition 5.0.

with black 19-inch alloy wheels.

Into the boot went his suitcase and carry-on, the battered guitar case went on the back seat before he got behind the wheel. His eyes travelled over the navigation system, CD/radio console. He could even heat or cool his seat, but all that really mattered was what was under that hood. Inhaling the leather smell of the seats, Thomas felt his smile break out for the first time in three months.

He started the engine and couldn't resist revving it a bit. His finger tapped in the address for the next stop on his route. He planned to travel across the country, sightseeing and stopping along the way until he got to his friends in Texas, where he would stay for a while before taking the trip back. He accelerated out of the airport onto the highway, *Maybe Rory had been right; this sabbatical was long overdue.* He gunned the engine as he roared down the fast lane and felt the vibration of the engine through the seat. *Maybe I should make it permanent.*

7:00 am, GMT-5. Toronto, Canada.

Kirsty woke up drenched in sweat. Another dream. Perhaps she should get those sleeping pills that her doctor prescribed. *More pills.* Wiping her eyes, she sat up, but a glance over at Jean-Pierre confirmed he was still fast asleep. At least he didn't seem to have any nightmares. His broad forehead, straight nose and long lashes that lay splayed across his cheeks were perused before her shoulders slumped. *What's wrong with me? All I want is a good night's sleep, is that too much to ask?*

Lifting the duvet off, she got out of bed before replacing it quietly, so Jean-Pierre stayed covered up. Her bare feet padded across the soft cream carpet. She pushed them into her woollen slippers by the door and headed downstairs to make tea. She liked a cup of Chai Rooibos tea in the mornings. Maybe Jean-Pierre would go out later to get their coffee.

Staring at the front door from behind the open-plan kitchen counter, she realised she hadn't left the apartment since the lizard episode. The knot in her stomach tightened.

Kirsty kicked off her slippers and pulled her legs up on the sofa, embracing her steaming cup of tea with both hands. She eyed the little blue amulet hanging from the bracelet on her wrist. *Fat help you are.* It was supposed to reject negative energies. The pretty woven American Indian pattern made her pause as a thought filtered into her head. *What if I have an inherited genetic condition the doctors are missing?*

Placing her cup down and grabbing her phone off the table, Kirsty made a call to her adoptive parents and arranged to go see them the following weekend. Her heart stirred as hope blossomed for the first time in three months.

As she disconnected the call, Jean-Pierre came in. She looked at his rumpled blue sleep shorts and naked chest covered in curly, black hair and smiled. *I love this man.*

"Would you like some breakfast?"

Jean-Pierre stretched out and looked at her with a scowl, "Who are you phoning so early on a Sunday morning?"

Kirsty walked over to him, "I've had an idea. I'm going to go to my parents this coming weekend."

Jean-Pierre lifted his eyebrows, "But…"

Kirsty impatiently shook her head, "I know, I know, but it might be worth it. Do you want to come along?"

Jean-Pierre shook his head, "No way, remember last time?"

A giggle escaped from Kirsty before she could help herself. He gave a mock growl, "Are you laughing at me? I'll let you know, I'm very good at punishing people who laugh at me." He started chasing her around the room, and they ended up on the sofa where he tickled her until she squealed."

"Stop! Stop! I surrender."

Jean-Pierre looked down at her and tenderly moved the hair out of her face, "I…." his words seemed to dry up on his tongue.

Kirsty put her hand into his dark curls and pulled his head down to hers so that their lips met and kissed him long and hard. When they came up for breath, she groaned, "You're squashing me."

"I'd like to do more than that," he teased, before he sat up, pulling her up with him. He interlaced his hand with hers and looked into her green eyes, "Would you go on a retreat with me?

I saw this advertisement, for a week retreat on a ranch in Texas." His voice trailed away as her posture stiffened next to him.

Kirsty pulled her hand out of his and pushed her hair behind her ear, "I don't know, Jean-Pierre." She looked at him askance and saw his shoulders droop, "Hey, if you want to, why not? Getting a fresh perspective on things might be good. What is the place called?"

Jean-Pierre looked at his lap, cleared his throat and said, "New Beginnings."

Kirsty's cheeks coloured, "Should I book for us? When do you want to go?"

He stood up, walked to the kitchen, and turned around to rest against the counter, "Why don't you fly there straight from your parents, and I'll meet you at the airport? We can rent a car for the week."

"Sorted." Kirsty gave Jean-Pierre a small smile, and he returned it before turning away from her. He got a pan out for frying eggs and bacon. Still sitting on the sofa, Kirsty bit her lip as she stared at his broad back. She squared her shoulders, lifting her chin. *I can do this.*

CHAPTER 2

12:50 pm, GMT-8. Saturday, 9th of January. Oregon, USA.

Kirsty drove up the sweeping drive flanked with poplar trees in the small Lexus that she had rented at the airport in Portland. The day was cold, but bright and sunny without a cloud in the sky.

Her parents lived in Happy Valley in Oregon. Happy Valley was only a few miles' drive away from Portland nestled amongst the hills. It had taken almost five hours to fly out here. She started at nine that morning but thanks to the time zone was arriving on time to have lunch with her parents.

Their home was surrounded by a few acres of land with woods behind it. This was the only home Kirsty had ever had. They adopted her when she was a baby.

As her eyes surveyed the large house, she felt the familiar thankfulness that her biological parents gave her up for adoption. She used to imagine they gave her up because they were poor, and they wanted to give her the chance of growing up with all the riches and opportunities she had had as a child.

The door opened before the engine's sound died away, and Maria, their longstanding Siuslaw Indian maid, ran out the door, "Miss Knight! Oh, I'm so happy to see you!" She threw her hands in front of her face, beaming from ear to ear.

Kirsty got out, straightened her dress, smiled widely and greeted Maria, "I'm glad to see you too, Maria. You don't look a day older than when I last saw you!"

"Oh, Miss, that was ages ago. We miss seeing you!"

A shadow crossed Kirsty's face. She had, in fact, visited more than a year ago. The butler came out after Maria, he was someone new.

Maria turned towards him and said, "Kirsty, this is Brad Garvey, Simon retired earlier this year. Brad, won't you place Miss Knight's bags in the room at the end of the hallway upstairs?"

Brad quietly dipped his head at Kirsty and collected her overnight bag from the trunk and took it in as the women followed more slowly.

"How are they?" Kirsty asked Maria.

Maria shook her head, "Tsk, tsk, they're the same as always."

Kirsty laughed, "You mean Dad is grumpy and Mom is gossiping."

Maria's eyes opened wide, "That's no way to talk about your elders, young miss."

Kirsty's smile dropped, and she sighed, "I'm thirty-four this year, Maria."

Maria patted her shoulder, "I'm sixty-eight this year, Miss. Double your age."

Kirsty's face wrinkled, "Shouldn't you be retiring soon?"

Maria gave an audible sigh, "I must, but I've been with your family for so long it is hard to stop." She turned to Kirsty with a twinkle in her eyes, "How's that young man of yours?"

Kirsty blushed, "You make him sound so young. He's only five years younger than me! He's painting away as usual. Selling more every year."

Maria stifled a laugh, "I'll never forget his visit."

Kirsty rolled her eyes, "I don't think he'll ever come again." She could still see in her mind's eye her parents shocked faces when Jean-Pierre had had a few bottles of wine too many and walked through the house stark naked, fixing the hideous pictures on their walls with a paintbrush.

They entered the sunroom where her parents enjoyed lunch in the winter. They were both seated at the table as she came in. She was a few minutes late. Kirsty walked across the modern wooden floor, her heels clicking loudly in her ears. She kissed her mother and father on the cheek, "Sorry I'm late, the flight was slightly delayed." She sat down at the table with them, and Maria disappeared off somewhere.

Her father cleared his gruff voice, "Pleased to see you. Flights aren't dependable these days."

Her mother chimed in, "Hello, dear, you look so thin. Hope you'll like the lunch. Dolores has been coming up with experimental dishes lately."

"It's because you've been pecking at your food." Her husband chided her.

"Nonsense, Harold, I'm a bit bored with the food, that's all. I like the new dishes." Her mother smoothed over her grey, permed hair. Her make-up and nails were immaculately done; Caroline Knight always looked smart.

Kirsty could see more wrinkles in her father's face. They were both reaching their eighties soon. They had one biological daughter fifteen years older than Kirsty.

Her throat felt dry, *What if they get upset? I've never questioned them about my birth.* She squared her shoulders; *I need to know.* After lunch, they moved to the comfortable seating that looked out through the glass windows over the well-kept gardens. With a warm cup of coffee in her hands, Kirsty took the bull by the horns.

"Dad, Mom, I need to ask you a favour."

They both turned towards her with eyebrows raised. Kirsty unclenched her hands and blurted out, "I want to know who my birth parents were."

Silence filled the space. She glanced up at them and saw them give each other a quick look. *What was that about?*

"It isn't because you haven't been great parents, it's more of a biological reason. I need to find out more about my inherited DNA."

"Are you sick?" Her mother's voice had a slight tremble in it.

"No, Mom. Don't worry, I'm fine. We've been struggling to fall pregnant and I need to find out if there are any inherited conditions in my family line."

Kirsty lifted up her chin and sat back.

Her father cleared his throat, "We don't have much to tell you I'm afraid. The agency doesn't exist anymore, they were small to begin with. They never shared with us where you came from."

Kirsty looked up and saw her mother frown at her father. "Mom, do you know something more?"

Her dad gave her mom a stern look and she seemed to retract into herself, "No, sorry love, I don't know anything else."

Kirsty inclined her head, "I guess I could do one of those popular DNA tests. That might help me track down any blood family I might have."

"No!" Her father's shout came out unexpectedly, "Why do you need to mess with those things. Leave the past in the past. Haven't we given you all you need? Why don't you adopt children? You don't have to have your own."

Kirsty felt her lip quiver, "I want my own children, Dad."

Her father harrumphed and turned away from her. Her mother's eyes were downcast. She was uncharacteristically quiet.

Kirsty stood up, "If you'll excuse me, I'm going to walk off that delicious lunch." She left through the front doors after grabbing her jacket off the hook without looking back. The fresh, cold air hit her in the face. She wandered until she found herself at the base of her favourite old oak tree in the grounds. Many hours were spent daydreaming underneath that tree. Kirsty sat down resting against its sturdy trunk.

That evening she found a little note underneath her door that read: *Meet me at the olb Oak at ten tonight. I can help you.* Kirsty re-read the note, confused. Old not 'olb'. She hated it when the dyslexia, she'd worked so hard to overcome, still tripped her up. Her thoughts sprang to her childhood. Growing up rich had provided her with the best tutors that money could buy and it helped that she had an above average intelligence. She'd rather forget the cruel taunts of the children at school. They were all put to shame anyway when she was accepted into that fast track elite program.

Kirsty crumpled the note. *Who could have written it?* The

handwriting looked familiar.

The old oak stood sentinel in the icy darkness, but the next moment a person appeared, startling Kirsty where she stood waiting. The person had a black cloak covering their head, but Kirsty would recognise Maria's distinctive round form anywhere. "Maria! Why are you meeting me here?"

"Shhh! Miss, what I want to tell you can't be heard by anyone."

"How do *you* know I want to know about my birth parents?"

Maria shifted her feet, "I listened at the door."

Kirsty shook her head, "What can you tell me?"

Maria looked around before moving closer to Kirsty. The faint moonlight shone on her face, making it look all theatrical. "I was there when it happened. They swore me to secrecy but I'm retiring soon, and I've always thought they made a mistake by not telling you the truth."

Kirsty felt a coldness take hold of her insides. "The truth, Maria?"

"Miss Knight gave birth to you when she was fifteen. They covered it up with the adoption story to avoid a scandal. She had slept with their gardener's teenage son. They promptly dismissed the gardener and sent the family away."

Kirsty shook her head, "That's impossible." She could feel empathy radiating from Maria, who had been more of a mother to her than her own mother. *My adoptive mother is my grandmother.* The stark truth punched her in the stomach.

"I've kept their details in case you ever asked. I felt it only fair that you knew the truth." Maria's voice faltered slightly, "I'm sorry I didn't speak up sooner. I needed the income…"

Kirsty placed her hand over Maria's, squeezing it in the dark, "I know, Maria, you had mouths to feed." In a shaky, disbelieving voice she said, "I can't believe that Emma is my mother. She…"

This time Maria pressed Kirsty's hand, "I know, love, I think she couldn't face the lie, so she pretended it was true."

Kirsty balled her fist as the coldness spread throughout her body, "I barely know her, Maria, she's always shunned me."

Maria exhaled slowly before saying, "She changed after

the whole affair. She used to be sunny and happy. He was her first love. She retracted into herself and when she emerged, she wasn't the same."

A flash of empathy shot through Kirsty before anger threatened to unleash hot tears through her eyes, "How could she lie for so many years? How could *they*?"

Maria pulled Kirsty towards her and in the safety of her shoulder, Kirsty cried. When her sobs subsided, Maria patted her on the back. Quietly she said, "His name is Lewis Pictou. He was sixteen at the time. His father's name is Warren Pictou and his wife, Olive. She sent me a letter after they left to let me know where they went. We were friends, she and I. She was the daughter of the then-current Grand Chief of the Mi'kmaq people. A Benjamin Sylliboy if memory serves me right, but it might have changed by now." Maria reached into her pocket and handed Kirsty a little envelope. "Inside is the letter with the address."

Wordlessly, Kirsty took the envelope and stuck it deep in her coat pocket. Maria gave her hand a last squeeze and then disappeared into the darkness.

Kirsty felt frozen inside and out. Knowing the garden like the back of her hand and with the moonlight bathing everything in silver, she walked across the lawn around to the back of the house keeping well away from the motion sensors of the lights. Reaching the rear garden, she entered a piece of woodland at the edge of their property.

Once, when Kirsty was around ten, she discovered a tree house built up in the trees in the thickest part of the forest. It became her fort where she hid from the world. It was there where her feet led her in the still of the night, while her heart tried to sort out the lies of her childhood.

At the foot of the tree she looked up. It seemed much smaller than she remembered. A noise behind her made her jump. Everything was still, except for a few branches rustling in the breeze. A twig snapped again, and Kirsty swivelled around to face the path she had come on.

"Who's there?" Her voice sounded small to her ears.

The shadows seemed to merge into the form of a lion

walking towards her. Kirsty froze. *It's him.* Of all the things she saw as a child, he was the only one who didn't scare her. But when she told her psychiatrist about her imaginary friend, he very gently but firmly told her that he wasn't real either and that she had to stop imagining him too. She started seeing him shortly after she had watched the film, 'The Lion, The Witch and The Wardrobe.' Enthralled with Aslan, she guessed that was what set her off imagining him.

She watched as he came nearer till he was touching distance from her. *I haven't seen him since I was little.* Tonight, she didn't have the strength to resist, she longed to put her head in his mane tell him all her fears and let him calm and comfort her like he did when she was young. Before she knew what she was doing, she knelt in front of him and looked into his golden eyes which seemed to glow even in the dark.

"Did you know?" The nonsensical words spilled out of her.

A soft growl emitted from the lion before he touched her face lightly with his nose, "I did."

The pain of betrayal twisted Kirsty's heart tighter, "Why?"

"You will see in time, little one. There is a purpose in it all."

Kirsty shook her head as tears fell from her already red and puffy eyes. She closed them and felt the lion's mane as he put his head over her shoulder. Her hands crept up around his neck, and she held on for dear life, allowing her need to override her logic. *I'll hold on to you for the last time.* Warmth seemed to come off him in waves, bathing her in acceptance and love that she had no words for. How her mind could conjure up something so real wasn't a fact she wanted to explore.

Excruciatingly slowly, one by one, the most powerful families in the world started discovering that someone had opened backdoors into their secret files, copied them and were releasing them on the internet for all to see. Governments started panicking as their secrets became public knowledge too.

Their best way to handle it was to deny it all and start a

rumour that an extremist had gone and written false files to create chaos. All around the world, people worked around the clock to erase it, but it felt like every time they deleted one item, two more popped up in another place. It was an unprecedented leakage of sensitive information and those in charge needed to find a scapegoat.

5:00 am, GMT-8. Sunday, 10 January. Oregon

Kirsty left early on Sunday morning before the household woke up. She left a note apologising for her hasty departure citing an emergency and changed her flight to the earliest one out that morning. It so happened that Emma Knight – her sister, no, her mother - had a residence in Austin, Texas, the same city in which she was meeting Jean-Pierre before they rented a SUV and drove to the ranch. The closest airport was San Antonio, but they had only five flights a week from Toronto, so she'd booked Austin which now worked out even better for her.

Kirsty shut her tired eyes on the plane and felt herself fall into a light sleep. Before she knew it, the four-hour flight was complete, and they were descending. Thanks to the time zones, time moved two hours forwards and she adjusted her watch accordingly. She had enough time to run her errand before meeting Jean-Pierre at two that afternoon.

Waiting until all the people had left the plane, she got up, smoothing the creases from her black top and wrinkled black jeans. She only had a light carry-on since Jean-Pierre was flying in with their bigger suitcase. Kirsty put on her navy down jacket, zipping it up before she walked off the plane and down the tunnel that connected the plane to the terminal. In less than thirty minutes she hailed a bright blue taxi.

She looked out at the sky appreciating the increase in temperature. The maximum temperature would reach sixty Fahrenheit that day, which was better than the minus forty-one degrees she experienced in Toronto on Saturday. Unzipping her jacket, Kirsty studied the buildings passing by. Austin was the capital city of Texas. A few tall skyscrapers filled the skyline impressing her with their modern look.

For the first time in her life, she regretted not having her sister's telephone number. Kirsty furrowed her brow. *My sister is my mother*. Emma Knight happened to be one of the most famous actresses of their day. Getting an audience with her wasn't as easy as knocking on the door, which is precisely what Kirsty had in mind.

The taxi deposited her in front of a property in Escala Drive with a thick iron gate and high walls that stretched in both directions. Kirsty spied a little intercom on the side of the pillar and pressed the button. Nothing happened so she pushed it again. A camera was facing her from atop the pillar and Kirsty looked up into it.

The intercom crackled and a male voice said, "Miss Knight's residence, may I help you?"

Kirsty inhaled and said, "Could you tell Miss Knight that Kirsty Knight is here to see her?"

There was quiet for a moment before the voice replied, "I'm sorry but Miss Knight does not see people without proper appointments."

Kirsty could feel her face get hot. *I need to see her.* "I'm her sister. If you don't tell her I'm here, I'll make sure she hears about it and fires you."

It was a long shot and the intercom stayed quiet for what seemed like an eternity. *Maybe I should try scaling the gate.* She jumped as the motors started humming and the gate silently opened. Relief jostled with nervousness.

She walked up the drive, her eyes going wider as the house came into full view. Green shrubs surrounded a large fountain in front of the main entrance. Kirsty had checked out the four-acre property online before she came. The mansion was built in Mediterranean-style and cost around five million. The glass front doors opened and a butler with a stiff upper lip looked down on her.

"Miss Knight will see you on the patio. This way."

He turned around and left Kirsty to follow him through the

open door. A stunning curved staircase rose on the right side of the foyer with a trio of narrow arched windows above it. Kirsty took off her jacket before she entered the door. She kept it over her arm, picked up her carry on and followed the butler through a sitting room and out double doors onto a patio. The opulence of wealth did nothing for her nerves.

The outside area was covered in large terracotta tiles with massive pillars; iron tables and chairs stood around and a bar area with seats filled the left side. The butler stopped and Kirsty came to a standstill next to him. By the bar area, a tall, slim blonde woman dressed in white slacks and a bright blue top stood looking out over the pool area below the patio.

"Miss Knight, Miss Knight?" The butler stumbled over the double pronunciation.

The woman turned around and walked towards Kirsty, her high heels clicking on the tiles.

"Kirsten! What a pleasant surprise. What are you doing in the area?"

Kirsty received Emma's slight kiss on both cheeks and felt her heart flutter. Green eyes focused on her, framed by the face that had made her famous. At forty-nine years old, Emma's face showed no wrinkles. Kirsty bit her lower lip and looked down at her toes where her Doc Martins peered up at her from underneath her jeans.

Emma tilted her head sideways and her thin eyebrows went up, "Well?"

The carry-on felt heavy so she put it down and looked back up at Emma. "It's Kirsty, not Kirsten anymore." She bit her lip breaking eye contact. "I had some time to kill. I'm meeting my boyfriend later today. We're going to a ranch for a holiday in the hill country." Kirsty looked back at Emma. "I went to see our parents yesterday."

Emma smiled at Kirsty, "How are the old darlings? I'm hoping to go see them this year if my schedule will allow it." She turned around towards the bar and asked over her shoulder, "Can I offer you something to drink?"

The resemblance was there, but Kirsty had never noticed since she'd never looked. *We have the same-shaped nose and eye colour!* Fighting against the tightness in her chest, Kirsty took a few steps towards Emma and the bar. Seeing a chair by a low table, she sunk down in it clutching her jacket in her hands. "Just water, thanks."

She heard Emma get out a bottle of water from the fridge and empty it into a glass. For herself Emma poured pink gin mixed with ice. She placed Kirsty's water on the table in front of her and seated herself opposite Kirsty crossing her legs and swirling her glass of gin in her hand. Kirsty took the water and swallowed a small sip. Her hand was slightly sweaty. She felt Emma silently scrutinise her. It made her squirm, so she blurted out, "Why did you never marry and have kids?"

Emma's eyes widened at the direct question before her face fell back to its impassive mask. "The life of an actress isn't predictable. It doesn't offer a family the stability it needs, so I chose not to."

Kirsty felt her eyes drawn to Emma's as she said, "So you chose acting above children?"

She saw Emma's eyes narrow before she broke eye contact. "I guess, or you could say the choice was made for me."

Kirsty sat forward, placing her water back on the table, "Do you remember the big elephant you gave me when I turned five? I named him Dumbo. I still have him. He was the only present I got that year. My birthday never seemed to be a day to celebrate." It was her turn to study Emma; whose eyes were on her drink.

Emma shifted her shoulders and said, "If there is one thing life has taught me, it's that there's nothing to be gained from dwelling on the past. You have to let it go and do the best with what you have, here and now."

Kirsty clenched her fist, "Would you have changed anything if you could've?"

Emma took a sip of her drink before replying, "I don't know." She stood up placing her glass down in front of her. "I'll see you out, shall I? And a word to the wise, if you ever mention, whatever you think you know to anyone, anyone at all, I'll deny it and reveal your little secret."

A cold shudder ran down Kirsty's back. *How did she know about it? No one knew.* Wordlessly she followed Emma out, barely seeing the magnificent foyer this time. The door shut behind her quietly and an intense ache started in Kirsty's stomach. *She didn't want me. I shouldn't have been born. I'm a mistake.*

She looked down and in the flowerbed against the wall, a lone bluebonnet had sprung up. Its vibrant blue flowers were out of season since they usually came out in spring. Her nose caught a whiff of the sweet fragrance and with her throat thick, she started walking the long way back to the gate while she phoned for a taxi to take her back to the airport.

Emma Knight shut her bedroom door behind her with a soft click. Kicking off her high heels, she walked over to where her personal safe was hidden behind a portrait. On the bottom shelf lay a thick folder. She took it out and sat down on her bed with it. Carefully the contents were unpacked around her until she found what she was after. It was a small photo of her and Kirsty with a big Dumbo elephant. Staring at their happy smiles she traced the lines of her daughter's face, feeling her throat thicken.

Throughout the years she had kept tabs on Kirsty via a very discreet private eye. When Kirsty lost the baby girl three months ago, Emma had spent a night drunk all on her own. *Why did I push her away? She might never give me a chance again.* Emma pushed her hand through her hair, feeling a tremor in it. *She wouldn't like me anyway. Who am I kidding? I must be the worst mother in the world. Knowing where my child is and not...*

Fumbling everything back into the folder, she pushed it back into the safe, locking it. A decanter full of golden whiskey stood on her dressing table and she measured a double shot into her glass and downed it neat. It burned down her throat, but the pain did not surpass the searing inside her heart. Her image in the mirror caught her eye and she looked at herself. *I hate you.*

She shook her head as the vicious words slashed through her, turned and filled her glass again.

The online psychic checked her website for the last time. It had been fun to reactivate her lucrative side business, but she didn't have time for it anymore. Casually browsing through the messages, one caught her attention. She clicked on it before she could stop herself and felt her heartbeat increase. This wasn't someone wanting her to help find their missing cat or tell them whether they'll find love one day. This was a father searching for his daughter demanding that she helped him. *He must be frantic, but I couldn't possibly help him. The forces that guard this type of thing aren't ones you challenge whether real or imaginary.*

With a resolute face, the psychic wrote a message informing all her followers that she was suspending her business indefinitely for personal reasons. She moved the father and daughter to the back of her mind and logged out of her account. It helped that no one knew her identity. It added to the allure of her website and gave her more followers, but now it also meant she could shut it down without any repercussions in her real life.

8:45 am, Sunday. Undisclosed location.

There was a commotion outside the door, and Camille Molineux opened her eyes. Before they had fully adjusted to the light, the door opened, and a girl was thrust inside. *Another one.*

The door clanged shut, and the girl visibly trembled. She was tall, with light reddish-brown hair. She barely glanced around the room before collapsing in a heap. Camille felt a hundred years older than this girl although she probably only had a few years on her.

With an inward sigh, she got up and helped the girl to a nearby chair. Kneeling in front of her, she lifted the girl's chin and looked into her blue eyes, "Hello, my name is Camille. You're not alone in this. We're going to make it out of here. I promise."

The girl lifted her blotched eyes and looked around the large room observing ten other girls, of various ethnicities, some lying on the triple bunk beds that flanked the walls, some sitting around a table playing cards. Her eyes sought out Camille's before she said, "What is this place? Why am I here? I'm a nobody."

Camille took a fortifying breath, "Nobody's a nobody. I suspect we've all been chosen for a specific purpose. So far, they've only been taking our blood." Her thin eyebrows came together in a frown, "I don't know what it is they are after. It seems they are doing medical experiments."

The new girl trembled again, "I want my mom."

Camille patted her hand and in a feigned, optimistic voice said, "When we get out of here, I'll take you to her. Let's see if we can find you something to eat or drink, shall we? We have a self-catered kitchen here stocked with various good stuff."

Camille opened the fridge to get a drink out for the new girl, her long blond hair fell over her face, and she tucked it behind her ear. Her throat felt tight as she thought of her father, he was the only close family she had left in the world. *Why haven't you found me yet, Dad?* If there was any parent in this world who could move heaven and earth to find her, hers could and would. It had been ten long days; she'd been the first girl to arrive. Where they were, she didn't know, but she had a suspicion they were being held in a castle. At least they weren't in the dungeon.

She buttered a piece of toast for the new girl and placed it on a plate before putting some ham and cheese on it. *Some new year this is turning out to be.* Her blue eyes scanned the room up to the small barred windows set deep in the thick walls and back to the locked door. Being a doctor herself, even though she was only finishing her residency this year, she had the uncomfortable feeling these scientists weren't going to stay with only samples of their DNA. *Hurry up and find me, Dad,* she silently pleaded.

9:45 am, GMT+1. Outside Paris, France.

Leo Molineux hit the boxing bag with all the force he could muster. If it was a person, he would have beaten him to a pulp. With every punch the thoughts reverberated through his brain. *Who could've done it? Why no ransom money? Why aren't they finding her?* A vicious punch to the bag. *What more can I do? Is she still alive after ten days?*

With one last punch he hugged the bag with his arms and felt his tears mingle with his sweat. All his life he'd protected his daughter and in one instant she was taken away.

After a shower and a change, Leo sat down behind his laptop at his desk in his home office. His blond hair streaked with silver was still wet as he stared intently at the screen scanning the search results on how to find missing persons. One of the random sites looked promising, and Leo left a message there. At this point he would try anything.

He tried a search for the various methods of finding missing people when he came across an insightful document. He sat back and steepled his fingers together while his eyes digested the information on the screen. Now *this* was promising. According to the document, which looked like something that wasn't supposed to be available to the public, the CIA had a government-funded research department with a team of physicists who explored finding people through ESP.

Extrasensory perception, hmm... He knew enough to know that some of it was legitimate. He looked through the document which listed all the present and former people working at the department. One person stood out as having extraordinary skills in locating people during their experiments in what they called remote viewing.

Leo closed his eyes clearing his mind, and for an instant he could feel her presence out there and her cry for help. *I'm coming, Camille, hold on.* Picking up the phone, he made a call and within hours he was on his way to America.

CHAPTER 3

9:00 am, GMT-5. Toronto, Canada

Jean-Pierre rubbed his eyes as he stared at the departure board in the airport at Toronto. Quickly he found his flight to Austin, Texas, but his eyes lingered on a flight leaving for Bilbao, Spain. *Only a short connecting flight from Bilbao and I'd be home.* It had been five years since he and Kirsty went to his homeland. The memory of their trip ran through his mind. It was on that trip that they'd decided to start a family.

Exhaling, Jean-Pierre picked up his hand luggage and turned in the direction of the departure gate. The flight was under four hours long, plus the one-hour added on with the time zone, so Jean-Pierre found himself walking out into the large arrivals area just in time to meet up with Kirsty. He pulled their large suitcase behind him in his one hand and the smaller hand luggage in the other.

As he neared the Starbucks, Jean-Pierre saw her sitting at a table with her laptop open in front of her. She hadn't noticed him and he stood watching her. His heart twisted as the scene reminded him of when he met her. She'd been sitting in the same pose, behind her laptop, in an internet cafe/coffee shop that he frequented with his artist buddies.

For weeks he watched the beautiful, mysterious girl engaged with her work, never glancing up his way. One day he intercepted the waitress and took her coffee to her. Her hand came out to take it when she noticed the male hand holding it. Slowly her eyes travelled up his arm into his eyes, and he was smitten. Her deep green eyes revealed a person he wanted to get to know, and although it took him a long time to break through her defences, once she'd let him in, she did it wholeheartedly.

On a whim, he went to the counter and picked up a take-away flat white for himself and a cappuccino with coconut milk for her. The aroma of freshly brewed coffee filled his lungs. He left his luggage at the table next to them and walked over to her extending her coffee towards her. Her fingers stilled on the keyboard as she looked at the cup and then slowly travelled up until she found his face. For a full second she looked like the girl he met seven years ago before the walls came up and she smiled at him.

I'm losing her. Jean-Pierre felt his throat tighten at the unwelcome thought.

"Hello, care to join me?"

"Don't mind if I do." Jean-Pierre placed his cup down beside her laptop and pulled their luggage closer to them. "Have you been waiting for me long?"

Kirsty took a sip of her coffee while shaking her head lightly, "No, not long. I'm glad you're here now, I've already rented us an SUV for the week." She closed the laptop with a slight click.

Jean-Pierre studied her from underneath his fringe, "How did it go with your parents?"

She shrugged, "They don't know anything, but I did find some information that I intend to follow up."

He tilted his head as he watched her avoid his gaze. *Was she lying?* A disquiet settled in his stomach. Kirsty wasn't anything like his mother, so why compare the two? His brows furrowed together, and he clenched his jaw.

"Kirsty?"

"Hmm?"

"Let's go." He stood up, leaving his half-drunk cup on the table.

She took another sip before she slid her laptop into its bag, stood, slung it over her shoulder, grabbed her hand luggage and followed him to the car rentals.

10:00 am, GMT–6. New Beginnings Ranch, Texas

Emily placed her hands on her hips and took one last look around the treehouse. They had had it built one year previously and so far, it was very popular with their guests. She smoothed over the white duvet and checked the small shower room to see if the toilet paper and soap were refilled.

The treehouse incorporated the tree through the middle of the house; it was built like a platform right around it. Her hand touched the roughness of the old oak where it formed a part of the wall. It was ancient and towered high into the sky. You could gaze up into its bare branches through the Velux window in the roof, right above the double bed.

She gave the room a last sweep trying to see it through her guests' eyes. Warm dark red and orange were reflected in the decor through the pillows and a soft throw on the bed. There were two comfortable leather high-backed chairs in the corner, either side of a wood burner stove. A sliding door opened onto a porch on which were seats and a table, where you could have breakfast while looking out across the bushes, yard and hills in the distance.

Satisfied that everything was ready, Emily pushed her long brown hair back behind her ear, closed the door, and carefully climbed down the wooden stairs.

Although the tree house was less than a quarter of a mile away from the main building, it was completely private, nestled amidst a few trees. The surrounding fields were filled with bushes, leaving only the two-track path open which ended at the clearing below the treehouse.

She walked down the track towards their ranch house, the dead leaves crunching under her wellies, remembering a few date nights she had had with Luke there. It was a very romantic setting; she hoped her guests would enjoy their stay. Thankfully they didn't have many people arriving, only the couple who booked unexpectedly and a friend from the UK, whom they were expecting later in the week. Arriving in the yard, she glanced towards the stables where the horses were safely ensconced.

Changing direction, she walked towards it. The comforting smell of horses and straw filled her nose as she entered through the double doors. Emily found them in the last stall, the occupant was their calmest bay horse who stood complacently as two pairs of little hands brushed her.

She observed her twins, with their long brown hair in two braids, standing on a step stool either side of the mare brushing a flank each. Luke had a wheelbarrow outside the stable filled with old straw and horse manure. He was busy spreading the fresh straw in the stable. The horse gave a soft whine and looked at her with brown eyes that seemed to say: *Please rescue me*. Emily gave the horse's nose a rub before her family spotted her.

"Mommy, look how nice I've cleaned Rosie!"

"Look at my side, Mommy, mine is better!"

"No, it's not. Mine is better!"

"Wow, girls, you've both done an amazing job." Emily made a show of inspecting both sides, before ending up next to Luke. "What do you think?"

Luke grinned, "They're going to make excellent horsewomen. I couldn't brush a horse when I was four and a half."

The two girls grinned at their parents. Luke's gaze rested tenderly on them before he said, "Can you go put those brushes away in the tack room? Do you know where they go?"

The girls nodded and were off at the speed of lighting. Emily turned to Luke, and his dark eyes rested on her, "Shouldn't you be resting? I took them out so you could have a lie in."

Emily's mouth turned up on one side, "Hmm…the amount of noise they made woke me up, but I did have a peaceful cup of tea and then got a chance to inspect the treehouse for our guests."

Luke rested the shovel against the side of the stable and pulled her up against him, "I miss the mornings we could just lie in and cuddle together till whenever we felt like it."

Emily placed her hand against his rough, chequered work shirt, "I love you. We'll have those times again one day."

He nuzzled her neck, "I know. I wouldn't exchange it for

the world."

She placed a kiss on his short charcoal hair, her green eyes twinkling, "Soon we won't get any sleep at all, we should appreciate what we have."

He gave a low laugh, "Indeed. Sometimes I still can't believe it."

She shook her head, "Neither can I."

The pattering of running feet could be heard behind them which stopped at the entrance to the stall. "Mommy, Daddy! We're hungry!"

Emily turned around in the safety of Luke's arms and he held her tight against him before letting go. "Mommy's going to make you a snack now and I'll join you as soon as I've given Rosie some water."

The twins flanked Emily, each one taking her hand on either side and skipped as they made their way back to the house.

5:00 pm, GMT-6. The Hill Country, Texas.

Kirsty frowned as she looked at the navigational device and back at the road. This road turned off another road and it felt like the roads would never end. They had been driving for three hours into an area that felt wilder and wilder the deeper they went. She had never explored the nature parks in this part of Texas and found herself astonished at the landscape that didn't fit with stereotypical images in her head.

She glanced over at Jean-Pierre, "Take that smirk off your face. I don't like getting lost. The signal is sketchy, I don't trust it."

Jean-Pierre shrugged, "I kind of like getting lost. The adventure of discovering new places."

Kirsty rolled her eyes, "I bet you won't like it that much if we ran out of fuel in the middle of nowhere. When last did you see something that looked like civilisation?"

Slowly, she drove up a lane with oak trees standing sentinel on either side of the road. They came to a gate, and Jean-Pierre hopped out and opened it. Around a corner, a group of buildings greeted them surrounded by a tidy grass area. Kirsty drove until she was in front of the main house and parked next to another blue SUV.

They got out and after the slam of the doors, the silence struck Kirsty. It was so quiet it made her ears hurt. She left her jacket in the car as the sun was shining, and a comfortable sixty-four degrees made it feel like a summer day in Toronto.

A glance around showed scattered Mesquite trees between a few log bungalows built to the left side of the yard a comfortable distance from the main house. The brick-built ranch house had a grey shingled roof and an open stone-tiled porch with large white pillars that surrounded the house. To the right, a massive wooden barn with a tin roof housed stables and there were round corrals for the horses further on too.

A horse's neigh vibrated through the quiet and then she heard the pattering of feet and laughter before two little identical girls ran out the door, down the porch steps coming to an abrupt stop in front of her and Jean-Pierre. They looked at each other for a second. Barely contained excitement sparkled in the twins' dark eyes.

"Welcome to our ranch!" The one on the left said.

"I'm Mercy, and this is Grace." The other one said while she pointed to herself and to her sister.

"You must be Kirsty, and you must be Jean-Pierre," Grace said with a grin.

Jean-Pierre cleared his throat and hunched down on his haunches, "Nice to meet you Mercy and Grace."

Mercy inclined her head, "You're not American?"

Jean-Pierre shook his head, "No, I'm from Europe."

Grace grinned, "We're from Europe too, but Mommy and Daddy are from New York."

Mercy piped up, "Daddy's Italian though! Where are you from?"

Jean-Pierre laughed a deep laugh, "I'm from the Basque country, which is in Spain and France."

Grace's eyes widened, "I've never heard of that one!"

Kirsty took a small step closer to the girls, but steps behind her made her turn back. A tall, beautiful, younger woman had come out of the house.

She walked down the three steps and looked into Kirsty's eyes with an apology, "I'm sorry, my girls like to greet the guests first. I hope they weren't interrogating you. They're going through the question stage." At this she looked at the girls with a slight frown, but her mouth was trying to hide a grin.

Jean-Pierre stood up and stretched out his hand to shake with the woman, "No, they weren't. It's not a problem. I like being greeted by such a friendly welcoming party."

The twins' faces beamed up at him. "Do you want to see the horses, Jean-Pierre? Daddy is exercising them. We'll go show you." At this, they grabbed his hands and pulled him towards the stables.

Jean-Pierre grinned back at the women, "I'll see you soon."

Their mom shook her head, "Those girls, I wish I had half their energy."

Kirsty exhaled, "Me too. Hard to imagine we were once so young."

"I haven't introduced myself. I'm Emily Johnson. New Beginnings is run by my husband, Luke, and me. Do you want me to take you to your accommodation? We could drive closer and park by it if you wish?"

Kirsty looked towards the stables to where Jean-Pierre had disappeared with the girls and back to Emily, "Sure."

Emily got in the passenger seat and Kirsty behind the wheel. As she started the engine she glanced over to Emily and saw her with her hand on her belly. The distinctive roundness of early pregnancy that showed through her white cotton shirt made Kirsty put the car in reverse. Emily steadied herself with her hand on the door and looked at Kirsty with her head inclined.

Kirsty's cheeks coloured, and she stepped on the brakes changing it to drive. "Where to?"

"Just around the house to the left, down to that group of trees. It's less than a quarter of a mile away but very private. Meals are at the main house and the times are by your telephone. You can ring if you need anything else in between too."

Kirsty nodded and tried to swallow the knot away in her

throat, her knuckles white against the black steering wheel. She parked the car and peered up at the tree house built on stilts that showed between the trees. Aware that Emily was waiting for her reaction, she said, "That looks great."

Emily's eyes sparkled, "Come, I'll show you the inside."

Kirsty pulled her shoulders back, "There's no need, thank you. You can just give me the keys."

"Oh, okay." Emily got out of the car and met Kirsty on the drivers' side. She looked into Kirsty's eyes, and Kirsty felt herself cringe at the openness in the other woman's gaze. "The keys are inside the room. If there is anything you need, just give us a call. You'll find a list of the activities and services we offer inside the treehouse. You are very welcome to any of them, simply book a few hours in advance."

Kirsty dipped her head and Emily turned around, walking away while Kirsty opened the trunk and collected their smaller bags. She would leave the large suitcase for Jean-Pierre to carry up. Pausing at the bottom of the wooden stairs she took a deep breath, squared her shoulders and climbed up the stairs to their treehouse.

The fading sunlight streaked pink and orange across the sky by the time Jean-Pierre came up the steps of the treehouse with their large suitcase in hand.

"Kirsty?" Jean-Pierre opened the door, and his eyes fell on the queen-sized bed in the middle of the room. There was a chill in the air and the scent of wood and musk. He spotted the woodstove in the corner with a stack of cut wood stacked next to it. The room was empty with only Kirsty's closed laptop on the table and their hand luggage on the bed.

Jean-Pierre put down the large suitcase next to the bed and walked across the wooden floor towards the sliding door that led to a porch. He found her there sitting quietly in a chair. He pushed his hand through his hair before saying, "Sorry I took so long. Those girls wanted to introduce me to every single horse and tell me each one's history, likes and dislikes; the works!"

She didn't move, didn't look at him. Frown lines marred his forehead, "I'm going to light the fire, it's getting chilly." He turned around without waiting for a reply and knelt by the woodstove. Soon he had it stacked, and he lit the kindling.

The fire started slowly then blazed high. The flames licked at the wood blackening it. Jean-Pierre stared into the fire as he heard Kirsty's footsteps come in through the door and stop behind him. He stood up and turned around to face her, but was taken aback at the sight of her face which had black smears where tears had run down her cheeks.

She walked right into his arms, clutching his shirt in her fists, leaning her forehead against his chest, she took a shallow breath and said, "Why did you bring me to this god-forsaken place?"

Jean-Pierre cupped the back of her head with his palm and lifted her chin with his other hand, "We needed to get away, you know that?" With his thumb, he wiped away a smear on her cheek.

She bit her bottom lip, swallowing, "Did we have to go to the middle of nowhere? There is no internet. No mobile signal, no nothing."

He couldn't help the lifting of the corner of his lip, "What doesn't kill you makes you stronger, right?"

She shook her head, but a small smile started on her face. He inclined his head, "Are you hungry? Dinner starts about now I think."

Her smile fled, "No, I'm not. Will you bring me back something?" She turned away from him and unzipped their bag. "I'll unpack so long."

Jean-Pierre looked at her back, released a sigh and said, "Okay, I'll be back soon. Add wood to the fire if it burns low."

He climbed down the steps, stopped, started going back up, but then turned around and walked down all the way.

Kirsty looked around the tidy treehouse with a feeling of satisfaction. She always felt better after creating some semblance of home in a strange place. The toothbrushes were at the sink and the shoes beneath the bed, her feet snug in her slippers. She placed another log on the fire and stood to watch the shadows of the flames on the walls.

She breathed in the scent of wood burning and felt herself relax. *It's going to be okay. I'll avoid our hosts as much as possible and try to enjoy being with Jean-Pierre.*

A few leaflets and welcoming papers were on top of a small table that contained coffee and tea, as well as a kettle. *We have electricity and a working bathroom. We're not entirely in the sticks, thank goodness.*

She took the leaflets and papers and settled down in the leather chair before the wood burner. She skimmed across the safety notices, and her eyes landed on the extra services they offered. Her eyebrows pinched together as she read that Emily Johnson was a qualified psychiatrist and gave private counselling sessions. That was one service she was not going to use.

I had to forget the pills, didn't I. Annoyance flitted up inside her. Her plan was to start taking them again on this trip just to get herself back on kilter for a few months before they tried again for a baby. She figured if she took them for two months, they should get her back on balance and then two months off them before they went for another IVF treatment. *I need time to find more funds too. Maybe I could take them for three months.*

Kirsty felt a yawn well up, awareness of how tired her body felt spread through her. She looked around the treehouse. *There's nothing to do. Why don't I have an early night? Jean-Pierre might still be a while.* After changing into her PJ's, she snuggled under the thick duvet, enjoying the feel of the Egyptian cotton against her skin as she drifted off.

Something didn't feel right. Kirsty lifted her head feeling the roughness of the grass against her cheek. *Where's the pillow?* She pushed herself up, surprised to find herself surrounded by grass almost as tall as her head. She stood and saw that the full moon was shining down, lighting up the countryside around her which consisted of fields, bushes and trees as far as the eye could see. She turned 360 degrees and couldn't make out anything except the vast nature surrounding her. *Where's the treehouse? The stables?*

A small oak tree stood three feet away from her rustling in the wind. Kirsty hugged herself with her arms feeling the snap in the early evening air start to affect her. She rolled her eyes. *Of course, I'm having another nightmare.* Night terrors had plagued her from as young as she could remember. She never knew what was going to happen when she fell asleep. She'd learnt to cope, to hide it. From experience, she knew the best way was to treat it as real and be like the hero in the Hunger Games, fighting for her survival.

Right now, she had to move to stay warm and find some shelter. Without thinking about it, Kirsty set out towards the west where a faint light still showed the remnants of the sunset. Her progress was slow though, the hard, rocky ground hurt her bare feet.

A breeze rustled through the grass, dark shapes materialising around her out of nowhere. Faces slightly browner than hers with black tattoos in sharp lines across their faces stared at her unblinkingly. Their spears were held towards her, their stance clearly stating that they were treating her with distrust. Kirsty's body was taut with fearful anticipation, she held up her hands and spoke, "I'm not an enemy."

Her teeth were beginning to chatter from the cold. A man with more feathers in his short hair than the others spoke to the others in a sharp language. As one, they lowered their spears. One of the younger ones loosened what looked like a cape made of soft leather from his shoulders and draped it around her. She clutched the ends together, feeling the leftover heat from his body still clinging to it.

The leader gave a command and they started walking in a direction following a small trail through the bushes. Kirsty followed them as best as she could. They wore soft moccasins, protecting their feet against the frozen ground.

The leader barked again, and they stopped. Another young man bent over and removed his shoes. He offered them to Kirsty with his eyes downcast. She felt sudden tears well up in her eyes. Gratefully, she slipped them on, finding them fitting her perfectly. They marched on until they reached a stream where the trail led them onwards next to it. A small clearing appeared where a few tents were pitched around a blazing fire.

The men were quickly surrounded by a group of women and children, laughing and chattering excitedly. Kirsty was drawn to the warm fire and squatted as near to it as she could, grateful to find the cold thawing out of her bones. The American Indians kept giving her furtive glances, but she tried to keep her eyes on the fire. *At least this dream seems monster free, although I wouldn't be surprised if they end up being cannibals that want to roast me.*

There was a commotion at the tent furthest from the fire, and Kirsty looked up, her eyes widening at the sight of a beautiful young nun dressed in a white habit with a blue cloak walking towards her with a broad smile.

"Hola y bienvenido!" the nun said and stood still to look at her.

Kirsty stood up clumsily still clutching the cloak over her pyjama shorts and t-shirt. "Hola." Her mind scrambled to think of any other Spanish words she knew. "¿Quién eres tu?" *I hope that means who are you.*

The nun showed white teeth as she replied, "My name is Maria de Jesus. I'm from Agreda, Spain but visiting with my friends, the Jumano. This tribe here are on a hunting trip at present."

Kirsty felt her mouth open at the perfect English flowing off the nun's lips. She licked her own dry lips and asked, "Where am I?"

Maria inclined her head, her eyes twinkling with laughter, "A better question is, who are you?"

Who am I? Kirsty looked into her dark eyes, finding herself unable to answer. Her name was Kirsten or Kirsty Knight, but it was just a name. She felt like the nun had hammered her problem straight on the head; she didn't know who she was.

"I don't know," Kirsty answered, finding relief in saying it aloud.

Maria gently answered, "That is a good start, Kirsty. A good start. Being honest with yourself will lead you to some answers."

Kirsty felt a strange fear twist inside of her. *How does she know my name?*

Maria clapped her hands together, "I believe you've skipped dinner. Shall we eat and talk? Please follow me."

She led the way to the furthest tent, and Kirsty ducked in behind her. It was cosily arranged with a mat and furs for sleeping on one side and a round stump to sit on, on the opposite side. The nun went to the corner which had a large pot and various cooking utensils and came back with two steaming bowls. The fragrant whiff coming from the food caused Kirsty's stomach to growl. The nondescript mush didn't look very appetizing though.

The nun handed a bowl to Kirsty and proceeded to sit down with her legs crossed on her bed. Letting go of the cape Kirsty draped it around her middle like a towel before she sat down on the stump opposite the bed. Maria had taken a bite and was staring at Kirsty with that friendly laughter behind her eyes.

"Interesting clothes you have on for the middle of winter."

Kirsty glanced down at her white T-shirt, "It's my pyjamas."

Maria lifted her eyebrows, "Pyjamas?"

A blush crept across her face, "Clothes you sleep in." She glanced at the coarse material of the nun's dress. *I wonder if she sleeps in that.*

Taking a tentative bite, she found it to her surprise very tasty. "This is nice. It tastes like chilli."

"Yes, it's a special recipe of mine. They have some lovely beans here that I like to experiment with."

Kirsty chewed through another bite finding her hunger greater than she realised, "Where is here exactly?"

"The Americas. I do believe in the year 1623."

A piece of food went down the wrong way, and Kirsty had a bout of coughing. After it subsided, she dared a look towards the nun who still sat calmly eating her dinner.

The nun met her gaze and lifted her eyebrows, her dark eyes almost shining in her white face. "I take it you are from another year?"

Kirsty took a fortifying breath before she said, "2016."

It was Maria's turn to look astonished, as her mouth widened into a circle, "Well, that's surprising, but I guess not impossible." The next moment she gave a little chuckle.

A frown creased Kirsty's forehead as she stared at Maria, "I don't get what's funny. Nothing about this dream's been funny."

Maria shook her head, "I remember praying yesterday for the world to be saved wondering how long it still has left and here you appear out of 2016. I guess there's my answer right there."

She inclined her head, "What makes you so sure you're only dreaming?"

Kirsty shrugged her shoulders, "I've always dreamed a lot. Some vivid like this, some not, nothing is really real. All I remember going to bed and starting to fall asleep."

"Hmmm…I've often travelled when I start falling asleep. Interesting. Now tell me, do you believe in God?"

The direct question caught Kirsty off guard, and she spilt some of the red sauce on her T-shirt. Wiping it off with her finger she swallowed the different answers that wanted to well up in her. As she looked into the strange nun's eyes the words came out of her against her will, "I'm agnostic."

"What does that mean?" Maria took another spoonful of chilli.

"It means I believe that nothing can be known of the existence or nature of God."

Maria burst out laughing, this time she laughed so loudly, that she had to put her bowl down on the ground. "I'm sorry," she said, when she came up for air, "that's the funniest statement, I've ever heard."

Her annoyance with the nun grew, "It's not funny. It's true.

Scientific evidence proves..."

"Let me stop you right there." Maria interjected with a gentle voice, "I'm not interested in proof. If you do not believe, if you are not born from above, you won't be able to see the kingdom. So, for you to find proof you must first accept it."

Kirsty sneered, "Blind faith? I don't think so. All my life I've been told to face the facts. Reality is what I believe in, not dreams, hallucinations or anything weird."

Maria made a tsk sound with her mouth, "They used to tell me that too. When I was a little girl, I used to see things they couldn't, and they dealt with me harshly. Even when I became a nun the other nuns shunned my supernatural experiences. They said I was crazy."

Kirsty felt her throat thicken as she looked down into her bowl. Maria's voice had a sad tinge to it, but that changed as she said, "Do you know that I've never left my convent in Agreda, but I've been bi-locating for years? Sometimes in spirit only, sometimes physically too. A journey that takes months takes me seconds, and I can even bring things like rosaries with me."

She looked around at the tent with a wistful look on her face, "I love these Jumano people, I would give my life to save even one of them. Those sceptics all believe me now because some missionaries have met the Jumanos, I sent to them to get baptised. Now they believe me, but it matters not. What matters is that I've overcome the fear of man so that I could fulfil my purpose. There is a purpose for each and everyone's life, Kirsty. Your life has a purpose, and you need to find it, for there are people who need you in your world."

Unexpectedly, Kirsty's eyes filled with tears. Maria bent down on her knees in front of her and placed her hand on her shoulder. "Don't worry, He'll take care of you. Ask Him to show you the Way." Peace flooded her it felt familiar like the peace she experienced with her childhood imaginary friend.

Maria tilted her head as if listening to something, she stood up, "You need to leave. They will take you back to where they found you. I hope to meet you again in the future, Kirsty."

Before Kirsty could object, Maria bundled her out of the tent, called three of the Jumano men, to whom she spoke in their language, who marched back with Kirsty along the trail towards the fields. They were a few hundred feet away from where they found her when they stopped. Something seemed to be spooking them, she didn't know what.

Kirsty could feel the cold taking hold of her again, but she gave them back the cloak and the moccasins. Without a backward glance they vanished into the now dark bush leaving her alone. *I hope I wake up soon. I wouldn't like to dream how I freeze the rest of the night.* Kirsty hugged her arms around her. *At least I didn't get roasted.*

Jean-Pierre walked back after dinner still smiling from the antics of the twins at the table. It reminded him of home, having dinner around a table with family. Even after his mother left, his father's side of the family made up for it with plenty of aunts and cousins that regularly gathered to have meals together.

As he neared the treehouse, he could see a faint glow from within which had to be the fire still going. He stopped and took a moment to look up at the vast sky. The quiet, interrupted by the sound of a cricket, encircled him.

He tore his gaze back to the treehouse and pushed his hands into his pockets. When he saw the small bump, their new hostess sported at dinner tonight, the penny dropped. *No wonder Kirsty wants to tail it back home.* The stairs creaked under his weight.

Their hosts had assured him there were no real dangers out here except a few red longhorns in the next pasture, and they were reasonably placid. There were wild critters in the bush, but they generally kept clear of the areas where humans lived. He pushed the door open and found the room tidy with no sign of the luggage or suitcases. *Where is she?* At least he knew she didn't leave in the car since he'd walked past it.

He did a quick check of the porch and the bathroom, but Kirsty wasn't there. He placed another log on the fire seeing it was low before he zipped up his jacket higher and went outside again. He spotted a penlight torch on the side table, grabbed it and shut the door leaving the key on the inside.

Jean-Pierre lengthened his stride as he walked over to the dark stables. It wasn't like Kirsty to go out for a walk all by herself in the dark. She preferred to be holed up inside. Getting cold wasn't on the list of things she liked, ironic since they lived in Canada. He focused the light of the torch and felt the door of the stables.

It was unlocked so he pushed it open. The soft munching of the horses greeted him combined with the smell of hay and horse. He kept the torch on the floor as his eyes strained to see the silhouettes of the horses in the stables. The windows that laced the walls high against the walls of the barn let in a little moonlight, allowing shafts of light to infiltrate the darkness of the barn.

"Kirsty?" Jean-Pierre whispered loudly. The horse nearest to him gave a low whinny, and Jean-Pierre rubbed its velvet nose for a moment. It was clear she wasn't in here.

He left the stables and closed the door. The lights of the main house looked welcoming in the dark. Jean-Pierre rubbed his forehead. He was pretty sure she wouldn't have gone there but he had to check in case.

He knocked on the solid oak door and it opened in front of him straight away. Luke, the twins' dad, stood in front of him, his eyes black in the darkened foyer while light from the sitting room shone from behind him reflecting on the wooden floor.

Jean-Pierre cleared his throat, "Sorry, to bother you Luke, I wondered if Kirsty, my partner, came by here?"

Luke stepped out of the door and pulled it halfway shut behind him, "Sorry, Emily is putting the twins to bed. She hasn't been here that I know of. You left barely ten minutes ago."

Jean-Pierre pushed his hands deeper into his pockets and looked at his feet, "I'm sorry to bother you. Maybe she took a walk, I'll wait for her at the treehouse."

Luke shifted his weight and asked, "Is there another reason you're worried?"

Jean-Pierre started shaking his head no, but said, "She was upset earlier. Your wife is pregnant, and we lost a baby three months ago." He felt a firm hand grip his shoulder, squeezing it.

"Sorry to hear about that man. Do you think she was upset enough to do something irrational?"

Jean-Pierre clenched his jaw, "No. No, I don't think so. Kirsty is very rational; she likes order and control."

Luke let go of his shoulder and Jean-Pierre glanced his way to see him give a little smirk, "Women, you do your best to understand them, but sometimes you just have to love them."

Jean-Pierre dipped his head and turned away, "I'd better go wait for her."

"If she doesn't turn up in the next hour come get me, and we can do a search."

"I'll do that." Jean-Pierre trudged back to the treehouse, flashing his penlight into the bushes around him. Finding the treehouse still empty, he stood indecisively before going out again. He wanted to search around the bungalows on the other side of the yard.

His heart was beating faster than usual and despite the cold there was a faint sweat on his brow. Flashbacks of searching for his mother, when she'd gone off wandering, came back to him. Memories he would rather forget. *Kirsty, where are you?*

As he rounded the last log bungalow, backed by a large field, he flashed his faint light towards the area and saw something white. There was a gate. He opened it, took a few steps closer and started running.

Kirsty was standing barefoot in the middle of the field, in her white T-shirt and shorts, with her long brown hair trailing down her back. He grabbed her by the shoulders and saw her eyes were closed. *Was she sleepwalking?* He lifted her up into his arms, one hand under her shoulders and one under her knees. *She's light as a feather, has she been eating less?*

Her head hung back as if she was still asleep. *I hope I don't stumble.* Leaving the gate open behind him he took the shortest route back to the treehouse behind the main house. As soon as he had her inside, he started warming her up. Her skin was icy. He placed her down on the rug in front of the wood burner, grabbed the duvet off the bed and wrapped it around her.

"Kirsty, can you hear me?"

She stirred a little, he stroked her hair out of her face,

"Kirsty?"

Her eyes fluttered open, she looked dazed before she focused on him, "Jean-Pierre?"

"You're safe, honey. I've got you."

She looked around the room, at the fireplace and back at him, "I met a nun with a blue cloak and then the Jumanos left me."

His eyes widened. *What's she talking about?* Jean-Pierre cleared his throat, "You were dreaming and sleepwalking."

Kirsty blinked a few times and looked down at her lap, "I'm cold."

Jean-Pierre sat down next to her and pulled her into his arms, "I'll keep you warm."

She nodded against his chest and gave a sigh, "You do that." She seemed to drift off again.

He sat for a while until her breathing became regular then he moved her to the bed, got the duvet and covered her, her head barely showed. He changed into his pyjamas and slid in next to her pulling her against him, so that they lay like spoons. He hoped his body heat would help restore her temperature to normal.

She gave a small sigh and pressed closer to him. He slid his hand over hers and breathed in her scent. He'd never really tried to describe her smell. It was something wild like wildflowers and woods. Jean-Pierre lay staring into the dark worry gnawing away on his insides. *What if losing the last one had pushed her over the edge?*

His heart twisted in fear as he ran through all the types of mental illnesses you could get. Some were only temporary after severe trauma, some were hereditary. She was adopted so they didn't know if there was anything in her family. Mentally, he shook himself as his thoughts raced through his mind. *Get a grip, Jean-Pierre, this is Kirsty you're thinking about, she's your practical and logical girlfriend, there isn't anything crazy or weird about her.* He hugged her more tightly and willed himself to fall asleep even though he knew it would be impossible.

CHAPTER 4

Chris Smith observed the well-dressed gentleman sitting in his office chair as he entered through the door. He took a sip of the black brew that they called coffee here in headquarters and with a slight grimace, swallowed it down. The gold ring with the black onyx stone and emblem on the man's hand had his radars on high alert. The few times he'd seen that emblem weren't pleasant ones. It would explain why a stranger would have access to the head of the CIA's office before eight on a Monday morning.

The man stood, walked around the table and extended his hand. "Leo Molineux. You are Director Smith?" Chris nodded, noting the French accent and the strength of the man's grip. "Please sit down." Leo pointed to one of the visitor's chairs in front of the table before he settled in the other.

Chris complied, taking another sip of the black brew. He could feel dark storm clouds starting to gather on the horizon.

"I want you to find someone who used to be part of your ESP program."

Chris tried to feign innocence, "Our ESP program?"

The other man scoffed, "Don't pretend you don't have one. The information is all online, although how you can have such a security breach is beyond me. It's beside the point though. I want you to find the woman and bring her in. My daughter is missing, and she's going to help me find her." He handed a slip of paper with a name on it to the Director.

Chris felt his face pull tight, "I'll pull up her file. I've heard of her, but she worked for us before I became Director."

Leo's face hardened, "I don't care. Find her and bring her in as fast as you can. Time is of the essence."

He didn't waste his breath to find out who Leo was to be ordering him around. Leo produced papers from inside his jacket that he placed on the table. With a malicious look he said, "There is your paperwork." Chris glanced over at it and saw the official seal of the President's office, feeling his heart sink even more.

Leo's voice had lowered an octave as he said, "You'll make this your first priority, right?" The threat radiating off the man made Chris's scalp prickle.

"I'll get right on it." He placed his coffee down, took the papers and moved to the seat behind his desk.

Leo Molineux got up and walked over to the door. He turned and said, "My contact details are on there, give me a call when you have her."

He disappeared through the door, closing it quietly behind him. Chris noticed he was clutching the papers in his hand, his knuckles white. He scowled and threw them on his desk. He'd better get to it then.

⊚

9:00 am, GMT-6. New Beginnings Ranch, Texas.

A low, unearthly sound vibrated right beneath the treehouse. Kirsty and Jean-Pierre woke with a start and sat up.

"What is that noise? Kirsty rubbed her face. Jean-Pierre got out and walked to the porch, he opened the sliding door and went out, but came back quickly.

"There seem to be cattle surrounding us." He went over to the wood burner and started packing the wood to light it.

Kirsty pulled her knees up and hugged them to her chest, "I wonder how the cattle got out."

There was a knock at their door, and Jean-Pierre opened it to find Luke holding a large hamper. "Morning! Hope the cattle didn't wake you. Emily thought you might like breakfast in bed, so she packed you a hamper. We need to round up the cattle before you can come down anyhow. Someone left the gate to their field open last night."

Jean-Pierre took the hamper from Luke. "Thank you, please thank Emily for us."

"Did Kirsty make it back all right last night?"

"Yes." Jean-Pierre glanced towards her quickly and then back at Luke, "I'm sorry about the gate. I left it open. I found her in the field sleepwalking and carried her back."

Luke's eyebrows furrowed, "Sleepwalking, hey? Well, no harm done. I'll see you guys this afternoon for the horse ride."

Jean-Pierre closed the door, placed the hamper on the bed and turned back to the woodstove. He could feel Kirsty's gaze on his back as he lit it. When it started burning, he padded back to the bed and got back in, his feet frozen.

He pulled the hamper closer and started unpacking it, "This is luxurious, having breakfast in bed. I hope you don't mind I arranged last night for us to go horse riding this afternoon."

Kirsty cleared her throat, "I don't mind." He handed her a plate. There was fresh juice and bagels with cheese and ham, blueberry muffins with butter and jam, a fruit salad, and dried jerky.

When they had finished most of it, Jean-Pierre placed their dirty plates and cups back in the hamper and moved it to the floor. He snuggled back down under the duvet, turning on his side to face Kirsty.

"You gave me quite a scare last night. Do you remember what happened?"

She shook her head where she sat, her long hair partly blocking her face. She twirled it in her fingers in front of her, "I remember falling asleep and waking up with you holding me."

"When I came back from dinner you weren't here. I searched for you in the stables and then asked Luke if you'd been to the house. I checked back here again before I searched around the other bungalows. My flashlight caught something white in the field, I went through the gate and found you standing in the middle of the field almost frozen. I carried you back and warmed you up. You've never sleepwalked before, have you?"

She sat very still her breathing quiet and regular, "Not that I know of." *Not recently, anyway.*

Jean-Pierre reached out and laid his hand on hers, "Do you remember something about Jumanos and a nun with a blue cloak?"

She jerked, "Why do you ask that?"

"You mentioned them when you came around."

Kirsty swallowed, avoiding his eyes she said, "I must have been dreaming. Maybe I read something about the history of this place. I don't remember." She squeezed his hand and moved so she was lying down facing him. "Thank you for helping me last night. I owe you one."

Jean-Pierre looked into her eyes, "You don't owe me anything."

"Well, I can try and make up for it." She moved closer, kissing him on the forehead and trailing her hand over his bicep.

"I'd like to see you try." His voice was warm and husky as he pulled her to him.

Kirsty picked up her white T-shirt off the floor. She was tidying up while Jean-Pierre took the hamper back to the house. Her hands trembled as she stared at the red mark on the white cotton. She felt like throwing the T-shirt into the fire, but that was irrational. She had to reason this out logically. The stain couldn't be from the chilli she had eaten with the nun. Bringing it to her nose, she sniffed it. Jerking it away again, her eyes widened. It smelt of chilli, this incriminating red mark on her T-shirt.

It couldn't be, she must have spilt something on it somewhere else. She thought, with rising hysteria, how scientists would laugh at her if she brought her evidence to prove she had travelled back in time. A chilli-smelling stain on her T-shirt; they would laugh her out of the building. But no matter how hard she tried, it stared her in the face like a blood stain. Evidence. Proof.

It's not real. I don't believe it. Not enough proof! Her thoughts screamed at the invisible entity who might be toying with her. She took the shirt to the bathroom and tried to wash out the stain with the handwash. It lightened but didn't disappear. Leaving the shirt to dry, she closed the bathroom door behind her.

A large engine revved outside, and Kirsty went out onto the porch. A yellow mustang had driven right up to the treehouse. The man inside spotted her and opening the car door, his curly, reddish-brown head ducked out as he looked up at her, "Hi! I didn't know Luke and Emily had other guests. I drove past the ranch house on purpose hoping they would hear the car but if they come out there won't be anyone. I wanted to surprise them and hide here. I'm Thomas by the way."

Kirsty laughed, "Hi, Thomas. She's a beauty. Is she yours?"

Thomas stroked over the roof and with a shake of his head said, "Only for a month. I rented her. I'm having a midlife crisis, as you can see."

Kirsty laughed again, "Well, it looks like you are making the most of it."

He grinned back up at her, "May I ask the name of the beauty in the treehouse?" His Irish accent made his words sound like music.

Kirsty had been leaning forward on the railing, but she stood up and pushed her hair behind her ear. "Kirsty Knight."

He made a mock bow, "Pleased to meet you, Kirsty Knight, I'm Thomas Quinn." He pointed down the track. "I'm going to go back and park like a civilised person instead of like a kid playing hide and seek. I hope to see you later!"

Jean-Pierre came walking back from the house, Thomas drove past him and neatly parked in front of the house. Kirsty waved at Jean-Pierre from the veranda.

"Who was that?" Jean-Pierre asked.

"I don't know. Says his name is Thomas Quinn, and he's friends with the owners. He's having a midlife crisis, so he rented the GT Ford for a month. He has an Irish accent."

Jean-Pierre joined her on the porch and placed his arm around her middle, "That's a lot of information out of a small conversation. I hope he knows you're taken?"

Kirsty batted her eyelids at Jean-Pierre, "Am I? She lifted her hand and wiggled it in front of him, "I don't see a ring."

Jean-Pierre growled, "If he comes near you, he'll have a thing or two coming."

"Ooh, I like it when you're a bit jealous. Maybe I should flirt with the Irishman so I can get a ring."

Jean-Pierre walked into the room, shaking his head, "No way, you are not putting a ring on me, woman. I'm a free spirit, not a traditionalist. Do you want to go for a walk?"

"Are all the Longhorns back in their field?"

Jean-Pierre nodded, "You should see those horns up close; they are enormous."

Kirsty's eyes were big. She didn't say it, but she had been in the same field as them for who knows how long. "Yes, to a walk. I'll put my boots on."

The temperature outside was rising by the minute, the skies bright and sunny. They walked all the way over to the field where the cattle were grazing. Kirsty leaned on the fence, staring at them. "They don't look that scary." As she said it, one bellowed out loud and made her jump.

They walked down to a river that ran a few hundred feet below their tree house. The water was crystal clear since it was spring fed. Kirsty trailed her hand through the water, finding it warmer than she expected. They walked next to it for a while in companionable silence enjoying the soothing murmur of the water.

On their way back, Jean-Pierre asked, "Are you comfortable going to the main house for lunch or should I fetch us something?"

Kirsty bit her lip before replying, "I think I'll be okay." Jean-Pierre slipped his hand into hers and said, "If you are okay, I'm okay. Okay?" A gentle smile spread on her face, "For a free spirit, you can be very traditionally romantic."

They shared a smile, and she gripped his hand more tightly.

11:00 am, GMT-5. New York.

With fast, jerky movements, Anna Martins walked up and down in the hotel room. *The arrogant, selfish bastard.* She kept seeing the face of her boss in her head wishing she could give him a piece of her mind. *I've worked my butt off to get my degree at the Milano Fashion Institute. Two years! Two years I've slaved away at his design firm in London, but I should have known all that glimmers aren't gold especially after what happened to Victoria.* She huffed her breath out and walked over to the window, staring out unseeingly, still clutching her suitcase in her hand. Charles Wade wanted more than an honest day's work from her. He wanted her.

It had all come to a head that morning when they booked into the hotel at the trade and fashion show in New York. They were a group of ten designers with Charles as their master designer and the rest of them next-level designers. He had booked them all into rooms in pairs to share. To her shock, he had calmly booked her in with himself as if they were an item. Not wanting to make a scene and embarrass him in front of everyone, she turned on him the moment they were in the hotel room. He laughed at her and said that she ought to be glad he picked her out of the crowd.

If she gave him what he wanted, he would make sure her name was the next big one in the fashion circles in London. Smearing honey around her mouth, he praised her designs and told her how much potential she had. She wouldn't want to throw all that away, now would she? He'd give her an hour to make up her mind, he said, before he gave her a kiss on the forehead and walked out.

Anna paused for a moment; her bright purple nails clenched tight around the handle of her suitcase. *The jerk. He has a wife.* Her nostrils flared as a tightness filled her chest. If she walked out now, she might never get another chance at her dream. At thirty-seven, she was already old to begin a career. She let go of the suitcase and rubbed her hand over her heart. Angry tears rolled down her cheeks. *Life isn't fair!*

Anna slumped to the floor of the hotel room. *I can't do it. It isn't worth throwing away my soul for my lifelong dream, or is it?*

Her thoughts jumped back to her one and only true love. He didn't recognise her when she accidentally met him after sixteen years, but she did. She would know him anywhere. There hadn't been a ring on his finger, but she kept as far away from him as possible. He walked out on her back then, so who's to say he ever really loved her anyway. Maybe he also wanted what Charles wanted and when he had that, he lost interest in her. Anna played with the silver ring on her finger. *I should have pretended that I was married. Not that it would have helped against the likes of Charles.*

She pushed her hands into her short, black bob and groaned. There had to be another way to fulfil her dream. Sleeping with her boss wasn't the way she wanted it to happen.

With the decision made, relief flooded her. She jumped up, grabbed her suitcase and left the hotel room. Her best friend lived on a ranch in the middle of Texas. She might as well go visit her, since she suddenly found herself without a job or plans for the immediate future.

She pushed the elevator button, waited for the doors to open and walked in. Observing herself in the full-length mirrors, she saw a short, slim woman dressed in colourful, fashionable clothes with white skin, red lips and purple fingernails. She made a face at herself. *I wonder what Ellie will think of this new development. She never liked Charles.* A pang of longing filled her for Ellie's soft arms around her. Maybe after Texas she could go back home for a visit. Wouldn't they love seeing her so soon after Christmas again.

1:00 pm, GMT-6, New Beginnings Ranch, Texas.

This was a mistake. As soon as they walked through the door, the twins had grabbed Kirsty by the hand and showed her where to sit, placing themselves on either side of her. Jean-Pierre sat at the one end of the table and Luke at the other end, with Thomas and Emily opposite Kirsty and the twins. The long rustic table was situated in a large room at the end of the house, opposite the kitchen. Kirsty was about to dip her spoon into the steaming bowl of vegetable soup when a small hand on her arm stopped her. "We haven't said grace!" The whole table heard Mercy say that and Kirsty's cheeks went red. Luke cleared his throat, "Let's do that, shall we?"

Everyone took hands, and Luke's deep voice said, "Father, thank you for friends, new and old. Bless this food to our bodies. Amen." The girls chorused his amen loudly and then started fighting over who had the most bread rolls.

Kirsty concentrated on her soup and listened to the conversation around her, glad that the girls were next to her.

Emily was laughing, "Thomas, we can't believe you are here. It feels like you married us years ago."

Thomas rubbed his chin, "It's been years, five to be exact."

Kirsty's head jerked up. *The Irishman is a minister?*

Jean-Pierre said, "So are you a religious man?"

Thomas met Kirsty's eyes for a second as if sensing his answer mattered to her, "You could say so. I've been a Methodist Minister for most of my life, but I'm on a semi-permanent sabbatical. I need a fresh perspective on things." He looked at Luke and Emily, "Thank you for having me. I needed a place to let my hair down."

Luke cleared his throat, "After what you've done for us, you will always have a home here."

Emily gave a little laugh, "I think the Mustang suits your new beginning. All you need now is a woman next to you."

Thomas' soup went the wrong way. He coughed and said, "I might have to drive to Vegas to find one, but I'm not that desperate. The Mustang is plenty of excitement for now."

Jean-Pierre lifted his eyebrows and said, "Yeah, safer too, I reckon."

Kirsty looked at Jean-Pierre and he shrugged.

Thomas' soft voice floated her way, "What do you say, Kirsty, should I stick to the Mustang?"

Kirsty bit her lower lip before saying, "She's a safe bet." She looked into his blue eyes and saw the mischief there which suddenly made her smile. Inclining her head, she said, "I could always help you sign up for an online dating service. I hear it is the way to get a wife these days."

Thomas' eyes widened in mock shock, "No ways, I don't think I would have the guts to meet strange women. Nobody would want to date a forty-year-old guy without a job, anyhow." The last bit was said in jest, but an undertone of bitterness laced his words.

Kirsty lifted her shoulders, "You'd be surprised. I've designed a dating site for a company, and I still do maintenance for them. There are all types of interesting people on there, and the matches they make are amazing. Their success rate is very high."

Emily grinned at Thomas, "Maybe you should give it a go. We have traditional dial up in the office. It couldn't be any worse than how Luke and I met, now can it?" She looked at Luke, her eyes warm with affection, "And just look how well, we turned out."

Grace piped up, "Mommy and Daddy met on a ship full of sharks and bad guys!"

Mercy not to be outdone said, "Yeah, and they had to run away and hide. That's when they fell in love."

Grace giggled, "They got married and got us from Romania."

Kirsty's mouth was hanging open as her eyes met those of Emily's, whose green ones were filled with laughter, "That's the gist of it. You girls got it right. Now, quickly go wash your hands so you can help Daddy get the horses ready for the trip." The girls left the table in a rush, and Kirsty found Emily studying her, "I couldn't have children. That's why we adopted them."

Luke placed his hand over Emily's and said, "They're such a blessing."

Then why does she have a bump? She felt Jean-Pierre's hand on hers, "Shall we go get ready for the ride too?"

Kirsty nodded and then looked at Thomas, "Are you going to join us?"

He grinned at her, "I think I will."

Jean-Pierre tugged at her hand, and she followed him out.

Thomas changed into suitable clothes for horseriding and looked around the bungalow. He could have stayed in the house, but he wanted some space so he'd chosen the furthest one out of sight from the main house. He eyed the battered guitar case on the bed. *I wonder if I'll remember how to play.* The case was covered in stickers from his teenage days. Good thing he'd bought some fresh strings to put on his boyhood plaything.

The yellow pine bungalow had two single beds on either side with a small kitchenette in the corner and a bathroom. What he liked best was the porch overlooking the fields. Two comfortable reclining chairs with a low table between them made a cosy spot.

He thought of Kirsty Knight's green eyes so alike to someone he knew long ago, and his shoulders dropped. *She's taken, go figure.*

Along the way, he'd bought himself a proper cowboy hat and boots and these he now donned before he made his way to the stables.

Luke whistled as he saw Thomas come through the door, "You look the part, brother, but can you ride the part too?"

Thomas gave a loud laugh, "Don't tell anyone, but I've never been on a horse before. You better give me your tamest horse the opposite of my car."

Luke grinned, "That would be Rosie. I think you'll get along well as long as no rattlesnakes cross our path."

"Rattlesnakes?" Tom's face scrunched up in alarm.

"Yeah, they can frighten even a tame horse, but we don't have many around. You're more likely to see a gopher. Your saddle has a hook in front that you can grab and hold onto if your horse ever gets spooked."

Thomas swallowed and said, "Maybe I should rethink this."

Kirsty and Jean-Pierre came in behind him, "Rethink what?" asked Kirsty. "You're not scared of a little horse-riding, are you?"

Thomas shook his head, "No, are you?"

She stroked the nose of the nearest horse, it was snow white, "No, I love them, I used to ride when I was a kid. Could I have this one?" She looked over at Luke.

Luke walked over to her and patted the horse's neck, "Lucy's a good horse, but she tends to be a bit skittish and nervous. Are you sure you can handle that?"

Kirsty rubbed the mare's white nose looking her in the eye. "We'll be fine, her and me."

Jean-Pierre chose a big bay horse, and Luke saddled them all including his own favourite dark gelding. The girls had helped him with the small tasks before they skipped back to the house to go play as they weren't big enough to go along on the long horse rides.

"Anybody want a hat? It helps to keep the sun out of your eyes," Luke looked at Kirsty and Jean-Pierre.

Kirsty lowered her black sunglasses and gave him a thumbs up. Jean-Pierre shook his head, in his comfortable Levi's he looked the part of a cowboy without the boots and the hat. They rode single file down a well-trodden path that led down to the river, the same one Kirsty and Jean-Pierre had walked along that morning.

Speaking over his shoulder, Luke said, "I'm going to take you on an hour trail. You all have water on your saddles and some jerky. If you need anything, just ask."

Once on top of Rosie, Thomas found the ground further down than he thought. *I hope I don't look like a novice.* The motion of the horse beneath him took some getting used to, but he found he rather liked the rhythmic movement. The bushes were thick in some places, leaving barely enough space for them to pass.

They rounded a bend in the river, and Luke pulled in his horse. He looked back over his shoulder, "You can't see anything, but this used to be a stopping place for the Jumano Indians when they came hunting in these parts. They've found spearheads and pieces of pottery around here." Kirsty paled slightly; glad the sunglasses could hide her expression. She felt Jean Pierre's puzzled gaze on her.

Turning away from the river they crossed a field towards a rocky outcrop. There was a small structure against the hill. As they neared it, Kirsty gave a small gasp. Jean-Pierre looked at her with a frown and then at the structure which was a sculpture of a nun inside a protective hollow wall. The inscription read: 'In honour of the Lady in Blue, who brought faith to our land.'

Luke pointed at it and said, "I don't know if you've heard of her, but she is a mystical nun from 1600 who reportedly travelled here via bi-location and brought faith to the Jumano tribe amongst others. Even the national flower of Texas, the Bluebonnet, is named after her as legend says once she levitated into the air and left a trail of these flowers behind her. You won't see them this time of year, but come springtime, and they spring up everywhere. It is quite a sight."

Thomas happened to glance over at Kirsty and Jean-Pierre and saw Jean-Pierre look at Kirsty with a strange look on his face, while her face looked pale like she'd seen a ghost.

Luke said, "From here it's a straight path back to the house so if anyone fancies a run you can let go of your horses now."

Kirsty pulled her horse around and kicked it in the sides taking off at a gallop. Thomas whistled, "Wow, she sure knows how to ride a horse."

Jean-Pierre grunted, "Yeah, just something else she neglected to tell me." He flicked the reins on his own horse and started on a slower gallop after her. Luke stayed with Thomas as they started walking back. After a few minutes of silence, Thomas cleared his throat, "You have a beautiful ranch here."

Luke looked at him sideways, "Yeah, my dream come true. I'm astonished at how many people we've been able to help get their lives back on track just by offering them a safe, quiet place like this."

Thomas looked down at Rosie's black mane, she flicked her tail at an imaginary insect, "I can't lie, I feel like I need something to help me get back on track too."

Luke cleared his throat, "As a wise minister once told me, all you need to do is take one step, He'll do the rest."

A chuckle escaped Thomas' throat, "Use my words against me, won't you."

A grin spread over Luke's face, "He also said that he would be there for me, night or day, and I'll extend that invitation now to you. I'm here for you, anytime."

Thomas felt his throat tighten and he nodded. He gripped the reins tighter as Rosie had increased her pace. She'd spotted the stables and was heading for her warm stall.

"I want you to go see Emily for a counselling session." Kirsty felt her mouth open and close at Jean-Pierre's unexpected statement.

"Why?"

"Do you really want an answer to that?"

She flinched as if he'd struck her. Jean-Pierre turned his back on her and put extra wood on their wood burner, he dusted his hands off and turned around, "I'll go see her too if you want."

Kirsty made a strangling sound, "How can I go talk to her about losing my baby, while she has one in her stomach. I can't do that." Her voice rose in anger.

They both turned at the sound of someone climbing the stairs of the treehouse. Emily appeared in the open doorway with a tray laded with biscuits and muffins.

"I'm sorry, the girls baked these for you this afternoon and I wanted to bring them over." She paused, "I didn't mean to overhear you, but I know what it feels like to lose a child."

Jean-Pierre walked over to her and took the tray, "Won't you come in?" he asked, his eyes pleading with her.

"Sure, if you'll make us some tea?" She walked over to one of the seats in front of the fireplace and sank down into it. Kirsty still stood frozen to the spot across from her as Jean-Pierre walked over to the kettle and filled it with water.

Emily rubbed her hands on her jeans and said, "I haven't shared my story many times, but sometimes it helps to know you are not alone in your pain. I was raped at fourteen, fell pregnant, and secretly aborted the baby which gave me scars. They said I'd never have children."

Kirsty felt herself move forward and take the seat opposite Emily.

Emily was staring into the fire as she said, "I'd given up on the dream of marrying and having children, but God had other plans and brought Luke across my path who took me as I was." She looked at Kirsty and smiled, "We adopted Mercy and Grace, calling them that to remind us of the mercy and grace we had found in our lives."

"I don't understand. Why are you?" Kirsty struggled to say the words.

Emily placed her hand on her bump and said, "I know, it's impossible but true. A few months ago, we visited my parents in New York. We attended their church who happened to have a faith-healing evangelist visiting. At one point he thundered out a prayer for healing over the whole congregation and I felt this warmth in my belly. I didn't make anything of it at the time, not even thinking of the scars. We came home, went on as usual and then I started feeling sick. When I didn't get any better, we took a trip to the doctor and he took blood and congratulated us. We were blown away."

Kirsty placed her hands on her own stomach, her jaw clenched. Jean-Pierre handed Emily a cup of tea and offered one to Kirsty. She took it with shaking hands. He brought the tray with the muffins and biscuits and put it on the low table between them, settling on the floor in front of the fire.

"Why do you believe in God?" Kirsty asked, and Jean-Pierre looked up at her, his dark eyes searching her face.

Emily frowned, "I grew up in church, but only when I went through trauma in my life, did He become real to me."

Kirsty shook her head, "I don't want to know a deity who throws such things at us."

Emily cleared her throat, "Without getting theological I'd like to point out that we live in a free world with free choices, in a world tainted by darkness. God is the light that destroys the darkness."

Jean-Pierre looked at Emily, "Light and darkness. Like the yin and yang. The one can't exist without the other, right? So, God created both and is in both?"

Emily took a muffin from the tray and bit into it, she stared into the fire, "I don't have all the answers and maybe no one has, but I believe God hates evil. Evil has perverted what God created as good and ultimately, He is going to destroy it. He is good. I believe that with all my heart. Look how he restored my womb and gifted us a child without me even asking."

She looked at them both with warmth in her eyes, "Thank you for the tea. I need to go rest before dinner. Luke is cooking his famous stew tonight. If you want any sessions, you know where to find me. This one is on the house. She winked at Kirsty and Kirsty gave her a small smile back.

Jean-Pierre walked with her to the door, handing her the empty tray, "Thank you."

She started going out the door but stopped, "I forgot to tell you, Luke is going into San Antonio tomorrow. I have an unexpected friend arriving, whom he's picking up at the airport. If you need anything you can give him a list." She zipped up her jacket and trudged down the stairs. Jean-Pierre closed the door behind her and stood still for a moment before turning back towards Kirsty. He walked over and took the seat Emily had vacated.

Kirsty sat staring into the flames.

"Kirsty?"

She turned towards him, "Yes?"

The firelight danced in her green depths, and he took a deep breath, exhaling he said, "I'm tired of pretending."

Her eyebrows lifted and she tilted her head, "Pretending?"

He tore his eyes away from her face and focused on the fire, his hands clenched on his lap. "Pretending that everything is fine when it's not. Pretending that I still want to try for children when I don't."

Kirsty struggled to get the words out, "You don't?"

He shook his head, his throat thick, "I can't go through this again. It's destroying me, you, us."

"But we want children? Don't we?" Kirsty's voice wavered; her hands clenched tighter on her lap.

Jean-Pierre stood up and placed another log on the fire, he stayed standing with his back to her, his shoulders slumped. "Why don't we adopt, Kirsty? Look at Mercy and Grace, adoption can be great."

"I don't want to adopt. I want my own family."

"I'm starting to feel like the only reason you're with me, is to have children. What if you must choose between having children and me? What then?" He turned around, staring down at her. "If I'm just a sperm donor, you could go get sperm at any sperm bank in the country. You'd be spoiled for choice."

"Don't be ridiculous. You mean much more to me, than jus-just that." Kirsty licked her dry lips, her face stormy.

Jean-Pierre crouched down in front of her, forcing her to make eye contact, "Can't you see that you've become obsessed with it? You're sleepwalking, for goodness' sake and thin as a rake!"

He heard her breath hitch, felt her body go rigid in front of him, "Why did you look like you saw a ghost when you saw that statue today? You said you didn't remember your dream, but you did."

"It was a silly dream. Not worth mentioning." She closed her eyes breaking their connection. *Stop asking me!*

"It seemed to shake you up. Why not tell me about it? Why won't you tell me what you found out about your birth at your parent's house either?"

Her hands clenched tight in her lap, her silence stretching the distance between them.

"Tell me!" Jean-Pierre's voice jarred through her.

She shook her head, "I don't want to." *I can't.*

He looked at her his eyes blazing, "Why not?

Kirsty's eyes were downcast as she sat with her hands balled on her lap, "You'd think I'm crazy." *Tell him.*

Jean-Pierre's pupils dilated, "I know all about crazy. Why don't you try me?"

She shook her head, "It's not real, Jean-Pierre. It doesn't matter."

Jean-Pierre felt like a punch hit him in the stomach, with barely controlled breath he said, "What's not real, Kirsty?"

"The dreams, the things I see." *Oh no!*

His hands were shaking as he got up and paced away from her a few steps, he pushed a hand through his hair, "Do you see things? Things that aren't real?" *This can't be happening.*

"No, I meant the things I see in my dreams." She bit her bottom lip and rubbed the back of her neck. *Please believe me.*

Jean-Pierre looked at her, his face tight, "I think we both need help and maybe," he paused and inhaled, "time apart."

"Are you serious?" Kirsty tensed up, "You drag me all the way out here to tell me this? You could have told me in Toronto!"

Jean-Pierre rubbed his forehead, his brows pulling in.

What've I done? Kirsty stood up and walked over to him, placing her hands against his chest, "Don't do this, we can work it out. I'll go see Emily if that's what you want."

He stood, his muscles taut, "It's not about what I want. You need to realise what you want, and for that to happen I need to go away."

"I want you!" Kirsty's eyes pleaded with him.

His forehead pressed against hers for a moment, his eyes closed, "I'm sorry." The words bled through his lips. "I'm going to go to town with Luke tomorrow and fly out to Ugarte-Garcia." Part relief, part anguish rushed through him as the words left his mouth. *I've got to get away.*

He moved past her and retrieved his hand carrier out from under the bed, filling it with a change of clothes, pyjamas and his toothbrush. The zip of the bag sounded metallic in the air as he shut the case.

"Jean-Pierre, don't do this." Her whisper barely reached his ears, as he walked across to the door, opened it and closed it behind him. He went down the stairs, planning on asking Luke to let him sleep in a spare bungalow. Wiping his face with his sleeve, he found it wet. Scowling, he walked down the path towards the ranch house trying to ignore the ache that grew with every step he took away from her.

CHAPTER 5

6:45 am, GMT-6. Tuesday, 13th January. New Beginnings Ranch, Texas.

Kirsty woke up early. She lay still for a few minutes listening to the birdsong in the trees. The bed felt empty without Jean-Pierre. *I miss him already.* A deep sigh escaped her, she turned over on her stomach. *He thinks I'm going crazy.* Kirsty shivered. *If he knew...* A pang of loneliness shot through her at the thought of him leaving. *What if he never came back?* She felt a numbness take hold of her.

She got up, dressing quickly for the room was chilly; the wood burner's fire had died hours before. She tied up her hair, rolled her tight shoulders and looked at the time on her phone. The battery was going down fast even on aeroplane mode. It surprised her that it was still before seven in the morning. Breakfast wasn't until eight. Luke had brought her a bowl of his stew the night before for which she was grateful. Taking the empty bowl and spoon she zipped up her jacket and walked over to the main house. Everything was quiet and deserted.

Kirsty's heart pounded as she imagined finding Jean-Pierre and begging him not to leave. Her throat burned. *He could have anyone he wants, maybe he'd be better off without me in his life.*

She found the front door open, silently she slipped in and left the bowl in the kitchen. On her way out again, she saw a side table with paper and pen. On impulse, she scribbled a note on it before she let herself out and went over to the stables. In no time, she had Lucy saddled and led her out of the stables. The horse was frisky as if she felt the same need to get out. Kirsty walked her the first few hundred feet, and then they took off on a fast gallop down the trail that led towards the hills. No one saw them leave.

Luke frowned at the note and looked up at Emily who stood waiting for him in the hallway, "Kirsty's taken Lucy out for a ride on her own."

Emily lifted her eyebrows, "Does she know what she's doing?"

Luke rubbed his chin, "Yes. She looks like an experienced rider, but I still don't like it."

Emily's face crinkled in a smile, "Don't worry. I've gone out on my own plenty of times. I think she needs space."

Luke walked over to her and tucked her against him kissing her on the mouth. "I'll be back this afternoon. If there're any problems ask Thomas to help you, okay?"

She pursed her lips, "I'll miss you, but I'm so excited about Anna coming!"

Luke rolled his eyes, "I might need to go stay with Thomas for a night and let you girls have a girls' night."

Emily giggled, "That would be weird."

He laughed, "Yeah, I did say nothing would ever get me out of your bed again, Señorita. You two just need to do all your talking in the day."

There was a sound at the door, and they turned to see Jean-Pierre with his hand luggage. Luke let go of Emily and said, "Ready to go?" Jean-Pierre nodded and gave a small wave in Emily's direction before he turned around.

Emily bit her lower lip; she wanted to plead with him to stay. Running away wasn't ever a good idea, but she knew she had to keep quiet and trust that things would work out for them.

They got in the pickup and were gone in minutes. Emily

walked into the large farmhouse kitchen and started preparing breakfast. It wouldn't be long before the twins would rush in, ready for food. She looked out and saw a few clouds beginning to drift over the blue sky. Hopefully, Kirsty would be back long before they had any rain. Emily closed her eyes and breathed a prayer for the couple.

Thomas opened the guitar case and took out his old guitar. The previous day he'd changed the strings and they looked shiny and new on the old instrument. He took it outside to the porch where he had already placed a bottle of Irish Whiskey and a glass on the table. Tentatively he started strumming and before long, his fingers flew to familiar places like long lost friends coming home.

Thomas was so absorbed in playing that he didn't hear the soft footfall that came to a standstill at the bottom of his porch steps. The sun was setting in fabulous colours of red, orange and pink across the field in front of him. As he glanced up, he saw her standing there listening to him. His fingers came to an abrupt halt his breath hitching. He stared at her.

Realizing he was staring he cleared his throat, "Hi."

"Hi, sorry, I didn't mean to disturb you."

"It's okay. Did you want something?"

Her head shook, her long hair swinging to and fro, "I went for a walk, heard you playing and found myself here."

A small grin tugged the corners of his mouth, "I'm rusty. Do you play?"

She pushed her hair behind her ear, giving him a shy smile, "In my teens, last."

"Me too. Want to have a go?"

"I don't know."

"Come on." He stood up and held out the guitar to her. She took a step closer and took it by the neck. Sitting down on the top porch step with the guitar on her lap, she gave a few strums before she started playing a haunting sad tune. Thomas sat down opposite her his gaze fixed on her. When she stopped, he gave a small clap, "That was beautiful. Who wrote it?"

Her cheeks coloured, "My teenage self." Standing up she placed the guitar carefully on the seat, turned and pushed her hands into her pockets. The sunset arrested her eyes, it was fast disappearing leaving a few stars coming out in the blackening sky. Her gaze came back to him, "I guess I should be going."

He unfolded his tall frame from the steps pushing his hands into his own pockets, "Do you have plans for tonight?"

Taking in the bottle of whiskey on his table the corner of her mouth lifted, "I see you have plans."

His hand wiped across his face, "Just giving this midlife crisis a run for its money."

She rocked back on her heels pushing her hands deeper into her pockets, "They say it's not good to drink alone."

A little snort escaped him, "I wouldn't know." His face lifted hopefully, "Do you want to join me? I could find another glass?"

A few different emotions flickered across her face before she shrugged, "Sure, if you don't mind sharing."

A smile spread on his face, "I think a bottle is enough between us? Come, sit down. I'll find a glass."

Two hours later, Kirsty sat snuggled up with blankets on the chair with a glass in her hand, Thomas sat across from her, the brown blankets draped around him like a cloak. He looked across the low table at her, "You're pretty, you know that?"

Her lips pouted, "They say so. Not as pretty as my mother though."

He rubbed the back of his neck, "Here I am forty and single, chatting up a woman almost ten years younger than me."

A giggle erupted from her, "I'm only seven years younger."

Rolling his eyes, he said, "I feel old. Like life somehow passed me by."

She gave a slight shake of her head, "I wish I could swap places with someone else."

Glancing over at her before taking another sip of the golden liquid he asked, "What would you change if you could?"

Her eyes stared out into the darkness, "To be normal. Not have the ability to see things others don't."

Thomas stirred in his chair, "That sounds boring."

A shudder went through her, "If you know the things I've seen, you wouldn't say so. Everyone says it isn't real, just hallucinations, but it feels so real, so scary."

"Are you talking about demons?"

Kirsty looked over at him, barely making out his features in the dark, "Have you seen one?"

He took another sip and shrugged, "I wouldn't say so per se, but I've seen them at work. I believe they're real."

"It's impossible. Scientifically impossible. Ghosts, demons, those things are figments of our imaginations."

His eyes closed, "Who says so?"

"They do. The scientists, physicists, people who study our world. I studied it myself. It defies the laws of our universe."

"Do you think they know everything? How many dimensions and unseen worlds could there be?"

"That exist at the same time and place as our world? Intertwined?"

Silence filled the space around them. Thomas refilled their glasses.

"You know, for a minister you believe some weird things."

A low laugh rumbled out of him, "I'm Irish remember, we grow up being taught about spirits and stuff. It's part of our culture."

She shook her head, "When I grew up, anything remotely spiritual was unrealistic nonsense."

He could feel her eyes on him before she said, "What would you say if I told you that I met with that Lady in Blue the first night I was here? I lay down on my bed and the next minute I woke up on grass, 400 years back in time. The Jumanos found me and took me to their camp. She was there with them. She fed me chilli beans and talked to me about how she used to see things her parents didn't believe was true and how I needed to find my destiny."

Kirsty took a breath, "It was so real, Thomas, as real as me sitting talking here with you. The next morning my shirt had a red stain where I had spilt some of the chilli. How can that be?"

Thomas swallowed the lump in his throat, "Would you

believe me if I told you I'm jealous?"

"Jealous?"

"Yes. I've followed God all my life and never have I had an experience like you. I learned about the Lady in Blue in Seminary. To meet her and talk to her, wow!"

"That whiskey has gone straight to your head. I'd give my ability, gift, curse, call it what you like, to you in a heartbeat."

Thomas laughed, "You're not wrong, it has gone straight to my head. Lucky I'm not a minister anymore."

"You're not?"

"Nope, I got fired."

"Why?"

"Because they wanted a couple instead of a bachelor. After ten years I wasn't good enough anymore. Maybe never was."

Kirsten took a careful sip of her whiskey and then whispered into the air, "Why didn't you marry and have kids?"

Thomas sat quietly before replying, "I wish I could say I never met the right girl, but I did. She was too young and Catholic. Her family said they would kill me if I ever came near her again. She had five brothers, so it wasn't an idle threat, but some days I wish I'd grabbed her and ran away."

"Why didn't you?"

Thomas gave a self-deprecating laugh, "I was nineteen and penniless." He inclined his head, "Your eyes remind me of hers."

Kirsty sat forward, "Did you ever go back? Try and find her again?"

Thomas shook his head, "They used to be our neighbours, but they moved and I didn't know where. I think I was afraid of finding she'd moved on. Forgotten about me." He turned his head in her direction, "Why did Jean-Pierre leave?"

Kirsty sat back and emptied her glass, "We lost a baby three months ago and since then…." her voice trailed away.

"I'm sorry."

"So am I."

Placing her glass on the table, she tried to stand up, finding her balance not quite there. Thomas stood too and caught hold of her arm, they stood holding each other steady.

"Your Irish Whiskey is something else."

"It is." Thomas looked down at her. He cleared his throat, "Do you want to bunk down here? There are two single beds? I don't think I'd be able to escort you over to your treehouse and find my way back."

She giggled and tried to let go of his arm but found the world swaying. "It sounds like a plan."

"Hold on, I'll lead the way." They got hold of the blankets on their chairs barely staying upright, navigated the doorstep and closed the door behind them leaving the room dark. Thomas helped her to the left single bed, on which she sat down. He gave a mock salute clutching his blanket with the other hand, "I'll see you in the morning when hopefully the world won't spin anymore."

He stumbled over to his bed, spread the blankets over it, kicked off his shoes and crawled in without bothering to put on pyjamas.

"Thomas?" her voice floated out to him in the darkness.

"Hmmm?"

"Do you really believe God exists?"

Silence lasted for a few seconds from the other bed.

"Yes."

Kirsty stayed quiet for a long time.

"Thomas?"

"Hmmm?" His voice was sleepy.

"Do you think if you asked Him, He might help me?"

"I'm not exactly speaking to Him."

"For me?"

"For you."

"Thanks."

9:00 am, GMT-6. Wednesday, 14th January. New Beginnings Ranch, Texas.

Anna sat around the breakfast table, enjoying the chatter of the twins, who'd taken to her like ducks to water. They wanted their nails painted like hers and wanted her to help them make dresses for their dolls. *Like Ellie, when she was little.* She felt a pang of longing in her heart for her own daughter.

"Come on, girls, give Anna and me some time to chat. You can go draw what you want to make for your dolls in the playroom." They jumped up and ran out of the kitchen like little whirlwinds and Anna shook her head, "You sure have your hands full."

Emily smiled as she watched their departure, "I know, full of blessing." She poured coffee into their cups and sat down at the table. "Now, tell me all your news. How's it going at your dream job? I was surprised that you'd get leave to visit me on such short notice."

Anna's smile fell, "It's not. I quit."

"Why?" Emily looked at her best friend with concern.

"You remember our landlord in Milan?"

"Yeah?"

"Well, his type parade around in business suits too. Only some of them will evict you if you say no."

"Oh, honey. I'm sorry. You've worked so hard for this."

"I know, but somehow I feel okay. Almost free. It wasn't worth selling myself for, anyhow."

Emily placed her hand on Anna's, "If it's any consolation, I'm there for you. You are an amazing fashion designer; I'm sure God will make a way for you."

Anna laughed, "It means a lot to me. I thought a few days here with you and Luke should help me recover before I fly back home. I miss Ellie."

"How's she doing? Is she still studying music?"

"She is. Her second year is going well. You should hear her play the violin. It is beautiful."

"I'll never forget that holiday I had at your home. Your family is so close-knit and warm."

Anna looked around the large kitchen. "You've created a lovely family right here. I thought you had guests that eat with you?"

Emily stood up and collected their empty cups, "We only have two guests, Kirsty Knight from Toronto and Thomas Quinn from England. You remember the pastor who married us? He is on a sabbatical and drove all the way from New York to us in nothing other than a Mustang. I expected them for breakfast, but with guests you never know."

Anna had gone quiet and when Emily looked over at her there was a paleness on her face. "Anna?"

Anna shook her head and stood up, "Sorry, I think I need some fresh air. I'll go for a walk."

Emily watched her leave with a slight frown on her face.

Anna slipped into her boots and zipped up her jacket. It was nearing ten o'clock, and the ground was starting to defrost as another bright sunny day unfolded. She headed in a random direction her thoughts scrambling. *Thomas Quinn. The one man I didn't want to see ever again.* She walked around the bungalows noticing how tidy they were. She rounded a corner and saw the door of the last bungalow open.

Upon instinct she held back, half hiding behind the wall of the fourth bungalow, A woman with dark brown hair and American Indian features came out first, zipping up her jacket. Behind her followed a tall, reddish-brown haired man she recognised instantly. The woman stopped, and they spoke to each other before the man gave her a quick hug. The woman walked away, and Anna pulled back behind the wall afraid of being seen. Her heart was beating wildly in her chest as it squeezed in pain.

4:00 pm, GMT+1. Ugarte Villa outside Vitoria Gasteiz, Spain.

Jean-Pierre placed his hand luggage down on the red-tiled floor and stood in the entrance of his family's villa. The usual quiet sounds of the countryside drifted past him from behind. Vineyards and fields surrounded the old place. The family's limousine had collected him from the airport in the capital, Vitoria Gasteiz: *It's good to be home.* He found his father in his home office, at the back of the villa.

"Jean-Pierre!" He raised his large frame from the chair

and clapped Jean-Pierre on the back, "When I heard you were coming, I thought I heard wrong. Are you home to stay?"

Jean-Pierre flexed his shoulders, "I don't know. For a few weeks at least." He took in his father's dark tanned face that had a few wrinkles added to it since he last saw him. His black curly hair was thinning, but other than that he looked the same.

His father raised bushy eyebrows at him, "Where is that Kirsty woman from the North? The one keeping you there in the cold?"

Jean-Pierre rolled his eyes, "She doesn't keep me there, dad." He hesitated, "She and I are having a little time apart."

"Good, good." His father gave him another clap on the back. "Maybe if I can introduce you to a few warm-blooded women from your own country, I could entice you to stay."

Jean-Pierre walked over to the window and placed his hands on the thick balcony railing, staring out over the brown vineyard below. "I'm not here to find a woman, I want to focus on my art. Hire a studio or set one up here."

"Humph! You can always paint later. You have a family to catch up with and don't you want to see how your inheritance is doing? A lot has happened since you've been here. Come let me give you a tour."

Jean-Pierre clenched his jaw, turned and followed his father out of the office.

1:00 pm, GMT-6. New Beginnings Ranch, Texas.

Thomas walked into the house whistling a tune. Despite waking up with a headache, he was feeling fine. Down the long hallway to the dining room on the right, he strode looking forward to lunch since he'd missed breakfast.

The twins were seated at the table and he sat down across from them, nodding hello to Luke at the head of the table just as Emily came in with a bowl of delicious smelling spaghetti and bolognese. He dished up his plate high and could barely wait for

Luke to finish his prayer before he dug in.

Footsteps sounded outside the door, and he saw Kirsty hovering as if uncertain. He jumped up and pulled out a chair for her. Her face brightened as she came in and sat next to him.

"You don't want to miss this. Emily's outdone herself again." He gave her a reassuring look.

Kirsty glanced at Emily and dished up her plate, "Thank you, Emily."

Emily smiled at Kirsty and then said, "My pleasure."

Grace piped up, "This is mom's specaltee."

Mercy giggled, "You mean speciality." She stretched the word out, syllable by syllable.

Grace rolled her eyes, "You know what I mean." She looked at Kirsty with twinkling eyes, "It's my favourite."

Kirsty's eyes widened, "It's one of my favourites too!"

Grace's face bloomed.

Thomas swallowed a mouthful of spaghetti and looked around the table, "I thought you had a friend arrive yesterday?"

Emily's forehead creased, "Yes, she excused herself from lunch, she isn't feeling well. Anna was my maid of honour at the wedding, she also made my wedding dress. Do you remember her, Thomas?"

"Anna?" Thomas squinted his eyes, "I thought she looked familiar at the wedding, but never got a chance to talk to her. Where do you know her from?"

"We were flatmates in Milan when I was working as a model and she was studying clothing design."

"Where's she from?"

"Why all the questions?" Emily playfully pulled a face at him, "Are you interested in her?"

Thomas shook his head and rolled his eyes giving Kirsty a grin.

Emily inhaled and said, "She's Irish like you and comes from Londonderry. I visited her once, lovely place."

Thomas had stopped eating and sat staring at Emily as if made from stone. Everyone at the table looked at him, sensing his change in demeanour. He cleared his throat twice before croaking out, "What's her surname?"

Emily licked her lips, "Anna Martins?"

Thomas's face turned the same shade of white Anna's had that morning as he mutely repeated, "Anna Martins."

"Do you know her?" Emily ventured; her eyes big.

Thomas pushed his chair back leaving his half-eaten plate, "I might. Sorry, I need to get some air." Like a man in a daze, he turned and walked out of the room.

Luke looked at Emily with raised eyebrows, "What was that all about?"

Emily shrugged, "I don't know. Anna had a strange reaction this morning when I mentioned him as if she knows him too."

Kirsty's eyes went big, but she kept quiet. She had an inkling of who Anna might be.

After lunch Luke, the twins and Kirsty went to the stables. The twins had their weekly riding lesson and Kirsty was going to take Lucy out for a ride.

After clearing up the kitchen Emily went to Anna's door and knocked. Her muffled voice answered. She opened the door and found Anna lying on her stomach, her face in her pillow.

"Anna? Do you know Thomas? I told him your surname and where you're from, and he looked like he'd seen a ghost."

Her friend sat up, her face streaked, bringing her legs close to her chest she whispered, "He's Ellie's dad."

Emily sank down on the bed next to her, "Oh, Anna!" She placed her arms around her friend and let her cry on her shoulder.

CHAPTER 6

4:00 pm, GMT-6. New Beginnings Ranch, Texas.

Luke heard the noise of a pickup coming into the yard and wiped his dirty hands on his jeans before closing the stable he'd been cleaning. He walked out of the barn and scrutinised the unknown black pickup with the tinted windows. *Government issued. I wonder what it's doing here.* Tipping his cowboy hat back he walked towards it. Four men in suits climbed out, and his senses went into high alert.

"Can I help you fellows?"

One of the men with blond hair and blue eyes took him in as if assessing him before saying, "Luke Johnson?"

"That would be me. Who are you?"

"Special Agent Lewis Carter with the CIA. We are looking for someone called Kirsten Knight. Our intel shows that she was last headed here."

Luke crossed his arms. "There is a lady called Kirsty Knight staying here."

The agent stepped closer to Luke, "If you could direct us to her accommodation, please?"

Luke inclined his head, "I know it's none of my business, but the CIA doesn't normally send a task force to find an innocent civilian on holiday, on a ranch in the middle of nowhere."

Agent Carter's face remained impassive, "It is none of your

business, Mr Johnson. Sufficient for you to know that we need to locate her and bring her in."

Luke uncrossed his arms, "Well, you'll have to wait. She took a horse out and might not be back for two hours. In the meantime I might make a few phone calls to find out if you guys are legit."

A twitch appeared in the corner of Agent's Carter's cheek as he clenched his jaw, "If you could show us the direction she took, we might try to track her down."

Luke laughed, "She has a head start of at least an hour and could have gone any direction. It would be easier to wait for her. You are welcome to have coffee with us. I'll let my wife know."

Agent Carter shook his head, "Thank you, but we will wait in the SUV after you've shown us her accommodation."

Luke shrugged, "Suit yourself."

He gave them directions to the treehouse before striding into the house, straight to his home office. After half an hour he came out, the frown lines etched more deeply on his forehead. Emily, Anna and the twins were in the kitchen making pancakes.

Mercy ran up to him and he caught her in his arms, "Who are those angry-looking men in the car, Daddy?"

Luke's eyes connected with Emily before he said, "They're government men, here to talk to Miss Kirsty."

Grace frowned as she sat at the table with a plate of pancakes in front of her, "I don't like them. I waved at them out of the window, and they ignored me."

Luke patted her head as he walked past and sat down at the table, "I don't blame you. Who can ignore such a cutie pie?"

Emily placed a plate in front of him, her eyes troubled, "Could you find out anything?"

Luke shook his head, "My contact said I must stay out of it. There is nothing I can do. It appears she used to work for them."

Anna shook her black bob and sat down next to Luke, "It's strange that they would come out all the way here to find her. Maybe she's hiding something."

Grace piped up, "I like Miss Kirsty. She's just sad."

Mercy added, "Maybe she's a spy?"

Luke shook his head at the girls, "I'm sure Miss Kirsty is a normal lady, who just needs our prayers."

Kirsty reigned in Lucy as she crested a small hill that overlooked the ranch. She stared across the bushes, her eyes finally resting on the buildings down below. There was a black pickup that wasn't there before. Something uneasy shifted in her stomach. *It's them. I know it, but why? Had my activities been noticed? Surely, it's far below their interest.* The urge to flee welled up strongly in her, but she resisted. *If it's them I'm glad Jean-Pierre left.* She wiped the sweat of her brow, moved her shoulders back and started down the hill, her chin set.

Dusk was settling in as she neared the stables unseen, having dismounted a few hundred feet away. She patted Lucy's hot flank murmuring her thanks to the horse for the ride. Leading her into the semi-dark stables, a black figure appeared out of the shadows.

""Hush, Kirsty. It's me, Thomas."

"Thomas?"

"There are men outside waiting for you?"

Her movements paused and her head bowed down, before she led Lucy into her stable and started unsaddling her. Thomas came into the stable and stood by Lucy's head.

"Anything I can do?"

Kirsty shook her head.

He cleared his throat, "Remember that girl I told you about? The one I loved when I was young?"

Kirsty's eyes settled on him, "Anna?"

He nodded, his jaw clenched, "She knows it's me. I know it."

Kirsty started brushing the sweat of Lucy with methodical strokes, "Give her a chance, Thomas. Don't jump to conclusions."

His body relaxed as he stepped nearer to her, "Are you going to be okay? Should we make a getaway in the Mustang?"

That got a small smile out of her. She focused her green eyes on him, "I wish. They must have a reason. I used to work for them."

Thomas cleared his throat, "I've asked Him to help you."

Before Kirsty could reply footsteps could be heard outside the doors and the next moment the barn filled with men in suits.

"Kirsten Knight?"

Kirsty stilled before continuing to brush the horse.

The leader of the men stepped up to the stable door, his hard gaze fell on Thomas who retreated to stand next to Kirsty.

She stopped brushing Lucy and turned towards the man at the door, "I'm Kirsty Knight. Kirsten Knight doesn't exist anymore."

"I'm Special Agent Lewis Carter, and I've been instructed to bring you in. You resemble Kirsten Knight, so I'll presume Kirsty and Kirsten are one and the same. Will you please come with us?" The last sentence was said like an order.

Kirsty handed the brush to Thomas, "Will you please finish brushing Lucy?" Wordlessly, Thomas took the brush, his hand squeezing hers as he did. She turned towards Agent Carter, "I can assure you that whatever reason you have for taking me in, it's going to prove fruitless. Whatever I did for your agency in the past, I can't do anymore."

Agent Lewis looked into her eyes, he licked his lips and said, "I'm only following orders, Miss Knight. It would make my job easier if you came willingly."

She rubbed her brow and walked towards him, "I want to collect my stuff in the treehouse."

"We've already collected it for you."

Kirsty narrowed her eyes and made as if she wanted to say something but then pursed her lips, "Okay, Agent Lewis. Can I say goodbye to my hosts, at least?"

He dipped his chin. She turned towards Thomas, gave him a small farewell smile and wave which he reciprocated before she walked out of the barn. The men fell in around her like four bodyguards.

At the steps to the porch they stopped, and she went past them up the steps. The door was open and in the twilight two little bodies came running out. "Auntie Kirsty!"

She bent down and hugged them both at the same time, "Hi,

Mercy and Grace. I'm going to go away, but I'll never forget you two." Mercy cupped her mouth with her hands and whispered loudly in Kirsten's ear, "Are you a spy?" Kirsty laughed and shook her head, "Nothing as glamorous as that. I'm good at doing some things that help them find bad people, but that was a long time ago. I'm not sure I can do it anymore."

Grace put her hand on Kirsty's head and patted it, "Don't worry, ask God to help you. You can do anything if He helps you." Kirsty gulped and looked up as Emily and Luke filled the doorway. She let go of the girls and stood up, pushing her hands into her pockets, "Thank you for having us, me. Will you please arrange with the rental company about the car? I'll pay the extra costs."

Luke extended his hand towards Kirsty and shook it, "It was a pleasure having you. If you need anything, please contact us." His eyes conveyed a message to her, and she gave a slight nod.

Emily came forward and hugged Kirsty, "You are so precious, Kirsty, don't forget that."

Sudden tears wanted to spring up in Kirsty's eyes, but she turned away and climbed into the SUV with the men. They drove away and disappeared out of view.

7:00 pm, GMT-5. Hotel in Langley, Virginia.

Leo Molineux received the phone call on Wednesday evening. They found her and were bringing her to a secure facility. He arranged to meet them there first thing on Thursday morning. Walking over to the window, he stared unseeingly out across the busy street. *Every hour they wasted was another hour I might never find Camille.* His stomach recoiled at the thought. *I must find her.*

Something was bothering him about the whole thing. When he enquired from their family connections and organisation, there had been very little response. *They know something they aren't telling me.* His fist clenched at the thought that the organisation might be behind her abduction. He would rather it be terrorists or fanatics than them. Hope seemed to be ebbing out of him like a leak he couldn't stop.

That psychic was a dead end too. He turned back to the table where Kirsten Knight's file lay open. He'd studied the file and although he didn't understand everything, it seemed clear that she had a gift. He rubbed over his face. *I wonder if she'd use it to help me. It's been a long time since she worked for the CIA. She's changed who she is and what she does entirely. At least she isn't crazy anymore which is what I'm starting to feel like.*

He closed his eyes and rested his face in his hands. *Why, out of all the women in the world, did they have to take my only daughter?* His face hardened as he pulled the file and his laptop closer to him. *Who are you Kirsty Knight? I'm going to find out everything about you, so you won't have any choice but to help me.*

10:00 am, GMT+1. Thursday, 14 January, Ugarte Villa, Spain.

Jean-Pierre approached the one-roomed building slowly, only lifting his head when he reached the door. It had almost fallen to disrepair, cracks showed in the walls, and the roof was overgrown with moss. Several ivy plants were starting to squeeze the life out of it. He lifted the stone on the small porch and found the rusty key still there. It took a bit of effort, but he managed to get it to turn in the lock. Tucking the creaking door open revealed the dusty interior. He pulled at the light switch and bright light filled the rectangle room.

It had two large windows filling both side walls, but they were dirty and covered with the creepers. His throat closed as he surveyed the interior. As far as he knew, nobody had been in here since the day she left. His father had built this studio for his mother before he was even born. Although Jean-Pierre was built like his father, short with broad shoulders like a bullfighter, a fact his father liked to remind him of; his heart and character had always taken after his mother, whose love of painting had rubbed off on him. They'd spent many hours here happily painting together.

His stomach clenched and a faint sweat gathered on his forehead. *Maybe I shouldn't have come here.* His dad wanted to destroy it long ago, but he'd begged him not to. He took a step across the tiled floor nearer to the two easels set up in the middle of the room. One large and one small, each portraying a half-finished painting of a glass vase with roses in it. Opposite them, a low table stood with a vase and dead, dried out roses in it.

His eyes focused on something yellowish white, folded and pushed in under the vase. His eyes were glued on the piece of paper as he took a few steps closer to it. *Could it be? The one thing I searched high and low for when she left?* The memories of that day came flooding back with a vengeance, as it had for years in his nightmares.

His beautiful mother making him breakfast and seeing him off to school with her usual kiss and hug. His nine-year-old self running to catch the school bus and waving back at her as he boarded. Then coming home finding his father sitting on the steps with a look of despair on his face that he had never seen before. First he thought she'd died, but it was worse. She'd met someone, fallen in love and left them; at least, that's what his father told him.

His hand trembled as he reached for the fragile paper. He gently blew the dust off it and opened it up. His mother's flowing handwriting filled the page, and his eyes swam making it hard to read. Furiously he rubbed the tears out of his eyes and focused on the words.

'Dear Jean-Pierre,

When you read this I'll be gone and for this I'm saying sorry. You are such a good boy with such talent in painting which I hope you will not give up on account of me. Your father is doing what he thinks is best and after I almost set fire to our villa with you inside, I'm inclined to agree with him.

I'm having a rare moment of lucidity today and the thought that I could have harmed you compels me to have myself taken in. One day you'll understand. You'll live on in my heart with the

fondest memories for as long as I still have them.
  Love you forever, Ama.'

When he was eighteen, his father confessed that he had lied to Jean-Pierre, and that his mother had been institutionalised because of her psychotic disorders and schizophrenia. He hadn't wanted Jean-Pierre to go visit her and keep seeing how her condition worsened.

Jean-Pierre, who hadn't really understood the extent of his mother's condition and adored her as a boy, found it very hard to comprehend why his father did what he did. Only after visiting her where she didn't even recognise him, did he understand that in his own way his father had been protecting him.

He read up on mental illnesses and suddenly certain things about his mother started to make sense. How she could be so happy the one moment and furious the next; how she could forget to pack his school lunch or go wander off in the middle of the night.

Jean-Pierre realised that the sobs he was hearing were his own, racking through his chest. He placed the letter back on the table and sank down in the dust allowing himself to grieve, but the angst in his gut at the thought that Kirsty might be losing her sanity stayed lodged in him.

Later that evening, around the dinner table he watched as his father filled their wine glasses with deep red wine. "This here, my boy, is one of our finest wines harvested five years ago the same year you were here last. Do you remember? We had a record harvesting year, thanks to a glorious summer. I know you prefer the white, but this one's my favourite."

Jean-Pierre took a sip, appreciating the sharp taste that filled his senses. "I remember." He looked at his father at the head of the table. *He's not going to like this.* "I want to renovate the old studio and use it to paint in."

His father's bushy eyebrows pulled together in the middle, and he grunted, "Must you?"

Jean-Pierre cut into the piece of steak on his plate and lifted it to his mouth.

His father stared at the tablecloth before raising his head, "On one condition. You come to all the social gatherings I've

arranged. I won't have you holed up in there for days so that I don't see anything of you."

"Thank you." Jean-Pierre took another sip of wine. *That was easier than I thought.*

After a few minutes of quiet his father spoke, "I sometimes wonder, if there was something more I could have done; been there for her more."

Jean-Pierre turned his head to look at his father finding him with his head bowed showing a bald patch on top before he looked up to meet Jean-Pierre's eyes.

Jean-Pierre shook his head, "She was sick, Aita."

His father frowned, "But did I love her as much as she needed me to? I was so intent on expanding our business, winning the prizes…"

Jean-Pierre clenched his jaw, "You can only love someone up to a point. You did the right thing."

Rubbing his hand across his face his father said, "If I had given up the business, brought in carers, devoted all my time to her…"

"Stop it!" Jean-Pierre stood up. "When last did you go see her? There is almost nothing left of the woman we both loved! It would've destroyed us if you kept her here."

Bending forwards his father said, "I guess you're right, but sometimes I still miss her, wishing things could have been different."

Jean-Pierre started walking past his father but hesitated next to him. He rested his hand on his father's shoulder. "I'm sorry. Maybe it's time that you find yourself a hot-blooded woman."

A gruff laugh escaped his fathers' lips.

"I'm turning in for the night, I want to start working on the studio tomorrow morning." He left his father at the table, his steps echoing in the empty hallway.

1:00 pm, GMT. Undisclosed location.

Camille sat in the corner biting her nails. She observed

the other occupants of the room feeling their communal stir-craziness driving her up the stone walls. *I need to do something.*

"Girls! Gather round." She strode into the centre of the room ignoring the cameras pointed at them from the ceiling.

"It's time we did something, and I propose exercise. Any of you any good at aerobics?"

A thin girl, with the build of an athlete, put up her hand, her Russian accent clear as she said, "I'm a gold medallist in gymnastics. I could lead us in some warmups?"

Camille nodded her approval, "That would be great, Yodska. Now, anyone good with doing a beat? Maybe we could make up some music as we go along?"

A few of the girls smiled, enthusiasm starting to fill the ranks. They pulled the table and chairs out of the middle of the room and soon they were stretching. A few were singing a popular pop song with some adding in beats. After half an hour they sank down to the cement floor, exhausted but happier than they had been. Yodska knew how to get their blood pumping as she had soon moved from mere stretches to jumps and push-ups.

Camille had gotten to know most of them well enough, but a new thought struck her.

"You know girls maybe if we shared some stuff about ourselves, we could figure out why they chose us? There must be a reason. Let's put our heads together, shall we?" The women looked at each other and moved closer to her.

She looked at Baya, an African girl as dark as the earth itself. "Baya, is there something specific that you are good at? A special talent or ability?"

Baya scratched her chin, she looked down for a moment and then slowly said, "I'm not sure if this is special, but I come from an old tribe in Africa, whose roots go back a long, long way. We've kept our gene pool quite small, not intermarrying with other tribes. As a tribe we are known for being connected with the water spirits of the land. Whenever it is dry, they come to us, and we do our thing and the rain comes." Baya kept her head down after her long speech.

"Thank you, Baya, don't feel shy. You might be right about the specialness of your people's gene pool."

"Maybe that's what's special about me too?" A girl piped up from the outskirts of the group. She had chocolate-coloured skin and long black hair. Her dark eyes sought Camilla's as she said, "I'm Aboriginal, from Australia. From a tribe that's also been around for thousands of years. We're also connected to the waters of the land and have special rituals and sounds and songs that we sing."

Camille's eyes widened, "Who else is from an ancient tribe?" They found they had a Jewish girl, an Indian girl, a Chinese girl, an Irish girl. It seemed almost every nation in some way or another were represented by their group.

A sigh escaped Camille, who knew that her own bloodline came from a unique German and French combination going back many generations. "That seems to be a special link that we all have. Let's see if there is something else. Do you have special talents? We know we have a gymnast, what does the rest of you do?"

They found that almost all of them had some skill or another, one excelled in languages, one in mathematics and so forth.

Camille's eyebrows raised, "Say, how many of you have done this new DNA testing, where you send in a swab of your DNA to trace your ancestry?"

As one their hands raised. The room grew quiet as they realised what this meant.

Camille spoke for all of them when she said, "That is how they tracked us."

"I don't understand. What could they do with our DNA? Why do they need us?" A small American Indian girl whispered.

The door opened and twelve pairs of eyes turned to the man standing in the doorway. His white lab coat hung loosely around him. He looked like the crazy professor from the movie Back to the Future. Rubbing his hands together in front of him, he said, "Would you like to find out? Come, follow me." With that he turned around leaving the door open behind him.

Camille swallowed away the fear in her throat and stood up, "Come on, ladies. At least we'll have answers."

They followed the man down the long corridor through a door and up some steps. There wasn't any doubt left that they were in a castle. Men were stationed along the way, their guns clearly visible on their belts. The cold stone walls of the corridor led past a window through which they glimpsed a rocky green field which ended at a cliff. The dull sound of the surf reached their ears.

They entered an enormous room which had laboratory equipment, desks and computers on the far-right side. There were other scientists there working away intently on their work, but what caught the women's attention was the sight of something they had never seen before on the left side of the room.

Huge iron bars ran the width of the room from floor to ceiling which formed a cell, backed by the thick walls of the castle. The walls had four huge pillars which extended into the room that created alcoves each fifteen feet wide. One of the alcoves of the cell held a large trolley type of bed. They stumbled to a stop in front of the cage their eyes glued to the thing on the trolley.

"Well, ladies. Here he is. The reason you are here. We've managed to recreate one of his kind from isolating and combining specific molecules from each of your DNA. At first we copied your DNA from the samples you'd sent in to make sure we'd have enough and started our research. Everything was going well and you would've been none the wiser, but we encountered a problem."

The man pushed his hand through his long grey hair. "Our subject developed a rare blood disease, so we needed to collect your blood. We thought we'd only need some of you, but it turns out that we had to combine all twelve of your blood types for his body to accept it. We can now supply him with blood transfusions. If we continue to harvest your blood, we can make enough for him."

He rubbed his hands together, his face full of glee, "Isn't he marvellous?"

He grinned at the trembling group of women, "You should be honoured. Your DNA has brought man into a new era. We've been searching for all the right components for quite some time and hit the jackpot with you twelve."

He clapped his hands and turned to a guard standing by the wall. "Show is over, please take them back to their room and prepare them for drawing more blood. I'd like to fill up our tanks for the next batch. " He walked off towards some place in the lab, and the girls found themselves being led back out of the room.

Camille cast one last glance back finding herself suddenly staring into huge dark eyes. He looked at her and Camille felt drawn to him almost like Beauty and the Beast. She blinked, and his eyes were closed again.

What if? She turned towards the way the professor had gone and spoke up, "Professor? I'm a doctor, isn't there something I can do? I could be useful in more than one way?"

The professor looked up from his table a frown on his large forehead, contemplatively he said, "Our last doctor met an unfortunate demise, we are waiting for a replacement. You might be able to help in the meantime. I was going to send Martin, our nurse in, but if I lose him, I'll have no one left. Although we can't afford to lose your supply of blood just yet either." Camille took another step towards him, "Let me help."

He shrugged his shoulders, addressing the guard, "Okay, first let Martin draw her blood and then bring her back here. Let's see if Subject 107 likes her better than the last one."

8:00 am, GMT-5. Secret facility for ESP Research, Langley, Virginia.

Kirsty opened her eyes as the light flickered on in the room. She was in a large warehouse where they'd set up a research facility of some sorts. It reminded her of the place where they used to do their experiments. The CIA team that brought her in drove to San Antonio where they took a flight to Langley, Virginia. They then took her in a car with no view of the outside and deposited her in the building, leaving her in a large Faraday cage, luggage and all.

After pacing for hours, she knew every inch of the 15 feet length and ten feet width of her new lodgings. The cage consisted of a special, fine see-through mesh, making her visible to everyone in the facility. There was a small wet room with a door where she could escape prying eyes. The door opposite the wet room sealed her in like an animal in a cage. She kept testing it in the night, not believing that they'd locked her in.

The cage was in the corner of the large warehouse well away from the desks and computers that filled the other half. The bare, concrete floor added to the impersonal feeling of the place. Kirsty pulled her knees up to her chin where she sat on the bed.

She grimaced. *I had to forget my pills, didn't I.* At least with the meds in her system, it would've been harder for her to activate her senses. As it was, she could already feel her body respond to the clean air surrounding her. A Faraday cage was one of the last places on earth where you could be without any interference, no waves, no electronics. Nothing could penetrate it.

The knot in her stomach clenched tighter. *I don't want to be here!* In the end she'd gone to sleep in her clothes and felt wrinkled and in desperate need of a shower. The facility started filling up with people, scientists by the look of them. It looked like a team studying extra-sensory perception, much like the ESP team she used to belong to. They ignored her and went on with their business as usual.

The main door opened and the hair on Kirsten's neck rose, she could feel the man's energy from the other side of the room. *Who is he?* Another shorter man escorted him, they walked across stopping in front of her cage. She stood up facing them.

The shorter man cleared his throat, "Miss Knight. Thank you for coming. This is rather a matter of urgency so please excuse our lack of diplomacy. My name is Director Smith, and this is Leo Molineux." He looked at the other man for a second and then back at her, "Mr Molineux needs you…"

"To find his daughter." Kirsty turned away from the men and sat down on the bed, facing them, her hand grasping her elbow.

The two men looked at her with frowns, "How do you know?" The Director asked.

She shrugged, "I just do."

Director Smith opened the gate with a key and allowed

Leo to go inside. "I'll leave you to talk. Ask Dr Lemming to let you out." He pointed to an older man at the nearest table, turned around and left the building at a clipped pace as if washing his hands of the whole thing.

Leo stood still, his blue eyes studying Kirsty's pose on the bed where she sat still, her eyes downward. Opposite the bed there was a small, dark mahogany desk and a green vinyl chair. He pulled the chair out and sat down.

"Would you like me to call you Kirsty, Kirsten or Doctor Knight?"

She looked up at him. "Kirsty."

He dipped his chin, "Yes, I've read your file and the things that Kirsten or Doctor Knight went through would make a name change desirable. Well, Kirsty, you already know what I want you to do. The question is can you do it?"

She moved back against the wall, tucking her legs up against herself with her arms around them. "No."

"No, what?"

"No. I can't do it. I can't help you."

She could feel the tension increase in the man opposite her as he said, "I find that hard to believe. Your track record shows that you were highly successful in finding people. In fact it was your speciality."

"That was then and this is now. I'm sure my file also told you what it'd cost me."

He folded his hands in his lap and regarded her, his face tight, "Do you know how much it has cost me to keep my daughter safe? She's twenty-eight, her name is Camille. Her mother died when she was young. She's all I have, and I'm not about to lose her." He sat forward leaning towards her, "You'll find her for me, or you'll wish you had never been born."

Kirsty looked down at her knees, "Who says I don't wish that already?"

Leo raised his brows, "What's your price? I could fund you with a lifetime supply of IVF's?"

A tremor ran down her spine. She kept quiet.

"Do you know who I am, Kirsty? No one, and I mean, no one says no to me." Leo balled his fists.

Kirsty dared a look at him and shrank back at the unexpected sight of a snarling face, merging with Leo's features. She shut her eyes tight and wished she was a praying person. "It's not real, Kirsty, it's not real," she mumbled to herself.

"What's not real?" Leo's quiet voice broke into her thoughts.

"What I see."

"What do you see?"

"A snarling face merging with yours." Kirsty didn't look at him.

A snort escaped Leo, "Oh, he's real. One of my familiar spirits. Interesting that you can see him."

"You believe in spirits?"

"Yes. Spirits, aliens, the world is much wider than your limited belief."

Kirsty opened her eyes. With relief, she saw he appeared normal again. "Do you believe God exists?"

"There are many spiritual powers out there, gods if you like."

"What about the Christian God?"

Leo's eyes squinted as he observed her, "I don't. Do you?"

Kirsty shook her head and bit her lip, hesitantly she said, "I'm starting to wonder. If these spirits are real, maybe He exists, too?"

Leo shook his head, "If He is, we are like ants to Him of no consequence." He stood up and looked down at her. "I'm going to let you think about helping me. I'll be back with some persuasion." He turned and nodded at the scientist at the table who had been keeping half an eye on them. The man got up, walked over and opened the gate.

Kirsty watched him leave the room, fear clutching at her throat. Memories of looking in the mirror and seeing things in her own eyes like what she saw in Leo's face clawed their way to the surface. She'd worked so hard to forget, to put it behind her, although deep down inside, if she were honest, she knew it was all still there, no matter how hard she tried to pretend it wasn't.

I'm going to go crazy again. It's going to destroy me. Logic and reason had failed her in the past, there had to be something else she could turn to, but what? What could help her out of this mess? *I'm all alone.* Kirsty shivered and crept under the navy duvet, faking sleep. She decided to shower later, aware of the people in the room throwing curious glances her way as if she was a rare new specimen for an experiment.

CHAPTER 7

2:00 pm, GMT. Thursday, 14 January. Undisclosed location.

Camille walked back into the main room flanked by a guard. She felt slightly dizzy from the blood they had drawn earlier. Scrambling her memory for everything she had ever heard about this extinct race; she could only come up with a few random facts mostly from an article she had read in the National Geographic. It wasn't much to go on. Repressing a shudder, she remembered the photographs of the massive skeletons they'd unearthed.

The professor came towards her, "I haven't introduced myself, I'm Professor Demid Petrov. Subject 107 needs his blood pressure checked. We also need to draw some blood to check the counts and make sure they are doing better after his latest transfusion."

Camille's heartbeat sounded loud in her ears as she followed the professor towards the cell where the giant man lay inert on the trolley. The professor handed her an oversized blood pressure monitor and a large syringe. He looked at her with a frown, "Think you can handle these?" She swallowed, her mouth and throat bone-dry, while she dipped her chin.

"Okay then." The professor slid a key card across the massive iron door and without ceremony, pushed her inside, shutting it behind her with a clang.

"Wait!" Camille turned towards the gate grabbing it with one hand, the other clutching the equipment. The professor was already striding away not minding her. The desks and equipment were all at the far end of the room as if they wanted as much distance between them and the giant as possible. She heard something stir behind her and she twisted around, facing him.

He had turned his head which was the furthest away from her. His eyes were open, watching her with a flicker of interest in their depths.

He could crush me with one hand, what was I thinking? Camille tried to stand taller although she was 5'8, she would barely reach his middle. He'd reach almost twelve feet when standing!

"Hi, I'm Dr Camille. I need to take your blood pressure and a sample of blood to check that your count is healthy. Would it be alright with you if I did that now?" She spoke fast trying to intone her calm hospital bedside manners.

The giant's eyes blinked then he moved and sat up, the trolley groaning underneath his weight. Camille couldn't help backing up, so her back was against the gate, the cold steel pressing into her shirt. His hands were resting on the trolley, her eyes fell on them and grew larger as she realised he had six fingers on each hand, she glanced down and saw six toes on each foot too.

"You're different." His low, rumbling voice was gruff.

"You talk?" Camille spluttered.

The dark eyes regarded her impassively. "I do."

They stared at each other. Camille licked her dry lips, "Do you have a name?"

His wild brows bunched together, and he said, "Subject 107."

"That isn't a name." Camille tried to steady her breathing, "Would it be okay if I gave you a name? What about Trojan?"

Something that almost looked like a smile flittered across his stoic features. Softly he said, "You want to name me after a Trojan horse?"

She focused on his face, "They used it to overcome a city, surprising everyone by what was inside."

"Killers were inside. Not a good surprise." His voice was a

whisper through his tangled beard.

"Yes, but it doesn't always have to be that way."

His hands seemed to clench the trolley, keeping his voice low he said, "You don't know what you're saying. My kind is what you humans base your folk stories on. The ones about trolls, giants and flesh-eaters. You're fools to bring us back to life."

Camille gulped but said, "I'm not one of them. I'm held captive like you. They used my DNA, along with eleven other women here to create you. Now they're using our blood to help fix yours."

He stared at her, "I'm not entirely human, little girl. If I was made from your DNA then you mustn't be fully human either."

She took a little step nearer to him. "How's that possible?"

He looked down at his feet, his skin was pale and bruised, with angry red-looking rashes showing beneath a massive hospital gown.

"My kind was created when the fallen ones saw the women of earth and liked them."

A dangerous look filled his eyes as they flicked back to her, "They mated with them and produced offspring. Us. The Creator condemned what they'd done and they were banished. My kind was slowly hunted, but we lay with the people of earth so our DNA became part of humankind, interspersed enough that our features didn't show up anymore. Hidden but still there. These foolish men have brought us back and they'll regret it."

Camille taking another step closer, halted. "Why?"

He gave a gruff laugh and before she had time to respond he grabbed her, his hand going almost right around her. He lifted her up close to him, growling into her face with a menacing voice. "Because we're evil. There's no good in us."

Camille had given a yelp when he grabbed her, but for some insane reason her fear fled. She placed her palm on the part of his hand that held her. "I don't believe that. I believe everyone has a choice, no matter what their DNA is like. For now, Trojan, can I be your doctor and take care of you? I can see your skin is looking sore. If I can find some cream it will relieve the soreness, but first I have to take the blood and the pressure for the professor."

The giant's eyes had widened in confusion at her gentle

touch, and he inclined his head as if bewildered. Suddenly he lowered her down, released her and turned his arm towards her, "Take your blood, Dr Camille."

She took the blood, taking care to insert the needle as gently as possible. He didn't move a muscle. She took the pressure, and when she was done, she found herself standing in front of him. "Thank you, Trojan. I'll go find that cream now and I'll be back. I'm glad I got to meet you."

Turning, she banged on the gate, someone ran over and opened it for her. Trojan watched her walk across the vast room and talk with the professor, giving him the sample of blood and the reading of the blood pressure. He saw the professor shake his head, and he saw her gesture with her arms as if angry.

To his astonishment he saw the professor bark out a few orders, and Camille followed another man into a storeroom. A little while later she came back out with a few tubs in her arms. She walked straight back to his cage where someone let her in.

When they were out of earshot he asked, "What's that?"

She placed the tubs on the floor and started opening the first one, "This is aqueous cream, it's all they have, apparently someone here has sensitive skin and washes with this. Have you ever had a bath? Anyhow this can be put on dry skin and should at least soothe it a bit." Walking towards him with the cream, she looked him over as if she didn't know where to start. "Would you mind lying down on your stomach for me? I could do the back of your legs more easily that way."

He complied and she started applying the cream, gently and soothingly rubbing it in. He had never felt anything like it. To his surprise, he felt moisture in his eyes. She had him turn around and started doing the front of his body. When she came to his face, she patted it around his eyes and ears. He watched her broodingly. His hand came up and caught hers between his finger and thumb. "Doctor Camille, why are you?"

"Why am I what?" She bit her lip trying to hide that her insides were quivering in fear.

He inclined his head, "You're the first person not to treat me like a monster, yet I am one, and you are afraid, but still you treat me with kindness? That's not normal."

Camille rested her eyes on his massive bicep and exhaled, "I grew up between monsters. Not outwardly but inwardly. I realised early on that I could choose, would I become like them, or would I choose to be someone who sees the good in people and help others. I chose the latter. I chose not to become what I was predestined to be. When I see you, I see someone with a choice. You are a person, fully human or not."

Trojan let go of her hand and touched her cheek with his thumb, "I can see why the fallen ones mated with womankind. You're beautiful."

Camille's cheeks flushed, "Thank you, Trojan. I hope your skin will feel better tonight and that they will let me see you again tomorrow."

He watched her leave, his eyes never leaving her until they led her out of the room.

2:00 pm, GMT-5. Secret ESP Research Facility.

Kirsty was coming out of the wet room, pushing her feet into her comfortable slippers, when she heard the door open. The older scientist had brought her lunch. She thought back to lunch at the ranch and missed the twins' chatter. It looked like a giant burger with fries and a coke.

"Thank you," she said to the man. He looked at her, his eyes an unusual grey, his face betraying his age as past fifty. He brought it over, handing it to her. She took the tray, sat down on the bed and placed it on her lap. She could feel him looking at her, so she looked up again.

His face was troubled, and his hand kept fiddling with the tag on his white coat. "I'm Dr Lemming. Paul Lemming. I've heard of you, Dr. Knight. Your studies on ESP were amazing, ground-breaking even."

Kirsty looked away from him and took a sip of the coke, "Thank you." *Why isn't he leaving?*

He cleared his throat uncomfortably, Kirsty looked at him

again, "Is there something you want?"

The man produced a tissue from his pocket and wiped across his forehead, "Actually I wanted to ask you a favour, but I'll understand if you say no. It's Leila, my dog you see. She ran away on Sunday, and I've been frantic the whole week. I live alone, it's just Leila and me. She's never gone off before like this."

Kirsty saw real tears appear in the man's eyes. She shifted on the bed. *My burger is getting cold.* "I'll see what I can do."

Thank you, Dr Knight. I've brought her favourite toy in case it helps." Dr Lemming produced a tattered yellow bear and placed it on the bed next to Kirsty.

The door shut behind him and Kirsty bit into her burger. *Wow, this is nice. Can't believe I've deprived myself of fast food for so long.* She frowned as she looked down at the offending toy next to her. *Why did I say I'll help him?* In honesty, she was bored and finding a dog wasn't nearly as dangerous as trying to find a missing person.

Kirsty finished off her meal, placed the tray by the hatch where they could take it and crept back under the covers with the toy in her hand. It felt like the old days when she used to enjoy doing their experiments. She used to practise different types of ESP like precognition, retrocognition, telepathy, clairvoyance, psychometry, but she was best at remote viewing.

First she had to tap into her naked awareness and to do this she had to clear her mind which she did as effortlessly as if she had never stopped doing it. Within a few seconds a picture appeared in her mind's eye. She saw a small brown dog with a white patch on one eye, a Jack Russell, inside a house looking out of the window. She zoomed out so she could see the house and street name. The dog barked as if he could see her.

Her eyes opened and Kirsty sat up. Shaking her head, she inhaled a deep breath and looked into the room, catching the eye of Dr Lemming who seemed to have been watching her while typing at his computer. He walked over and picked up the tray. She ambled over, handing him the toy through the hatch. Quietly she said, "House no. 15, Beaumont Drive. Jack Russell, brown with a white eye patch?"

Dr Lemming's eyes went wide, "Thank you." He dropped the tray on the nearest table and hastily left the building. Kirsty watched him walk out with a smile on her face which vanished as she saw Leo Molineux walk in through the door. She turned her back on him and sat down on the bed, crossing her arms.

He walked until he almost touched the mesh of the cage, "Have you reconsidered?"

Kirsty shook her head.

"Well, then I have a guest for you. Maybe your mother can talk some sense into you."

"My mother?" Kirsty visibly paled.

The door to the facility opened, and two men in black suits accompanied Emma Knight who was protesting loudly, "I'll let you know that I'm going to sue you for forcing me to go with you against my will. This is unheard of in our democratic country. I'm well-known, you know; you won't get away with this."

Leo turned around and walked towards her, "Ah, the famous Emma Knight! Pleased to make your acquaintance. I need you to talk some sense into your daughter."

Emma turned a darker shade of red as she stared at him, "I don't have a daughter."

He lifted his eyebrows at her, "Oh, I thought Kirsten Knight was your illegitimate daughter. The one that you had at fifteen with the gardener's son which you and your parents covered up by pretending she was adopted? In any case, mere specifics. I want you to talk sense into her because if you don't I'll make sure every news agency in the world know your story with proof, birth certificates, the works."

Emma Knight had gone pale, "I don't know what you're talking about."

Dr Lemming opened the cage, and the men led Emma into it and shut it behind her. Leo looked at the two women, "I'll give you half an hour then I want an answer."

He left with the suits and Emma looked around the cage and at Kirsty with disdain, "What is this, this place?"

Kirsty had pulled up her knees against her chest. She shrugged, "It's a Faraday cage. It keeps most interference out to help when you're doing experiments with ESP."

Emma looked at the green vinyl chair and sat down on the edge of it. "Why did you tell that man? Didn't I tell you not to tell a soul?"

"I didn't tell him. I haven't told anyone." Kirsty's voice had gone hard.

Emma gave her a piercing look, her forehead in a frown, "Who is he then? How could he know?"

Kirsty shrugged her shoulders again, "I think he is one of them. You know, the ruling families."

A shudder went through her mother's frame. Her voice was different, softer when she said, "Well, in that case, why don't you do as he asks?"

Kirsty shook her head, her jaw tight, "I can't. I'm not going to go crazy again."

Emma inclined her head, "What does he want you to do?"

Kirsty stood up and started pacing up and down, "Find his daughter via remote viewing. She's been kidnapped."

Emma's eyes went wide, "Can you do that?"

Kirsty stopped and faced her, "Yes."

"But...how?"

"You know I used to be a doctor in physics who specialised in extra-sensory perception. I worked in a unit like this one and was very good at finding people."

Emma folded and refolded her hands on her green capris, "What changed?"

Kirsty started walking up and down again, "I started seeing things that weren't real during experiments. Scary demon-like beings, especially when I tried to find people who were kidnapped. I'd always had night terrors, but then I started seeing monsters in the daytime and they harassed me. It was as if I'd opened a door and they could attack me anyway they liked. Real or not, it was enough to drive me over the edge."

Emma followed her with her eyes, her face in a frown, "So you're saying that if you help him find his daughter it might open this door and you'll go crazy again?"

Kirsty stopped pacing and fell on the bed again. "Yes." *I've already started seeing things again.* Her face pulled tight, "Now I suppose you're going to say I might as well take a chance and do it, since if I don't he's going to destroy my life and possibly yours."

Emma wiped her hands on her slacks before fiddling with a golden, diamond-encrusted ring on her hand, avoiding eye contact. Kirsty looked down at her own empty fingers, plain blue T-shirt and comfortable old Levi's all the way down to her woollen clad feet. *Can't believe we're related.*

"I…" Her mother looked around the room and out at the scientists before she looked back at Kirsty. "Why did you study physics?"

Kirsty studied her hands, chewing on her lip, "I guess since I've always dreamed of and saw unusual things as a kid it interested me. The universe, how the world works."

"Lewis used to be interested in that. He had such a vivid imagination." Emma's voice was soft, quiet.

Kirsty sat up and looked at Emma's bowed head, "Was he clever?"

Emma nodded almost imperceptibly, "He was. If he had the opportunity, he could've been anything he wanted to."

Her eyes had a faraway look in them, "I packed my bags and tried to run away from home after they sent them away. I planned on following them, finding them and living with them. His parents were so warm and loving, I was sure they would've taken me in." She shook her head, "I didn't make it past the front door. My father caught me and confined me to my room locking me in for a week. I had no way of knowing where they went, no way to contact him. He didn't know about me expecting."

Kirsty swallowed at the tightness in her throat, "Why do you hate me?"

Emma turned her green eyes on Kirsty and gave a sad smile, "I never hated you. I resented you at the beginning. If it weren't for you, Lewis wouldn't have been sent away. My mother, though, she took over and barely gave me a chance to bond with you, be near you. They made me feel bad, like I'd done a horrible thing, and now I had to make up for it. I worked hard, poured myself into my studies and tried to forget that you were mine."

They became aware of someone approaching, and mother and daughter looked at each other as Leo opened the cage door.

"Well?"

Emma stood up, she looked Leo in the eye, "I'm sorry to hear about your daughter, Mr Molineux. Since I've only recently found mine, I can't force her to do something that might destroy her sanity. Do as you please with the information you have."

She turned back to Kirsty and there was a certain warmth in her eyes that wasn't there before, "Please contact me when this is over, maybe we could go for tea?" She rummaged in her small handbag, produced a golden pen, walked over to the table and scribbled something on a piece of paper that lay there. "There, now you have my number." She turned and walked past Leo out of the door.

He was clenching his jaw, his fists balled by his side. Kirsty sat with her mouth slightly open, her wide eyes following Emma as she walked out of the building. *What just happened?*

Leo turned on Kirsty, "Every hour we waste is one hour closer to my daughter's possible death. Do you realise that!"

Kirsty felt tears gather in her eyes, "I'm sorry Mr Molineux, I don't know how to help you. Those entities that guard that type of thing they're…"

"Monstrous?" Leo stared at her. "I know only too well. Why do you think I want to find her so desperately?"

"Is there no other way?" Kirsty looked at him, her body trembling.

He slammed the door shut. "I'm pursuing every angle. You are one of my best bets." He stared at her, "Your mother is too high profile to eliminate, but I've discovered we both know someone no one will miss except you. Maybe…"

Kirsty ran to the door, "Who are you talking about?"

"You'll see…"

5:00 pm, GMT-6. New Beginning Ranch, Texas.

Thomas pushed his hand through his hair, it was getting longer than he usually wore it, curling around his neck and ears. Maybe he should let it grow out like he had in his teens. His beard was already a thick reddish stubble; he hadn't shaved since he arrived in America.

He thought back to how Anna looked back in the day. She'd been avoiding him. He only got a brief glimpse of her when he went into the kitchen for a snack, but she scurried away with barely a glance at him.

Her short, black hair was long and wavy back then, a light brown that she now seems to dye. Must be wearing contacts instead of her glasses. No wonder I didn't recognise her. They were next-door neighbours as far back as he could remember. Although it was unusual for Catholic and Protestant families to live next to each other, a small section of Londonderry wasn't as segregated as the rest.

A wall and a river naturally divided the Protestant and Catholic sides. It was on this wall that they met for long walks when they reached their teens. It was their secret escape where they could pretend there wasn't any division between their families. One day their innocent friendship changed when they kissed. After that, it became harder than ever to hide their relationship.

He sighed, this cat and mouse game had to end. He'd have no peace until he spoke with her. He stomped up the stairs at the back porch and entered the kitchen. A pleasant aroma filled his nose and he saw Emily in front of the stove stirring something.

She looked up and smiled at him, "Hi Thomas! Dinner isn't ready yet."

He walked over and peered into the pot, "It smells divine. Bachelor fare doesn't compare to home cooking." He rested his blue eyes on Emily and asked, "Is Anna around?"

Emily's eyes grew wider, and she shook her head, "No, she went for a walk."

"Which direction?"

Emily looked out the window in the direction of the river and back at him. He started walking towards the door, "I'll see you later."

"Thomas?"

He paused with his hand on the door handle, inclining his head towards her, "Be gentle with her? She's been through a lot."

"Has she told you?"

Emily's cheeks flushed, "Not much, but I gather you know each other from years ago."

He tilted his head to the side, "I don't understand why, after so many years, she doesn't want to at least talk to me."

Emily looked back at the stove, "You'll have to ask her, but…"

"Be gentle. I heard you." Thomas walked down the path towards the river, his hands deep in his pockets. It was getting chillier, the sun closing in on the horizon.

He hadn't walked very far when he heard a soft moan coming from the side of the path, down between the rocks next to the river. A patch of bright red caught his eye and he veered off the track, climbing over a few boulders until he reached the river's side.

There sitting on the ground next to a large rock sat Anna with her one leg bent and the other straight. She looked up, the sunlight shining in her eyes from behind Thomas, blinding her, "Luke, is that you? I'm so glad you came looking for me. I think I've twisted my ankle; I can't step on it. I'll need some help getting back to the house."

Thomas stepped closer, squatting down beside her, "It's not Luke, it's me, Thomas. Let me feel your ankle." She had gone rigid as recognition struck her. He pulled her sock gently down, seeing the swelling already starting up.

"Ouch!" she exclaimed, as his probing fingers moved it around. He placed her foot down after covering it up with her sock again, noticing her impractical pumps, "These aren't shoes for walking in the bush."

She huffed, "Always preaching away. I wasn't planning on coming to the ranch, hence not the right attire. Are you going to help me back to the house now or not?"

He surveyed her face, feeling his heartbeat increase, "No."

"No?" She dared a look at him and saw that he meant it. "What do you mean no? I need to get some ice on this."

He casually sat down cross-legged observing her frowning face with a slight smile on his own, "I meant not straight away. I'm not giving up my one opportunity to have your undivided attention without you avoiding me."

Her eyes grew big, and she clenched her jaw, "I'd call that taking me hostage."

"Anna? Why won't you talk to me? It's been what, twenty-one years?"

She bit into her lip, avoiding his eyes, "There's nothing to say. You left and I got on with my life. End of story."

"Will you look at me please?"

She lifted her head and their eyes locked, "Why are you mad at me?"

She shrugged her shoulders, "I'm not mad at you. Why should I be mad at you? If you want to sleep with beautiful girls that's your problem."

His face clouded with confusion, "What are you talking about? I haven't slept with anyone..." his voice trailed away.

"Except me?" Anna's harsh laugh filled the air. "Likely story. I saw her leave your bungalow with my own eyes. You're no different from the rest of the men species. You just want one thing and when you get it, you drop the girl like a hot potato. " She looked out across the river; her face tight.

Thomas made a choked noise, "Is that what you think happened with us? How can you think that of me?"

Anna's eyes blazed as she bore into him, "What other reason could there have been? You lost interest in me. Didn't love me as much as I..."

Thomas moved forward on his knees grasping Anna's upper arms, "I didn't leave because of any of those stupid reasons!" He shook her lightly, "I left because your family threatened to kill me and throw you out of the house if I ever came near you again. I left because I didn't want to force you into choosing between your family and me. I couldn't take care of you or provide a home for you. You had big dreams; dreams you would've had to give up if you came with me. I left because it was the best thing for you!"

Tears were pooling in Anna's eyes and she said in a hoarse voice, "Let go of me, Thomas." He realised he was clenching her upper arms; he let go, his hands falling away into fists by his sides.

They sat in the quiet, the sun's last rays highlighting the

river with sparks of shiny silver. In a still voice devoid of fire Anna said, "I cried for weeks. You broke my heart."

Thomas wiped his hand across his face, "I'm sorry, Anna. You were sixteen. I felt so awful after what happened that night when we got drunk. I told myself you deserved a better man than me. I couldn't believe that I'd crossed the line and disrespected you like that. For me…doing that with someone meant you become one with them, marry them. That's why I've never again…"

"Never?" Wonder filled her voice as she looked at him, "But I saw Kirsty?"

He shook his head, "Kirsty and I shared a bottle of whiskey and some conversation and since it was late and we couldn't walk in a straight line, she slept in the extra single bed in my bungalow. Nothing happened."

Anna wrapped her arms around herself, moving her hands up and down over her arms. He looked at her in concern, "Did I hurt you?" She shook her head, "No, I'm getting cold."

He stood up and dusted off his trousers, "I'll help you get home." Gently, he helped her up. With her arm around him, her weight on her good leg and her bad leg in the middle between them, they worked out how to walk. It took them some getting used to, but the going was easier when they got to the path. Every few feet they stopped for a rest. Darkness was falling faster now. During one rest, Anna looked up sideways at Thomas, "Thank you."

He grunted and looked down, "Did you marry?" His voice was low, shy. Anna felt the warmth of his hand around her waist, glad the darkness was hiding her blush. "No. I pursued my dream. Studying hard, getting a scholarship. Studying even harder in Milan. Getting a job in London."

He gave a tight smile, "I'm glad it's worked out for you."

She swallowed the knot in her throat, "It hasn't actually. I lost my job this week."

"Why?"

"The boss wanted me to sleep with him or else…"

"That's disgusting."

"I haven't either."

"Wow." His stunned silence filled the air, something crackled between them.

They moved a few steps on before resting again. Anna pushed her hair behind her ear, her body trembling as she said, "There is something you should know."

"Yes?" His eyes turned towards her, looking down at her face. He was so close she could feel his warm breath. Her heartrate increased, her palms starting to sweat.

"Anna…" His face came nearer, hovering inches from hers. She licked her lips, and he pulled back, his arm gripping her tighter against him.

"I have a daughter. Her name is Ellie."

He froze and her heart twisted as blue eyes sought hers. "Ellie?" But you said you never?

She swallowed the knot in her throat and nodded. Thomas's eyes grew and in a low voice, he asked, "How old is she?"

"Twenty-one." Anna felt warm tears run down her cheeks as the man next to her stood still in wordless shock. "She has your eyes. She loves music and plays the violin. She is studying in Dublin." The words rushed out of her as if they had been kept in a prison for years.

He turned his face to her again, "How, why?"

She shuddered, "I'm sorry, Thomas. You left and my family threatened to throw me out if I told you. I didn't even know if you wanted me anymore. I tried once to go to your parents' home, but they told me that you were studying in England and wouldn't be home for another year. I had to do what was best for her and keep her safe in a family, my family. She was baptised in the Catholic church, and they brought her up as their own."

What have you told her about me?" The tremor in his voice betrayed the hurt.

"I told her only good things. That you left without knowing about her, and that I didn't know where you were."

"But five years ago, at the wedding, you recognised me? Why not tell me then? Why waste another five years that I could have known her?" His voice had gone hard.

Anna trembled again, "I couldn't face it. You were a pastor for goodness' sake. What would your church have thought if you suddenly had an illegitimate daughter? I don't know. Maybe I should have."

"You should have." Again, that hardness in his voice. They walked, hopped the last few hundred feet to the house in silence. Outside the door, Thomas paused, "I want to meet her."

Anna held her breath, "All right."

"I want to meet her as soon as possible. In fact, tomorrow. You are going to take me to her tomorrow."

Anna's eyebrows rose, "It will take days of travelling to get there. I'm planning to go home on Monday." He shook his head, "I'm not wasting another day. If you don't come with me, tomorrow, you can give me the address, and I'll go on my own."

"You are not meeting her alone."

"Then you are leaving with me tomorrow."

"What about my foot?"

"You'll manage. We can bandage it and get you some crutches; we can stop at the local hospital on our way to the airport if you want."

The door opened, the light spilling out highlighting them, Luke's tall frame filled the doorway. "Hi! Anna, what happened?"

"I was silly, I climbed on some rocks by the river and lost my balance. Luckily Thomas found me before you had to send out a search party. I think my ankle's sprained." Anne kept her face downcast.

Luke supported her weight on the other side, and they helped her into the house.

Later around the dinner table Thomas said, "Anna and I are leaving tomorrow. I appreciate all you've done. Hopefully, I can come back for a longer stay another time."

Emily looked at Anna and then at Thomas, "She told you?"

Thomas's face hardened, "You knew?"

"I only told Emily yesterday." Anna piped up defensively.

"Something I don't know?" Luke asked, sensing the tension in the air.

Anna tried to speak but her mouth was bone-dry.

Thomas looked at Luke, "We're going to go and see Ellie."

"Who's Ellie?" piped up Mercy.

Emily cleared her throat, "Ellie is Anna and Thomas'

daughter." Luke almost choked before turning astonished eyes to his wife and Anna, finally resting them on Thomas.

Grace was staring at them with big eyes too. "They have a daughter. But they aren't married?"

Mercy pumped her sister on the shoulder, "Shush, maybe they're divorced."

Grace pulled her little face into a pucker as she thought about it, "But if they're going together does that mean they're married again?"

Luke cleared his throat, "Mercy and Grace, enough for now. Let's go brush your teeth."

As he stood up, he rested his hand on Thomas's shoulder for a moment, giving it a squeeze.

"Thomas?" Emily willed him to look her in the eyes. "You'll take care of Anna for me, right?"

Thomas frowned, "I will."

Anna pushed her chair back and stood, forgetting about her ankle, "I've taken good care of myself all my life, I'm not about to start depending on a man." She became aware of the throbbing pain and awkwardly turned, supporting herself on the back of the chairs as she tried to make her way to her room. Thomas got up and stood looking at her back. He turned back to Emily and lifted his shoulders, "As she said, she doesn't need a man."

He strode out of the room. Emily rushed to Anna's side, placing her arm around her. They made it to Anna's room where she sank down onto her bed with relief. Emily lowered herself next to her and gave her a sideways glance, "Want to tell me about it?"

CHAPTER 8

One by one everyone left. The lights went off, and they left Kirsty alone in the cage. She had a small battery-operated lamp, and someone somewhere had placed a few books in the drawer of the small desk. She flipped through the meagre selection. *Boring. I don't like reading anyway.*

With nothing else to do she switched off the lamp and laid back on her bed, allowing darkness to fill the place. The windows had total blackout shutters. The complete quiet reminded her of the ranch minus the crickets. Kirsty turned over on her stomach. *Jean-Pierre, I miss you.*

She could imagine him in the sunshine, walking through the vineyards. *What I wouldn't give to be with him right now.*

She thought of her mother and felt her face smile. *Now there was a surprise, maybe something good will come out of this ordeal.* She turned back onto her back, wishing sleep would come but also dreading it. Once for an experiment she'd stayed in a Faraday cage for a whole month. The longer she stayed, the clearer her thinking and abilities became. She also started dreaming more vividly than usual. *If I start dreaming like that again, I might lose it. The nun dream was bad enough.*

Finally before midnight she fell into a slumber and to her alarm, she felt herself lift and leave the cage floating up, until she was hanging above the building. She glanced around, trying to work out where they were. It appeared to be in an industrial area on the outskirts of Langley. Her speed increased, and in a blur, she found herself travelling what felt like quite a distance before she slowed down, hovering over the lights of a suburb.

It wasn't very well-to-do, all the little box houses looked the same, but they were tidy. She landed in the street and looked up and down it, trying to figure out why she was there. The air was frigid, and a dusting of snow lay on the ground. *I need to start sleeping in warmer PJ's.*

The porch light of the small house opposite her came on and an American Indian woman opened the door. She came out and walked down the steps, her wrinkled face lighting up in a smile, "You've come! I've been waiting for you. Please, come in."

Strange, but it'll be warmer in her house. She looks harmless. Kirsty smiled back and followed her. Inside, the little old lady led her to a faded couch in the sitting room where a small stove was pumping out heat.

"Please sit, can I make you some tea? Oh, I haven't introduced myself. Do you know who I am?" She stopped, her grin showing a gap in her teeth.

Kirsty shook her head.

"My name is Olive Sylliboy, but when I married I became Pictou. My husband was Warren and my son Lewis."

Kirsty felt herself tremble, and she stilled her hands on her lap. *I'm dreaming of my American Indian grandmother.* "My name is Kirsty Knight. I think your son is my father?"

Olive threw her hands against her cheeks with a cry, "My Lewis had a daughter?"

"With my mom, Emma."

"Miss Emma, yes. Warren worked for the Knights and Lewis and Emma were friends. More than friends, it seems!"

She put her hands on both sides of Kirsty's face and peered into her eyes, "Yes, yes, I can see my Lewis in you. Now I know why they sent us away so sudden like. My, oh, my. When I dreamed of you coming, I didn't see this." She tucked Kirsty closer to her and embraced her, "My long-lost granddaughter. How happy I am to meet you."

Tears of gladness were running down her face, "Oh, I forget my manners. Let's make tea." She looked around, "Wait, I'll give you something to look at while I make tea." She quickly scurried out and came back with a large photo album. Placing it on Kirsty's lap she said, "This is your papa's photos. I think there's even one of your mother."

She left, and Kirsty could hear her getting cups out in the kitchen. She opened the album, mesmerised by photos of her father, from babyhood, to boyhood, to a teenager. She peered closer at one where he and a blonde-haired girl stood smiling in front of a garden full of flowers, recognising her mother. *Sometimes I wish my dreams were real.*

Her throat felt thick, and she paged over quickly, cutting her finger on the edge. She put her finger in her mouth sucking at the sharp pain, continuing through the album all the way to where her father was a grown man.

Olive came back, handed her a steaming cup of tea and sat herself down next to Kirsty, "Did you see the one of your mother and Lewis?"

Kirsty nodded, glancing down at the closed album on her lap. In a gentle voice her grandmother said, "You can keep it if you like."

Kirsty looked into her wise old eyes and blinked, "I have so many questions, but I don't know where to start. I only found out this week about my birth parents. Her parents, my grandparents, pretended to be my adopted parents. I had no idea she was my mom. I thought she was my sister."

"I'm sorry. If only Lewis were still around. He would've been so happy to meet you."

Kirsty looked at her with a frown. *Oh no!* "Is he, has he passed away?" Her words stumbled, her body going limp.

Olivia nodded her own eyes filling, "It was a car accident. They both got taken ten years ago."

Trying to gather herself, Kirsty asked, "Did he marry?" *It's just a dream, Kirsty, get a grip.*

Olivia shook her head. "He wasn't interested in girls, maybe he never got over your mother."

"I'm sorry."

Olivia patted her hand, "Don't be. We all have our paths to walk. I'm just delighted mine has crossed with yours now."

"But, I'm not..." Kirsty's voice trailed away. "Where are we?"

Olivia looked at her with eyebrows raised, "We are in the Sable River Village. It's an American Indian Settlement in Canada. I am of the Mi'kmaq tribe. It means the People of the Red Earth. My father was a saqamaw, a chief. Warren had to prove himself to get me."

Her eyes were warm, as she thought of the love of her life. She looked at Kirsty again, reaching out to touch a strand of her hair, "Your aura is so beautiful, green the colour of life. Our people believe that every being who comes to earth has a unique purpose. Your colour is connected to that purpose."

Kirsty shifted, moving a bit away from her, "I don't know about that. It's not as if my birth was planned or anything."

Olivia tilted her head, "Not planned by man, but definitely planned by Someone." Her eyes lit up, "I have something for you, wait here! She shuffled out as fast as her old feet could carry her and came back within minutes with something wrapped in a soft, red cloth. She pressed it into Kirsty's palm. "Keep this. It was sacred to your father and might help you on your journey."

Gently, Kirsty unwrapped the cloth, revealing a delicate, old silver cross. It had intricately carved patterns on it and fit snugly into her palm. "Thank you, it's beautiful."

Olivia's eyes glistened, "I gave it to him to give to his children one day, it goes back generations in our family. Some say all the way back to Grand Chief Membertou, who converted to Catholicism in 1610."

Kirsty looked at the cross and back up at Olivia, "I can't take this then, it's too valuable." She tried to put it back in Olivia's hand. "No, no, you must have it. It belongs to you, along with our family heritage."

"But, I'm not pure blood, I'm only half." Her grandmother laughed, "Why, that makes no difference! Even if you have only a drop of our DNA you are forever imprinted with it, part of our family."

Kirsty felt herself start to fade, "Thank you, grandmother."

The old lady reached out to her, "Please come visit me again soon."

"I'll try."

9:00 pm, GMT-6. New Beginnings Ranch, Texas.

Thomas heard a knock. With a grunt he got up and pulled open the door, Luke's tall form filled the door carrying two plates with custard pie.

"You missed pudding; thought I'd steal us two pieces for an evening snack?"

Thomas narrowed his eyes at Luke, "Emily sent you, didn't she?"

A violent shaking of the head on Luke's part came before he cleared his throat, "I figured you might need a sounding board."

The wooden floor creaked as Thomas turned around and walked back towards the small kitchenette in the corner. He filled the kettle, put it on and pulled cups out of the cupboard, banging them down with more force than necessary.

"I don't want to talk about it."

A chair scraped as Luke settled down at the table in the middle of the room, "Bring us some spoons, please."

Thomas brought two over and sat down opposite Luke; in silence they dug into the pie. He could feel Luke's dark gaze, a frown indented his forehead, "I don't want to talk about! All my life I did the right thing, except once! I stepped over the line and the results were a daughter that grew up without a father. I can't believe I had a living, breathing daughter somewhere in the world I didn't know about! I feel like, like I want to punch the wall!"

Luke lifted his eyebrows, "Why don't you? I know the owner, and he's quite handy at woodwork."

Thomas jumped up, pacing up and down, "It won't help, will it? I'll just injure myself."

Luke shrugged, "It might help you channel your anger. I've broken a few doors and walls in my time."

The stallion tattoo on Luke's bicep showed under his rolled-up sleeves and caught Thomas's eyes, "You know, I don't even have a tattoo. I've always tried to toe the line, be good, and what do I get for it?"

The sound of the kettle boiling filled the silence. Luke glanced towards it, "I'll make the coffee, shall I?" He got up and started on it while Thomas brooded behind him.

"It's not fair, Luke. All I ever wanted was a family."

A strong hand touched his shoulder, "I know it's tough man, but God can bring good out of anything. When Emily got kidnapped and it was my fault, I felt so out of control, but in it all God was there. He's with you. He doesn't love you for getting it right, He loves you because He died for you. For who you are, not what you do."

A deep moan came out of Thomas, "I'm a sinner, Luke, a self-righteous sinner."

Luke grabbed his shoulder more tightly, "Yes, your flesh is sinful, but Thomas by faith in Christ you are a son of God and by walking with Him your flesh gets redeemed. It's by faith, not works. You are His son, no matter what you do."

Tears formed in Thomas's eyes, and Luke pulled his chair up next to him, sitting beside his friend as he cried for what he'd lost.

1:00 am, GMT. Friday, 15 January. Undisclosed location.

Camille tossed and turned, struggling to fall asleep. Her encounter with the giant kept replaying in her mind. She didn't know what she felt about it. Terrified didn't begin to describe it, but exhilarating too. She shifted on her side, staring into the dark.

"Are you asleep, Dr Camille?" His gruff voice interrupted her thoughts, as clear as day.

Camille lay there stock still, stunned.

"Are you?" His voice sounded again, an impatient note in it.

"No." Camille answered in her head.

"Good. Neither am I."

"How are you?"

"Talking to you?"

"Yes."

"Telepathy is a higher form of communication than speech. It used to be normal for your kind, but it's another thing you've forgotten how to use."

"How do you know all of this?"

"The memories of your ancestors are stored in your DNA. I know how to access them."

"So, you know everything your ancestors knew?"

"Yes. I'll prove it. You said I have some of your DNA?"

"Yes." Camille touched her forehead, astounded at the conversation in her head. It was quiet for so long that Camille thought he was gone.

"Trojan?"

"Yes. I went to see what I could find about your ancestors. They are evil indeed. Trading with blood for power."

"You know that?"

"I know your mother ended her life when you were nine. Interesting that your father shielded you, gave you a chance to have a normal life."

Tears were rolling down Camille's cheeks, "He sacrificed his soul to protect me. I think the only good left in him is his love for me."

"Love. A strange concept. A willingness to sacrifice yourself for another."

"I know." A quiet settled between them as Camille wondered to herself whether he could read all her thoughts.

"I can." A low, grumbling laugh sounded in her head.

"I don't like it." She retorted.

"Who says you can't read mine? Why don't you try?" He said teasingly.

Camille focused her thoughts on him, imagining him lying in the cell. She tried to see what was in his head. A thought popped into her head. *I don't want to be here.*

"Do you regret that you were made?"

A sigh filtered into her thoughts. "Yes."

She bit her lip, before saying, "I'm not. You're amazing." Silence met her sentence. "I mean it. You know things about who we were meant to be. I wish I knew what you know."

"Believe me, you don't. It's the knowledge of good and evil that got men into trouble in the first place."

"What other knowledge is there?"

"Life."

"Life?"

"Yes. The higher way. The Creator's way."

"Do you mean God, as in the Christian God?"

"Yes. The way my kind rejected."

"And mine." Camille lay quietly, feeling her eyelids grow heavy. "Goodnight, sleep well, Trojan."

"Sleep well, Dr Camille." His voice had a softness to it that she didn't dare explore.

8:00 am, GMT-6. New Beginnings Ranch, Texas.

Thomas loaded his carry-on and battered guitar case into the Mustang. He left the large suitcase with stuff he didn't need to make space for Anna's luggage. He marched into the main house looking for her.

Emily came down the hallway, Thomas stared at her round stomach. *Anna carried my child.* A mixture of regret, anger and grief flooded through him before he shut it off, straightening his shoulders. "Where's Anna?"

Emily looked at him with a frown, "I haven't seen her. She must still be sleeping."

"Is this her room?" Thomas asked, pointing down a side hallway, with a door on its right. Without waiting for an answer, he walked down it and pounded on the door, "Anna, time to go."

A muffled response reached his ears, he clenched his jaw, "If you don't come out in five minutes, I'm coming in."

A soft hand grasped his elbow, "Thomas, come have

breakfast. She'll probably have a hard time getting dressed with her ankle."

Oh, the ankle. He followed Emily to the kitchen where she fried them up some eggs and bacon. His hands gripped his mug of coffee tightly, not feeling like conversing.

Emily sat down across from him, munching on some toast, "I'm so hungry now, I feel like I can eat a horse every day."

Thomas shook his head, "Luke wouldn't like it if you started in on his horses."

She smiled, but it didn't reach her eyes. She looked at Thomas, "Thomas, you can't blame Anna. She did what she thought was best."

He studied his plate his appetite gone, but obediently he forked a piece of bacon and placed it in his mouth.

Emily tried again, "I've counselled many couples, and I see time and time again how misunderstanding can cause hurt and separation. You must talk about it; get to the bottom of how you are feeling and why. Don't presume the other person knows."

Thomas' eyes blazed, "Anna's always done what Anna wants, when she wants, how she wants." His grip tightened on his fork as he speared another piece of bacon. "I'm sure you would like to blame me for that one-night stand and yes, I did have a choice, but she planned it. She coerced me into buying the alcohol, manipulated me by saying I was boring and no fun, that she would have to find another guy to hang out with."

Emily's soft sigh could be heard across the table, "Thomas, it isn't important whose fault it was. It is important how you go on from here. You have to forgive, let go of the past and make good choices here and now."

A smile lifted the corner of Thomas' mouth, "You would've made a good preacher, Mrs Johnson. That sounds like a line out of one of my own sermons."

Emily lifted her thin eyebrows and rolled her eyes, she reached her hand out and placed it on his forearm, "Thomas, Anna's done good, Ellie's amazing."

His jaw hardened again. "Yes, without me."

They heard a scuffling by the door and saw Anna standing there, dressed in a knee-length purple skirt and dark green, embroidered top. She had a black shoe on one foot, with the other in a bandage looking twice its size.

"Oh, Anna, morning! That looks worse. Is it sore?" Emily stood up and helped her friend to the table.

Anna sank down in a chair, her teeth clamped together. Emily placed a plate in front of her, poured her coffee, and got her pain medicine with a glass of water.

"Is your luggage packed?" Thomas asked, his voice clipped.

"Yes." Anna avoided his eyes.

He emptied his cup, stood up and looked at Emily, "Thank you Emily, I'm going to load her things, go say goodbye to Luke and then come help Anna to the car."

When he left the room, Emily took a seat next to Anna. "Are you going to be okay? I could ask Luke to talk to him?"

Anna took a fortifying breath and shook her head, "It's better to get this over as quickly as possible. Once he has something in his head there's no changing it. I think I need to get to a doctor with my ankle so it's probably a good thing to go into town."

"Yes, but travelling all the way back to Ireland with it?"

Anna shrugged, "At least you sit most of the way. I'll get a wheelchair or disabled service in the airports. I'll be fine."

"And you and Thomas?"

"For Ellie's sake, I'll be civil."

Emily gave a small laugh, "For Thomas's sake, I hope so too. He's a good man. Life has been hard on him lately."

Anna shrugged, "Life is tough."

Emily touched Anna's forearm, "I'll be thinking of you, and I'll miss you. Will you come to visit again soon? And bring Ellie?"

Anna's eyes filled, and she leant forward into the nook of Emily's shoulder. They held each other for a moment. "I will. You be good and don't do too much. I'm going to make your baby a few gorgeous outfits."

Thomas cleared his throat behind them and said, "Your chariot awaits you." Anna's cheeks turned red as she scooted back her chair and stood up on one leg. Luke and the twins trailed in behind Thomas. They all hugged her, the twins begging her to come back soon.

Thomas waited until they were done saying goodbye before he walked over, placed his arm around her for support, and helped her to the car. Once there, he carefully lowered her into the low seat. After hugging Emily, the twins and Luke again, he got in on the other side.

The engine growled to life and the taillights of the Mustang glowed red. Thomas drove off, gathering speed slowly. When they reached the main road, he put his foot down hard on the accelerator making the engine roar. Anna grabbed the door handle, but her face reflected her appreciation. He glanced over at her saw the smile which started one of his own. "She's a beauty, isn't she?"

Anna nodded.

The rest of the day passed in a blur. They found a hospital where they took x-rays of her foot. After an hour the results came in; she hadn't broken it but needed to keep her weight off it for a while. They re-bandaged it, gave her crutches, and she was good to go. They gave the Mustang back at the airport, booked flights, and before the day was done, they were on their way to Ireland.

Anna had decided not to forewarn Ellie, firstly because she didn't know how she would react and secondly because Ellie didn't answer her phone when she called. She left a message that she'd be there on Saturday, and that she was bringing a friend with her. It bothered her that Ellie wasn't replying to her messages as she normally replied straight away.

Finally on the international flight, Anna shifted her weight, her ankle throbbing. She couldn't wait for dinner to be served so that she could drink some more pain medicine. Thomas glanced over at her. "In pain?"

She nodded. He was silent. "Did it hurt? To have her?"

Anna grimaced, "What do you think?"

He frowned, "I just wanted to know if it went well."

Anna exhaled, "Sorry. You have a right to know about your daughter's birth." She proceeded to tell him in as much detail as she remembered about the birth pain that started the afternoon after she had eaten some muffins and tea. How she was in labour for three days wearied out beyond words. How her mother cried, and her father paced the hallway. How Ellie came out with a smile on her face, quiet with no tears.

In the middle of her story she looked at his face and saw the tears there; she wanted to reach out and wipe them away. This man that she thought hadn't loved her, this man that she'd wronged by keeping his daughter's life from him.

After she'd told him everything, he gruffly thanked her and turned away, taking a magazine and leafing through it. Anna swallowed down the apology that kept wanting to escape her lips. Instead, she asked for some water from the passing flight attendant and swallowed the pain meds on an empty stomach.

With her eyes closed, her head resting against the backrest, her imagination conjured up how different it would've been if he'd been there at the birth. *My parents would have thrown us out, Ellie would never have known them.* The realisation gave her a painful jolt.

Her throat felt thick as she contemplated the past. *Emily's right. I need to lay the past to rest.* She'd listened in on the conversation Emily had with Thomas. She also heard he thought that she always did what she wanted. *He's right. It was my idea. I don't regret it though. Ellie is the most fantastic thing that ever happened to me. It changed me from a selfish teenager to a loving mother, gave me purpose, made me strong. I don't regret having her, but I do regret losing Thomas. I can't believe he's right here, next to me. I never thought that would happen.*

She studied him, noticing he wasn't shaving, and his hair looked unkempt, a far cry from the tidy minister who married Luke and Emily. What happened to him? He looked up, their eyes meeting.

He lifted his eyebrows, "What?"

She shrugged her shoulders lightly, "I was wondering if you're still the minister at Nomansland?"

His eyes clouded over, and he looked back at his magazine. "No."

The cart rattled as their dinner came nearer and they had to choose between chicken or beef. Thomas chose beef and she chicken, while the aeroplane took them ever nearer to Ireland and to Ellie.

2:00 pm, GMT+1. Ugarte villa, Spain.

Jean-Pierre surveyed the room with a sense of satisfaction. His father had given him a few workers and they cleared the ivy off from the building. They cleaned out the dust inside, washed the windows and within a day the place was transformed. He had bought supplies; seven fresh, white canvases, paints and brushes and brand-new easels. He inhaled and looked out the window where the view ran out and down the hill over the vineyards.

Since they'd lost the last baby, he'd been dreaming vivid dreams of children, their faces laughing and singing. In his dreams he danced with them and played. It had become so recurrent that he started hoping he would dream about them. It felt like they were his. Maybe some of them were the ones they'd lost, three miscarriages and the girl, but he didn't try to understand it too much. He hadn't even told Kirsty about them.

His mother used to take him to the Catholic church down in the valley, but since she left, he never went again. He frowned. *Maybe I should visit the church on Sunday, but first I want to paint the children of my dreams. If I stop dreaming, I might forget what they look like.*

He thought of the large social gathering planned for the next day by his father, all the extended family and friends were coming to the villa. He wasn't in the mood for it.

He wondered uneasily if Kirsty was still at the ranch or whether she'd gone back to Toronto. She hadn't texted him or phoned him at all. Neither had he, but she was usually the first one to use digital communication. *You abandoned her. No, I didn't. She needs you. She doesn't.*

This internal dialogue caused a flitter of worry in his stomach, he took his phone out of his back pocket and stared at it. His fingers opened the WhatsApp application, and he found her name. Quickly he texted, *'Landed safely. Renovating my mother's old studio.'* He snapped a quick photo of the interior and sent it to her. The message showed that it wasn't delivered, and he frowned. If she was still at the ranch with no signal it made sense, but she always had her phone on in Toronto.

He found Luke's mobile number that he'd taken in case of an emergency. He texted him: '*Kirsty still with you guys?*'

The message got delivered and within seconds Luke read it and replied, '*No. She went with the CIA on Wednesday. She didn't let you know?*'

Jean-Pierre reread the message not sure he read it right. '*Do you mean CIA, as in Central Intelligence Agency?*'

'*Yes. She used to work for them? They needed her for something.*'

Jean-Pierre felt a buzz somewhere in his head. '*Are we talking about my Kirsty?*'

'*Yes?*'

Jean-Pierre held the phone in his hand, not knowing what to do or say; eventually he typed, '*Do you think she's all right? Her phone is not taking messages.*'

'*Should be. Try phoning her parents or family?*'

'*Ok.*'

Jean-Pierre put the phone back into his pocket. He didn't have her parents' telephone number. He pushed his hand through his hair, exhaling and inhaling slowly, trying to calm the worry that was escalating in him. He clenched his fist looking for something to punch. *Worked for the CIA? How come I don't know about it? What else has she hidden from me? What could she possibly have done for the CIA?*

Grabbing his phone out of his pocket again he Googled, 'Kirsty Knight'. Nothing unusual came up, her web design business, her Facebook page. He wiped his hand across his face and googled, Kirsten Knight, CIA. He scrolled down through the various unrelated items until his eye caught a news article. "Doctor Kirsten Knight finds missing diplomat's daughter and uncovers kidnapping ring in Mexico. The unusual process called 'remote viewing' produced impressive results, helping for the first time to uncover crimes."

It was dated nine years ago. She must have been twenty-four. He scanned the rest of the article. It said she held a doctorate in physics. *How could she have been a doctor in physics at twenty-*

four? Could this be my Kirsty? Mentally, he reviewed everything he knew about her past. She mentioned that she studied, but never elaborated, he thought she meant web design. She was dyslexic after all! He was twenty-three when he met her, and she was twenty-seven. She struck him as mature and settled, running her own business.

He ground his teeth. *Was everything about her a lie? Who's the woman I've spent seven years of my life with?* There'd only been one brief relationship before Kirsty, she was the first woman whom he truly fell in love with; body, heart and soul. What if she had a split personality, always showing him the one and hiding the other? Jean-Pierre felt nauseous, she always seemed so in control, so organised, as if she had it all together.

He placed his phone back in his pocket, resisting the urge to keep googling for more information. He took his pencil and started on rough sketches of the faces haunting his dreams. Seven children, four boys and three girls. Slowly, they took shape on the canvas. Jean-Pierre lost himself in the concentration of drawing from memory.

It was dark by the time he finished, realising with a shock that he was hungry and thirsty, having drawn for hours. He couldn't wait to start filling them in with colour, but first he had to find some food and water. He thought about Kirsty but pushed it aside. There wasn't anything he could do besides going back to America and trying to knock on the CIA headquarters' front door. His fingers tapped restlessly against his thigh, his gut churning at the thought that she might not be who he thought she was at all.

He locked the studio, the urge to get away welling up in him. Getting out his mobile phone, he phoned an old school friend, who was so excited to hear from him that he suggested he come pick him up straight away and take him out for dinner in San Sebastian where they could spend the evening. He texted his dad that he would be out, catching up with his friend until he had to be back for the get together the next evening, placing his phone on silent.

His friend picked him up within half an hour. They passed a car coming up their villa's drive on their way out. Jean-Pierre didn't wonder who the car belonged to, for the next twenty-four hours he was going to try and forget about every single one of his problems.

9:00 am, GMT-5. Secret ESP Facility, Langley, Virginia.

Kirsty was woken by the noise in the room. She opened her eyes and then shut them again, the bright light piercing her skull. Why did she feel so tired? Slowly she sat up, observing all the scientists already full speed at work in the facility. Her dream came back to her and she smiled. For a change it was a good one. Imagine if she really had a loving grandmother like that somewhere in the world.

Someone had left her breakfast pushed through the small slot in the wall above the table. She tucked into the still-warm baguette with bacon and cheese, relishing the freshly brewed, take-away coffee, not even minding the full cream milk.

There was a commotion in the corner of the long row of tables at one of the computers. Uneasiness stirred inside her as she observed everyone in the building standing around, gaping at something showing on the computer screen. After a little while, three of the people strode over to her cage and peered at her as if she was an anomaly.

Kirsty flexed her shoulders. "What? Stop staring at me like that."

Dr Lemming seemed to be the one in charge. "Dr Knight did you have an unusual experience last night?"

She shrugged taking another sip of her coffee. *Not unusual for me.* "No. Why?"

The three men looked at each other and back at her, a younger one with wild black hair spoke up, "We want to run some tests on you."

Kirsty shook her head, "I'm not letting you do any tests on me. I'm not one of your lab rats."

He frowned, "But Dr Knight, this could be a real breakthrough in scientific discovery. Aren't you interested in knowing more about your abilities?"

She rolled her eyes, "What abilities, Dr?"

"Black. Doctor Black."

"What abilities, Dr Black?"

Dr Lemming cleared his throat, "We have a surveillance camera for the inside of the building for safety. It has night vision capability and can pick up any movement even in the dark. It clearly shows your body moving up out of your bed through the roof of the cage and the roof of the building. Then an hour and a half later it shows how your body lowers down until you're back in your bed.

Kirsty's eyes widened. "But that's impossible."

"Did you or did you not have any strange experience last night?" Dr Black demanded.

Kirsty pursed her lips. "No. Just the usual dreams. Your camera must have a glitch."

Dr Lemming cleared his throat, "Thank you, Dr. Knight. Let's go."

"What? You're just going to let her lie to you through her teeth? We both know that camera doesn't lie! She translocated out and back into that cage. I'd bet my life on it."

"Quiet!" Dr Lemming stared down Dr Black. "Enough. She isn't here for our studies. We cannot do tests on her and that's the end of the story."

Dr Black threw Kirsty a dark look and stormed back to his computer station. The third man who'd been quiet through the whole exchange, hung back while Dr Lemming walked away. He quietly opened the cage to retrieve her breakfast rubbish and with it in his hands, he sank down on the chair looking at her. "I want to say; it's an honour."

Kirsty grunted, "Why?"

"You clearly have a supernatural gift or ability that very few people have mastered in our lifetime. I've studied gifted people, especially the Saints who had mystical abilities, trying to link it to ESP. We just don't have enough data to understand it."

Kirsty studied his earnest dark face and asked, "Did you ever hear about the Lady in Blue?"

"Oh, yes, I found her fascinating. Claiming to translocate to the American Indians for so many years, even taking things with her. There is overwhelming evidence that her story is true."

Kirsty rolled her eyes, "She's fascinating, also very annoying."

He dipped his head sideways, "You speak as if you've met her?"

Kirsty shrugged, "I might have. She might have fed me some of her chilli beans, which I spilt on my white T-shirt which had a stain on the next morning when I woke up. How do you think that would hold up as scientific evidence?"

He laughed, "Not very well. I see your point." He sat forward, "So it happens involuntarily, you cannot predict when or where to? Yet, it seems relevant to your life in some way. Fascinating. There must be a higher force, or if you will, God involved, for this to happen.

Kirsty gave a forced laugh, "Or my own psychic powers are propelling me to places, against my will."

He stroked his chin, "But you had no foreknowledge of the Lady in Blue?"

"No, I hadn't, neither did I with my grandmother last night."

His eyes grew big, "So you did have an experience?"

Kirsty scowled at him, "I didn't tell you anything."

"I'm John by the way." He extended his arm to her, and she shook his hand.

He pulled his arm back and rubbed his hands together. "This is so interesting. How can your psyche dish this up and or even transport you somewhere when you have no prior knowledge of it? It has to be orchestrated by something or someone."

Kirsty rubbed her face, feeling a sting on her forefinger. She placed it in her mouth, sucking it and the papercut she got in her dream came back to her. "No ways!" She pulled her finger out and looked at it.

"What is it?"

"My finger, it's cut."

He jumped up. "Did you cut it in your experience?"

She stared at him with a bewildered look on her face before she gave a slight nod. John let out a loud whoop! "That proves it. You must have been there physically."

She looked at him, suddenly afraid. "John, keep it down. I

don't want people to know about this."

"Sure, sure." He sat down, but he looked like a kid at Christmas. "Dr Knight, this is the most exciting thing I've encountered in my life as a scientist."

She shook her head, her face in a frown, "I don't understand it. It simply isn't possible. Natural law defies it. You cannot physically move through things and to other places."

John sat his one foot going up and down, "But they did it, the saints, even the people in the Bible. There was Philip who translocated and Peter who walked out of a jail cell."

"Only one problem; I'm not a saint. I'm not even a Christian."

John grinned at her, "I bet you that's going to change. Even your name is against you."

"What do you mean?"

"Don't you know? Kirsty or Kirsten means Christian."

"That is not funny."

Kirsty felt around under her covers, her hand touching something hard. She pulled it out and stared at the silver cross in her hand.

John sat forward, watching her intently. "You got that when you were with your grandmother? You brought it with you?"

Kirsty folded her hand around it and hid it under the covers again. She looked at John, her eyes troubled and afraid. "John, thank you for talking to me, but I don't want to talk anymore. Please leave me alone now."

He stood up; his tall frame almost as tall as the door. "Dr Knight, I don't know why this is happening with you, but I'll let you know I'll be praying for you. I know scientists aren't normally praying men, but this one is, and you sure look like you need it." He looked at her, his eyes kind. "Remember that He said, 'Look I stand at the door and knock. If any man opens for me, I will come in…'"

With that, he winked at her and left. Kirsty went into the bathroom to shower and put on new clothes. She placed the cross inside her handbag, not believing that it could really be there. The hows and whys were driving her up the wall. A chilli stain was one thing, the paper cut she could have gotten another way, but a physical cross that wasn't there before was quite another thing. *What about the video footage?* Her brain felt like exploding.

After her shower, she sat down at the little table and started to write down some of her theories and questions. After a few minutes she tore up the paper, crushing it into the bin. Her eyes strayed onto the blue amulet bracelet on her arm and she undid the catch. Holding it in her hand she frowned before she threw it into the bin on top of the crushed paper.

Walking over to her handbag she rummaged around till she found the slip of paper with the address Maria had given her. The words Sable River Village seemed to freeze her to the spot. *It's only a coincidence. My subconscious remembered the address and dreamed it up.*

She started pacing up and down, not caring what they thought. Stopping abruptly, she stared at the people in the room. There was one explanation she didn't want to explore. *It's happened. I've lost it. Maybe I'm imagining having the cross here, speaking to John.* Her eyes searched for him between the people, but she couldn't locate him. *See, you're hallucinating, Kirsty. You're going crazy.* Frantically, she searched in her handbag and brought out the cross. Its cold, solid shape was reassuring, but also disturbing.

She sat on her bed, knees pulled up, staring into the room. Her awareness of other things in the facility increased. A dark depression seemed to settle on her and she knew it was only time before she heard the voices, felt the attacks and the maddening fear of not knowing what was real and what was not. Without knowing it, her body started rocking back and forth.

The whole day nobody else came, and she wondered uneasily where Leo Molineux had gone. *Has he given up on me? How can we both know someone that I wouldn't want eliminated? Does he mean kill? I only love Jean-Pierre. I'm glad he went to the Basque country, far away from here; he'll be safe there. He abandoned me.* Kirsty cut off the last thought.

Around four o'clock, Dr Lemming brought over her dinner and quietly he said, "Thank you for finding Leila for me yesterday. She'd been found by someone who decided to keep her. When I knocked, Leila went ballistic and the person had to give her back to me."

Kirsty felt her heart warm at the gratitude in his eyes but shrank back as she saw a green frog-like creature on his head. It seemed to be covering his brain and without knowing how, she knew its intent was to deceive him. The black eyes stared at her insolently and with eyes shut, she asked, "Dr Lemming, do you know when I might be free to go? Is there a way you could ask the Director, Mr Smith?"

She didn't see his face become grave, and his hand fiddle with his nametag, clipped onto his pocket.

"I can inquire for you. No one knows what's going on, and no one wants to know. It seems your case is above even the Director's authority."

Kirsty sighed; she'd thought as much. "Thank you in any case. For earlier today and for dinner too."

"No problem." Dr Lemming turned to go, but Kirsty opened her eyes and said, while looking anywhere but at him, "Do you know what they did with my laptop and my phone?"

He turned back to her, fidgeting with his tag, "They gave it to me to keep, but I can't give it to you in the Faraday cage." His eyes darted around the room. "I can't let you out either."

Kirsty bit her lower lip, "Would you mind doing me a small favour? Could you charge my phone and send a text to someone called Jean-Pierre? Just tell him I'm all right, but won't be available for a while?"

Dr Lemming lifted his eyebrows but gave a small nod, before turning around and closing the door behind him. Kirsty released the breath she'd been holding.

Fifteen minutes later, Director Smith stared at the e-mail on his screen. He clicked on the attachment and felt sweat break out on his brow. At five minutes to five, he strode into the facility, just as the scientists were packing up for the day. He waited until they left before entering Kirsty's cell, seating himself on the chair.

She was sitting on the bed trying to read one of the boring novels, anything to distract her. She placed it down as he came in, hugging her arms around herself. The grey creature hanging on him like a cloak caused her only slight anxiety.

He cleared his throat, "As I said before, I'm sorry for the inconvenience this is causing you. As it is, we don't have a lot of say in whether you come or go. That's up to…"

"Leo Molineux…so I gathered."

The Director sat back, pursing his lips. "I don't like it any more than you do, believe me, but sometimes we just have to toe the line."

"I can't do what he asks." *Although it might not matter anymore.*

His face scowled, "That's between you and him, but whatever you do, do not disappear out of this Faraday cage. It is my responsibility to keep you safely available."

Kirsty's brows lifted and a half-smile played on her lips, "You saw the footage?"

His scowl deepened, "I don't know what I saw, but all I know is that if you disappear I'll have to hunt you down and it won't be fun for either of us."

Kirsty gave an impatient huff. "If it helps, I'm not doing anything voluntarily."

His eyes widened, "So you can't control it?"

"No! The only thing I can control is not doing what he wants, to try and protect my sanity." *Which I might have lost already.* Kirsty shivered.

Director Smith stood up and looked down at her, "I can't help you, Dr. Knight. You'd better figure out a way without disappearing."

She cleared her throat, "Director?"

"Yes?"

"He said he was going to find someone I love that no one would miss except me. It sounded like he was threatening to kill him or her?"

A flicker of distress passed over his face before he let himself out of the cage. He stood still, his hand on the handle, "I can't help you. I'm sorry, you're on your own."

As the door clanged behind him, Kirsty crumpled into a heap, crawling under the covers fully dressed. Curling up in a foetal form, she cried while clutching the old silver cross tightly in her hand. As hopelessness descended on her, the first prayer she ever breathed escaped from the depths of her soul: *God if You exist, let Me see you.*

CHAPTER 9

Kirsty woke with a start. She turned her head and saw a bright white room with nothing but a door on the one side. *Where am I?* A look down at herself revealed a white dress with her feet bare. She bit her lip, this dream felt different from the others. Another glance at the door. *Where does it lead to?*

She took a hesitant step towards it but a knock from the outside made her jump. Her heart beat in alarm, as an irrational fear seized her. She withdrew to the far corner of the room. The knocking stopped, and dead silence permeated the air. The scripture John quoted earlier came back to her, 'Look I stand at the door and knock, if any man opens, I will come in'.

Kirsty peered at the door, instinctively she knew that there would be no returning to blissful ignorance and unbelief once she opened it. Hours seemed to pass as she paced, the length and breadth of the room, which wasn't more than twelve square feet.

Sweat started to appear on her forehead, as the intensity of her inward struggle increased. She stopped in front of the door and as she paused, that gentle knock sounded again. Her hand reached towards the handle, her resolve not to open it weakening. She pulled it open fast, dreading who she would find.

In front of her stood her childhood lion friend.

"You?"

He stared at her with his liquid golden eyes, "Hello, little one."

She gazed into his eyes, finding his love warming up her insides and quelling her fears, "Why are you here?"

"This is my home. Do you want to see it?"

She stepped across the threshold, gripping his mane with her right hand like she used to when she was young. They walked together, the path leading towards a river in the distance. Kirsty marvelled at the bright colours in what appeared to be a garden. The leaves of the trees were silver, and fruit she had never seen before grew in clusters on some of them.

"Where are we?"

"This is the beginning of my realm, my garden." The low vibration of his voice seemed to carry into her and suddenly she stopped. He stopped too, looking up at her. She stared at him, her eyebrows bunched towards the middle, "Who are you, exactly?"

"Who do you think I Am?" He looked at her, his head slightly inclined.

Kirsty licked her lips, "Are you, you can't be, God?"

His lips pulled up in what appeared to be a lion's way of smiling, "Do you want to know who I Am, Kirsten?"

Her heart started beating faster, and she found herself kneeling in front of him. "I do."

"I am not a figment of your imagination." His warm breath blew on her face.

"I am the Alpha and Omega, the beginning and the end."

"I am the Way, the Truth and the Life."

"I am the living Word, the Lamb slain before the foundations of the earth."

As he spoke, his form started changing, and before her eyes he transformed into a man's form, with a brilliant white tunic, eyes like fire, scars on his hands and feet.

He's real! Kirsty knelt with her face at his feet. Trembles racked her body as deep sobs convulsed through her. She felt her unbelief draining out of her, her sorrow for denying His existence drowning out everything else.

When at last her tears subsided, she felt his hand resting on her head. "Kirsten Knight, I traded my life on the cross to save yours. Are you willing to trade in your life for mine?"

The last resistance in her crumbled away as she said, "Yes, I am."

"Then come, child, see My kingdom. Everything that's mine is now yours." With that, he helped her up and as her eyes locked with his, his smile radiated back at her.

I love you. She thought.

I've always loved you too, little one.

His answer came into her mind. It didn't surprise her that they could speak heart to heart without the need for words. What did surprise her was that there was no darkness or fear anywhere, not even inside her. She felt swathed in blissful, joyous love.

Hand in hand they walked down to the river that was glistening with gold and precious stones in water so crystal clear it looked like liquid glass.

Am I dreaming?

You're not dreaming. This is a real place, not an imaginary one. I was never a figment of your imagination either. He turned fiery eyes on her. *Unless you're born from above, you cannot see My kingdom. I'm the door to the Kingdom of Heaven.*

Kirsty blinked, tearing her eyes away from his. *It's beautiful.* She drank it in. Sounds seemed to come from everything, visible frequencies that radiated joy, peace and love. Inhaling deeply, the sweet fragrance of lilies filled her lungs.

She looked at him, and he read her thoughts again. *Call me, Yahshua.*

Yahshua. She liked the sound of it. She knew Him, He was the One who chased away the monsters who terrorised her in the night as a child. That is until she chose not to believe that He was real.

I couldn't help you anymore.

I know. Were You there when I went crazy?

He turned his fiery gaze on her, sending tingles of love into the fibres of her being.

I never took My eyes off you.

The thought that He was there during a time when she felt totally abandoned, filled her with a healing comfort, but nothing made sense to her anymore.

I don't understand.

Yahshua gave her a comforting smile. *It isn't what you know; it's Who you know. Come.* He turned and walked next to the river. Kirsty looked ahead and saw a bridge which had a person standing on it. Her eyes couldn't make out his features, but the sense of love she felt radiate out from him was stronger than anything she felt before. Her heartbeat increased; it was almost painful.

They approached the bridge and walked onto it, standing face to face with the person. His warm eyes rested on Kirsty. "Daughter, welcome."

Kirsty's eyes were wide; His presence so strong it made her knees feel weak. *Who are You?*

He gazed into her with eyes that were alight. "I AM. You can call me Yahweh."

She licked her dry lips, trying to speak. "Yahweh?"

Yahshua turned his head and nudged her hand. "My Father and your Father, I became the way so that you can know Him."

"Father." Kirsty felt the word on her tongue and a strange hunger took hold of her. "Yahweh?"

"Daughter?"

"I want to know You."

He held out His hand. "Come."

She placed her hand in his, feeling the security of His touch travel up her arm and envelop her being. Strength flowed into her. He looked deep into her eyes and said, "Would you like to see how you came to be?"

Kirsty's eyes grew wide, "Oh, I don't know."

He laughed a soft laugh. "No. Not that. Come, I'll show you who you are. Who you were, before you were born."

"Before?" Kirsty hurried to keep up with him, for he was moving across the bridge. Faster and faster they went, until their surroundings seemed to blur. Kirsty blinked and everything had turned dark around them.

She heard his quiet voice next to her but didn't see him. "The kingdom of heaven is outside of time and space. We are now before you were born, when you were an illuminary with Me."

She saw it then; a bright spirit being hovering slightly above her. The being was beautiful with a green glow around her. In her hands she held what looked like a scroll. Kirsty couldn't tear her eyes away from the sight. *That can't be me. I'm a mistake.*

"No one is a mistake." His words filled the emptiness inside her with love as hot as lava. She stared mesmerised at her spirit being.

What's on the scroll?

Again, He answered her unspoken question, "That is your destiny scroll. What you agreed with Me to go and do on the earth. When you're born it's within you, but from the moment of conception it gets overlaid with the layers of your parents' DNA and all your ancestors' DNA. You lose the memory of it and only find it again when you find me. If you allow me, I'll help you to unlock your scroll so that it can start fulfilling your destiny within you and reveal to you what you were meant to do."

I have a destiny? Kirsty stared at the glowing scroll, everything inside her earning to know what was written on it. "I want to know what it says, please, unlock it!"

"First, let's look at your conception." The scene changed, and she looked down seeing a little sperm and ovum as if enlarged under a microscope. Fascinated she followed the sperm as it outswam all the millions of other sperms to wriggle into the egg. The moment the two became one there was a bright flash of light, and she saw her spirit joining the tiny embryo.

That's me? The awe of the moment overwhelmed Kirsty, a moan escaping her lips.

She felt the warmth of His presence surround her, "Kirsty, you're a spirit being, who chose to go to earth to fulfil a destiny you agreed to, joined to a living soul and living in a body. When you accept My Son's sacrifice, you receive a new soul and regain access to where you came from."

His voice had a sad tinge to it as He said, "In the Kingdom of Earth, you're born in darkness, inside of time and space. If you don't find the light, everything you see is perverted, twisted."

Why did I agree to go there then? I don't like being there.

The scene changed in an instant and they were in front of a table on which a goblet filled with a red liquid stood next to a flatbread. Yahshua appeared beside her in human form. She couldn't see Yahweh, but she felt His presence around her.

Yahshua picked up the bread and turned to her. Breaking off a piece he said, "Part of the reason you went to earth, was to redeem your DNA. My body, my DNA is holy, redeemed. If you eat Me, your DNA will change to become like mine."

He took the cup and held it out to her, "My blood cleanses you of all unrighteousness which is everything in you that's not the way you were meant to be. When you take it on earth, at the same time, you can take it here in My kingdom realm, cleansing you, restoring you to your original estate."

His fiery eyes bore into hers, "You went to earth to redeem your DNA."

Kirsty felt her knees grow weak as the impact of His words filled her mind. "Are you saying that by eating and drinking of You, I can change my DNA into yours?"

He placed his hand on her shoulder, "Not just yours."

Kirsty bunched her brows as she struggled to understand, "Who else?"

"Everything you redeem, you redeem for your children and their children, too."

A sob escaped Kirsty as she spluttered, "But I can't have children. They keep dying."

Gently, he wiped the tear off her cheek and lifted her chin, "Have faith, Kirsty. Remember, every light being fulfilling their purpose on earth no matter how long they lived and afterwards they return to the Father of lights."

He took her hand. "Come, we'll show you."

They seemed to land in a vast open space, Kirsty could see a large city shimmering in the distance, but here between the fields and the trees, there were many groups of people enjoying the outdoors.

As they approached a group, a bunch of children broke free and ran in their direction. The leader, a girl, shouted, "You brought her! Thank you, Yahshua, Yahweh!" She came to a stop in front of Kirsty, the rest of the children bunching around her. "My name is Mia, and this is Jared and Nathaniel and Bethany."

Kirsty looked into her green eyes and knew without knowing

how that these were the children she'd lost. *You're the little girl I lost three months ago.* Tears started rolling down her cheeks.

Mia looked at her with a broad smile, "Yes, we're yours. Thank you for giving us life, and a chance to fulfil our destiny. We were willing to offer our lives to work out His purposes on earth. We're watching and cheering you on, Mommy. You're amazing!"

Kirsty knelt, and they crowded around her, touching her hair, kissing her. She held their young bodies tightly, crying and laughing at the same time for what seemed like forever, yet felt like only a moment.

When she finally looked up, she saw three other children shyly standing a bit apart. The oldest one appeared to be a boy with Jean-Pierre's dark hair and eyes. The second one was also a boy, with features and build more like Kirsty. The third was a girl, who had Kirsty's green eyes but lighter hair. Kirsty looked at them feeling a flutter of anticipation in her stomach. *Are they?*

Her eyes met Yahshua's, and He smiled at her. "Yes, they are yours too yet to be born. Caleb, Sebastian and Maria. In fact, Caleb is already within you."

Kirsty felt her stomach in wonder, she looked at them again and they gave her a small wave before they disappeared. Mia tucked at her arm. "See, Mommy, you wouldn't have made Caleb if I stayed." Their eyes locked, a peace settling inside her heart, she blinked and found herself back in the garden where she came in.

"No! I don't want to leave." Kirsty looked around her finding both Yahshua and Yahweh standing behind her.

"Kirsty, you never need to leave, but only to learn how to come and go and be in both places at the same time." Yahweh said, with a broad smile.

"I can come at will. Even when I'm awake?"

"Yes, you can. Everything that's mine is now yours. Ask, and you will receive, seek and you will find, knock and..."

"The door will be opened." Kirsty reached out to Yahshua, and he pulled her into a hug. "Beloved, all will be well. Trust Me."

She turned to Yahweh, hesitating, but He placed his hand on

her head. "Be strong, daughter, I'm with you, always."

Kirsty opened her eyes, and the electric lights of the facility stunned her eyeballs. She shut them again marvelling at the warmth she felt in her heart. *Was it a dream?*

The door opened, and she saw John enter with her breakfast. She sat up, keeping the duvet over her.

"Good morning, thought I'd bring you a present." John placed a small pocket size Bible on the tray with her muffins and coffee. He set it down on the table, turned around, looked at her face and stilled, "Dr Knight, what happened? You're positively glowing?"

She smiled from ear to ear, "I think He knocked, and I opened."

"Alleluia!" John shouted, causing the other scientists to look over in their direction.

"Hush." Kirsty said, her cheeks flushing.

"Will you tell me?"

Kirsty nodded, "Later. You won't believe the half of it."

John laughed, "Try me."

9:00 am, GMT. Undisclosed location.

Camille pulled on a soft pink sweater with her jeans and trainers on Saturday morning. She hoped that the Professor would summon her to work with Trojan that morning. The other girls hung on her lips when she told them about her adventure of the previous day, although she'd left out small details, like the fact that he was highly intelligent. Most of the women were terrified of him and couldn't understand how or why she would volunteer to do it. Camille's response was simple. "He needs doctoring like any other living creature."

Her face lit up when their door opened and the guard pointed at her. She followed him, her pulse hammering in her throat. As they entered the ample open space, her eyes sought out Trojan, but what she saw made her shudder. He was feeding on what looked like half a cow.

It was raw and the blood ran down his beard dripping on the floor. He turned towards her and slowly, deliberately took a bite, tearing out the flesh, chewing it, his eyes daring her to look away. Bile welled up in her throat, but she refused to break eye contact. He swallowed what he was chewing and turned his back on her as he finished off his meal.

"Ah, Doctor, your services are required again today. It seems our replacement isn't going to be here any time soon, so you'll have to do. As soon as Subject 107 is finished with his meal, I want you to take a blood sample and recheck the pressure."

"What's wrong with him, Professor?"

The professor shrugged, "It looks like aplastic anaemia. His bone marrow doesn't produce enough red blood cells. Our medications seem to be having no effect, but the blood transfusions are helping. Check his heart rate too. It's been beating irregularly." He thrust the equipment of the previous day, along with a stethoscope in her hands. After opening the cell and letting her in, he walked off.

Camille stood watching Trojan, who was seated on the trolley, his shoulders slumped, his breathing coming in short bursts.

Placing the equipment next to him on the trolley, she put her hand on his forearm, "Are you okay?"

He lifted his head, and she could see he wasn't feeling well. "Are you dizzy? Why don't you lie down?" Camille moved her equipment to the floor and watched him lower himself down.

Thank you, Dr Camille. She heard in her thoughts; his lips weren't moving at all. She replied with her thoughts. *Do they know how intelligent you are?*

No, and I don't intend to let them know.

You want them to think you are a mindless brute, like a caveman?

Yes.

Why? Her eyebrows furrowed. *Your knowledge could help mankind in so many ways.*

Would it? He turned his head towards her, his dark eyes searching hers.

She stilled and swallowed at the knot in her throat. *Maybe not.*

I didn't think so. Do your thing, Doctor Camille, I'm tired.

She took his blood and then the pressure. It was slightly higher than usual. There was a light bruise where she'd taken the pressure the previous day and she touched it. *Did you bruise from me taking the blood pressure? I'm sorry.*

He grunted, but kept his eyes closed. *Your rash looks slightly improved. Would you like it if I applied more cream?*

Camille kept talking to him in her head, ignoring the weirdness of it. *Yes*, his reply came fluttering through her thoughts. She got the extra pot that she'd stashed in the corner and had him turn on his stomach before gently rubbing it in the most obvious places. Camille eyed the gown wondering if he had rashes under there not daring to explore higher than his knees.

A low chuckle filled her mind, and she blushed red. *Why don't you? I'm sure it's sore, somewhere on my behind.* Camille gulped and straightened her shoulders; she lifted the gown up, aghast at the bruising and redness across his back and behind.

You bruise from lying down and sitting?

He kept quiet, but she wanted to swear she heard a murmur of pain when she touched a sore spot. She did his front too, not daring to explore his stomach and privates. He seemed almost asleep. His hand came up and scratched at his head, and she looked at the tangled mass of dirty, black curls. *I've got an idea. Wait here.*

She banged on the gate and strode over to the professor explaining what she wanted. He looked puzzled and then shrugged giving her a guard to help her get supplies. Before long she returned with a large plastic container filled with hot water and a bottle of peppermint shampoo.

She had to push the heavy container across the floor until it was positioned at the top of the trolley where his head was. The guard wasn't helping her beyond the gate to the cell. "There, that does it." She was a bit out of breath and stood still staring at his face. *Are you still awake?*

Hmmm…

Would you mind moving up a bit, I want to get all your hair hanging down.

His eyelids opened as if against his will and a slight frown set in on his forehead. *What are you doing now, Dr Camille?*

I'm going to give you a hair wash. You won't believe how much better one feels when one's hair is clean.

There was a slight roll of the eyes on Trojan's part, but he shuffled up a bit, and she moved his hair towards the back. She had a small cup which she used to wet his hair letting the excess water drip down into the container. When it was wet enough, she squeezed almost the whole shampoo bottle out onto his head.

Trojan sniffed the fragrance filling the air, while she started working it into a lather. She touched his scalp and gently massaged it, round and around in circles. A sigh of pleasure escaped his lips aloud and a smile played on her lips. She rinsed it a few times until she was sure the soap was out and then she towel-dried it with a towel that she had also managed to snag from someone. His dark beard got the same treatment with the last bit of shampoo in the bottle.

Being done she started moving the container towards the door, the water black as soot. She felt him move behind her and in an instant, he'd taken the container and placed it by the door. For a giant, he could be light on his feet.

His frame towered over her, and before she could do something, he picked her up, holding her on his forearm against his chest. She had to grab onto his hospital gown to keep her balance, her surprised eyes finding his dark ones.

Shock filled her at the change in his appearance, his shiny black locks made him appear almost regal. *He looks like a king.* In her head she said, *What are you doing?*

You're compromising my brute persona, Dr Camille. His dark eyes bored into hers, but there was something else in them that made Camille swallow her fear.

He turned around so his back was towards the room and she was hidden from their sight. No one seemed to have noticed that he'd grabbed her. *So, my new look makes me look like a king?*

A blush flushed her cheeks and she willed herself to relax allowing her hand to rest on his chest, while she tried to empty her thoughts.

I like it when you touch me. It's soothing. His voice was low, filtering into her thoughts. *Do you think they'd let me keep you as a pet?*

Camille shook her head. *I don't want to be your pet.*

What do you want to be? His other hand came up, and he stroked over her blond tresses, twirling it over his finger.

Your friend? Camille ventured, her heart beating loudly in her chest. She licked her dry lips and said with her thoughts, *We have a fairy tale called Beauty and the Beast. In it the selfish prince gets turned into a beast until he can make a true princess love him. Only then the curse can be lifted, and he can become a prince again.*

Trojan had stilled, inclining his head. *Not all the love in the world could change this beast into a prince.*

It's not all about looks you know. Camille gave im a pointed stare and then for reasons unknown to her, she placed a soft kiss on his chest where his heart was. *I forgot; I need to listen to your heartbeat for the professor. Will you put me down?*

Trojan gave her a look that spoke volumes, before he pretended to drop her, making her scream before catching her, leaving her on unsteady feet. A guard and Professor Demid came running. The Professor adjusted his glasses, "Are you okay?"

She nodded, although she was trembling, "Just need the heartbeat."

Trojan had lain down on the trolley again, feigning disinterest. She walked around to the other side and listened to the loud irregular beating of his heart, counting the beats per minute. In her thoughts, she said: *That wasn't necessary.*

It was. My image, remember?

Hmph... A thought struck her, and he answered before she could ask. *Yes, I can read their thoughts too.*

Do you know what they're planning with us, or you?

Perhaps.

Come on, Trojan!

She kept listening to his heart, pretending to need another minute.

They don't plan to release you or the others. They'll harvest your eggs and anything else they need from you.

At least they won't kill us, right?

Not soon. No.

And with you?

Silence met her question and she became aware that the professor was watching her intently. She took the stethoscope off his chest and walked around to the gate, gathering her equipment. Professor Petrov let her out, and she gave him her findings.

He stared at her for a long moment, and she looked away. "You seem to have a special knack of handling Subject 107. None of the other doctors have been so successful. I want you to do some more tests with him and record your findings." He clicked his fingers, and someone ran over with large index cards printed with pictures and words. He gave them to Camille, "Test his intelligence and try to teach him a few words."

"I think he's tired right now. Can we do that after lunch?" Camille said, glancing towards Trojan who was lying with his eyes closed.

"Very well. We need to draw blood from you too, to have enough for a transfusion tomorrow."

10:00 am, GMT. Dublin, Ireland.

It rained the day they landed. Tired wasn't enough to describe how Anna felt. Trying Ellie's mobile again, there was no answer. She left another voicemail, and they hailed a taxi to the Music Academy.

Being a Saturday, the grounds were less busy and they knocked at her dorm door finding no one around. They stood there waiting for someone to come, Anna resting on the low wall outside the door.

The door opened, and a short girl with a brown bob came out. Thomas caught the door before it closed behind the girl and they went inside finding Ellie's door on the first floor. Anna knocked but there was no reply. The door next door opened and another girl with long blond hair came out and looked at them funny. Anna turned to her, "Do you know Ellie?"

The girl looked between them and shrugged her shoulders,

"I haven't seen Ellie since last Saturday."

Anna's eyebrows rose, "Any idea where she might be?"

The girl shrugged, "You might like to ask her new boyfriend, Jake. He lives in House Beaumont down the road."

She walked past them, putting her earphones in her ear. Anna looked at Thomas, a bewildered expression on her face, "She has a boyfriend?"

"You didn't know?"

"No." Anna looked so upset that Thomas decided to let it go.

"Let's go find the guy."

They set off and before long they were knocking on the door at Beaumont house.

A short young man with spiky hair came bounding down the stairs. Thomas stopped him. "Hi, do you know a guy named Jake?"

"Yeah, I'm Jake?"

Anna came forward and looked into his blue eyes, "I'm Ellie's mum. We've come to visit but can't find her."

The young man put his hands in front of him in a gesture of innocence, "Listen, I don't know anything. We went on our first official date last Saturday. She went to the bathrooms and never came back. I asked around and apparently she left with some hunk of a dude, getting into his car willingly. I wasn't going to chase a girl who's double dating some other guy."

Anna pulled herself up to her full five feet two and glared at him, "Do you think Ellie is the type of girl to double date?"

Jake hung his head and shook it, "No, not really, but my last girlfriend cheated on me and I didn't know what to make of it."

"What about reporting it to the police?" Thomas almost growled at him.

"What do you mean, the police? Is she in trouble?" Jake looked worried; his eyes large as he stared at Thomas.

"We don't know, Jake, we've just arrived here, and it seems you're the last one to see her. The girl next door to her hasn't seen her since last Saturday."

Jake raked his hand through his hair, "I wondered where she was this week. She hasn't attended any of the classes we share, but I thought maybe she was sick or had taken off with this guy, I don't know."

Thomas bunched his brows as he focused on Anna's worried ones, "I think we need to find the Dean of the school and figure out if she's been to any of her classes this week."

"Can I come with you?" asked Jake. "I'd feel terrible if something happened to her."

"Okay, lead us to the Dean, please." Thomas and Anna followed him; Anna slow on her crutches but managing as fast as she could.

The visit to the Dean proved fruitless, he checked the class attendant lists, but she hadn't attended any classes that week. He phoned the house-mother, and she said that she'd received a typed note saying that Ellie would be away for the week, but it had been pushed under her door and she didn't know anything more.

Thomas could see the steam starting to come out of Anna's ears as she ranted against the Dean for not checking up on a missing student.

"Anna, we need to figure out what to do right now, it doesn't help we blame them. Let's go to the police."

The Dean apologised, saying that students weren't always predictable, and they would do everything in their power to make sure she was found. The police said the same thing and promised to investigate it. They had a whole wall of missing people, and Anna was starting to hyperventilate by the time they were done at the station.

Thomas took her by the upper arms and said, "Anna, calm down. Getting hysterical won't help. Let's go to the restaurant they were at last Saturday. Maybe someone working there saw something. It is worth a try; besides we haven't eaten since early this morning and it's way past lunch."

Mutely Anna relented, not knowing what else to do. Her insides felt frozen in fear and her brain terrified by the thought of what could have happened to Ellie. Jake had given them directions which they easily followed to the Italian restaurant which was walking distance from the campus.

They were lucky to find a table available without having

to wait long. A waitress with curly red hair that stood in all directions arrived with a notebook ready. Thomas saw that Anna was staring blankly at the menu, so he ordered for them both. When the waitress finished taking down their order he asked, "Were you working here last Saturday, night?"

"Yeah, why?" The waitress looked at Thomas with a question mark on her face.

"Well, we believe our daughter ate here that night with her boyfriend, but she seems to have gone missing since then. She went to the bathroom and never returned to the table."

Anna fumbled with her purse, getting out her phone and opening the photo album, scrolling to Christmas which was the last time she had a photo of Ellie. "Here, this is what she looks like." She showed the photo to the waitress, her hand trembling.

The waitress took the phone, squinting at the photo, "I remember them. The guy was quite upset when she didn't come back. He left without eating the meals they ordered. I think my friend went to the bathrooms same time as her and saw this big guy walk out with her, out the back door. She said he looked like a Russian thug, like you see in the movies. The girl was tucked under his arm though, as if he owned her."

Thomas took the phone back from the waitress, "Thank you. Is your friend working? Could you ask her to come and tell us what she saw?"

The waitress shook her head, "No, she's not on today, but I don't think she would be able to tell you anything more." She left to get their order.

Thomas took Anna's hand across the table, her eyes looked glazed, "Anna, don't worry. We'll find her."

He started scrolling through the photos on her phone, his eyes drinking in his daughter. A muscle twitched in his jaw, as he saw Anna and her having a family moment during Christmas.

"You know all I ever wanted was a family. Instead, I made the church my family, but they didn't feel the same in the end."

Anna seemed to shake herself out of her trance and looked at him, "What happened?"

"They wanted to exchange me for a couple, who could minister to their families in a more balanced way than a single bachelor." A bitter laugh escaped him, "Me alone wasn't good enough for them anymore. Ten years, Anna. Ten years of my life gone."

Anna placed her hand over his, "Not gone. I'm sure you made a difference in their lives for the better."

He looked at her, "But they let me go as if I didn't matter to them. Not family. Family doesn't just throw you out."

Anna bowed her head, "Sometimes they do. Mine would have if I'd gone with you."

"Would you have?"

"Gone with you?"

"Yeah."

"Yes. I think so."

"I'm sorry."

"Me too."

Anna turned her dark green eyes on him, "Where's Ellie, Thomas? I'm terrified!"

He tightened his grip on her hand, "I don't know, but we are going to find her, do you hear me? I'm not going to leave any stone unturned until I find my daughter."

Tears rolled down her face, "Can you forgive me?"

Thomas let go of her hand, "I'm trying, Anna. Give me time, please."

"What do we do now?" Anna looked around the restaurant, a feeling of hopelessness overwhelming her.

"Let's ask the owners if they have CCTV of the backdoor. You stay here." Thomas got up, leaving her at the table.

After speaking to the owners, they showed him the CCTV which didn't help much, there was a blue sedan parked in the alleyway, but its number plates were covered up. Bile rose up in Thomas' throat as he saw the man push Ellie into the back of the car.

He asked the owners to phone the police and give them the tape before going out the exit door at the back to have a look at the alley. It was too much to hope for any clues a week later, but he needed to try in any case. His stomach churned, and he kicked the large metal dumper, next to the wall. *Why?* He screamed inside. *First, I don't get to know her and now that I can, she's kidnapped?*

Footsteps sounded behind him, and he swivelled around to see a man approach him. There was something familiar about his face. He looked younger than Thomas.

"Hi, Thomas." The man stopped a few feet in front of him.

"Do I know you?" Thomas pulled back his shoulders staring into the man's friendly blue eyes.

"I'm your grandfather, Samuel Quinn. I've been watching over Ellie and want to help you find her."

Thomas shook his head, his mouth open, "My grandfather died when I was nine."

"Yes, I'm now part of the cloud of witnesses who cheer you on. You know the one the Bible mentions in the book of Hebrews?"

Thomas felt his body start to tremble, "I'm not sure."

His grandfather gave a low chuckle, "I know. Remember being jealous of Kirsty for her encounter? Well, here you have your own one. Heaven is helping you out, son. The question is, are you going to take it?"

Thomas felt a faint sweat break out on his brow, there was so much he wanted to ask, but Ellie sprang up in his mind and he said, "Do you know where she is?"

His grandfather nodded, his face grave, "I need you to take the first flight out tomorrow to Inverness, Scotland. Rent a car and start driving towards Kinlochbervie. I'll meet you there and show you the rest of the way."

Thomas gulped and found his grandfather giving him a look that he knew meant he needed to pray. Wherever Ellie was, it wasn't a good place.

He blinked and there was no one in the alley but him. In a daze, he made his way back inside to where Anna was impatiently tapping her bright purple nails on the table.

"What took you so long? Did you find out anything?"

He slid into the booth opposite her and took a sip of water, his throat suddenly very dry. Anna looked at him, "Thomas? Why are you so pale? It looks like you've seen a ghost."

His body jerked, and he locked eyes with her, "I think I did, kind of."

Anna's frown deepened, "What do you mean?"

"They have footage that shows her getting into a blue sedan with a guy back in the alley. I was looking for clues there, when a man appeared. He said he was my grandfather and that he's looking out for Ellie and wants to help us find her."

Anna's eyes had gone wide, her own face getting pale, "Are you serious?"

"He died when I was nine. This man looked younger than me, although he resembled me." His voice trailed away; his gaze distant.

"What did he say about Ellie?" Anna said, her hand fisted.

"That we should fly to Inverness on the first flight tomorrow morning, rent a car and drive towards Kinlochbervie."

Anna sat looking at him as if he had lost his mind, "I don't want to go to Scotland! I want to stay here in case she turns up."

Thomas' shoulders slumped, and he swiped his hand across his forehead, "Let's go to her dorm and look for clues."

On their way there he turned sideways to Anna, his face pulled tight, "Have you phoned your parents?"

"No, I don't want to upset them."

"They might have heard from her or received a note."

"A ransom note?"

Anna's fingers trembled as she fumbled around inside her handbag looking for her phone.

Within seconds she was ringing them, "Hi, Mom."

Thomas listened to the one-sided conversation wishing they could keep walking, but Anna couldn't use the crutches and talk on the phone at the same time. He pushed his hands deeper into his pockets, the rain had stopped, but there was a chilly wind nipping through them.

"Have you heard from Ellie this week?"

"Last Saturday?"

"I'm in Dublin."

"No, we aren't coming home for the weekend."

"She seems to have gone away for a trip or something, but she isn't answering her phone."

"Yes, young people lead their own lives, I know."

"No, you don't need to send Conor to come and fetch me.

I'll rent a car or something."

"I'll explain later. Got to go."

Thomas lifted his eyebrows at her. "And?"

They haven't heard from her, but they aren't worried. Apparently she phones them once a week and did so last weekend, telling them about her date with Jake.

"Maybe we should speak to him again, try and work out if anything out of the ordinary happened the week before she was last seen."

They spent the afternoon going through her room, the effort draining them both to the core. Jake thought he remembered a blue sedan parked across from their college the one day when they came walking out, but he wasn't sure. There wasn't much to go on. Nothing pointed to her planning to leave except the note to the house-mother, which could have been planted by her kidnappers.

2:30 pm, GMT. Undisclosed location.

Camille rubbed her arm where the needle had poked her. It wasn't a large amount of blood they took each time, but the site where they'd injected the EPO drug felt painful. They made sure they had a good supply of red blood cells by enhancing the girls blood regeneration with the drug. One of its side effects was allergy-like swelling at the site of the injection.

She was sitting opposite Trojan on a chair, he was settled on the trolley bed. The index cards were on her lap as she studied his face. In her thoughts she said: *Are you feeling better?*

Yes. Are they hurting you?

No, just where the needle goes in. I've never liked needles.

A doctor who doesn't like needles. He lifted his eyebrows at her, and she rolled her eyes.

Camille lifted the cards upright. *So, how are we going to do this?* She thought.

The old-fashioned way. He looked at the cards with a stupid look on his face, and she had to stifle a laugh.

Camille pointed at the first picture, "Apple. Say Apple."

"Apppla." He copied her in a loud baby voice. It took all her self-control not to laugh out loud.

You're so funny, she thought. The next one was cat. "Say cat."

"Caaat." He mimicked, a sly grin on his face.

You haven't told me what they're planning for you, she said with her thoughts.

His face turned serious; his dark eyes broody. *Do you really want to know?*

Yes? Her head inclined as she watched him.

They plan to mate my seed with your eggs to produce a better specimen of me. One that they can control and teach better. Ultimately, they want to learn how to incorporate our DNA with normal human DNA to enhance mankind.

Super soldiers. Camille frowned as she glared at the scientists in the room.

She looked back at Trojan. *But what will they do with you?*

Once they've produced successful offspring, they'll kill me off.

Camille's eyes widened. *You mean once they have children from us, they'll murder you?*

Does that bother you, Dr Camille? His voice was low, the thought barely registering inside her head.

I don't want to produce children, that are...

His face was a mask as he said, *Monsters?*

She shook her head, *Sorry, I didn't mean it that way.*

You did.

Yes, but no and yes, of course it bothers me that they want to murder you.

So, they shouldn't murder me, but you don't want me to be the father of your children? Trojan had leaned closer to her, and she became aware of the brute strength of his muscles as it bunched in his arms.

A blush crept up her cheeks as she fiddled with the index card, turning it over to reveal the next one which was baby. Staring at the picture, she retorted, *It isn't the same when they make babies in a clinical lab.*

He shook his head, *Really? But I was created in a lab, so then it shouldn't matter if they kill me off.*

Camille's cheeks flushed redder, and she fisted her hand. *I don't mean it that way. You matter. I guess…then offspring created in a lab…would matter too.*

She looked down at the card, tears welling up in her eyes. His thoughts flitted into her head, she realised she was reading his thoughts. *I matter to her.*

Yes, you matter to me.

She looked at him her eyes suddenly ablaze. *And why shouldn't you? But if you fathered my children, I'd rather it not be in a lab!*

His eyes widened in surprise, his mouth opening slightly, *Dr Camille, you are by far the strangest human I've encountered. Are you saying you would like a future with me if we were not here in this lab, but free to do as we please?*

Camille bit her lip as she realised what she'd said, her heart hammering in her chest. *Trojan…I don't know what I'm thinking. I need to go.*

She stood up, left the index cards on the chair and banged on the gate. Fiercely aware that he could stop her if he wanted to, she held her breath until they let her out, and fled to her room with a guard flanking her.

As soon as she was locked in, she climbed into bed, turned her back on the other girls, and hid under the covers. She hoped Trojan wasn't reading her thoughts all the time, for she needed to figure out what was going on with her heart.

CHAPTER 10

Jean-Pierre was hiding with a glass of wine behind a pot plant on the terrace. The onslaught of family and friends was too much for him. Arriving barely on time, he'd tried to keep a low profile, but everyone swarmed over him like excited bees. He sensed someone approaching, and he ducked his head even lower.

"Hello, Jean-Pierre."

He recognised that voice and looked up into the face of an old family friend whom he hadn't seen in eight years.

"Wow, Leo, you haven't changed at all. Long-time no see."

"I've been looking for you since yesterday." Leo sat down in a chair at an empty table next to them and Jean-Pierre joined him, studying the father of his first ever girlfriend.

"Sorry, I was out with a friend. How's Camille? Is she married yet?"

Leo gave a low laugh and retorted, "I wish. No, as a matter of fact. She's doing her doctor's residency in Scotland."

Jean-Pierre sat back and smiled, "She always wanted to be a doctor, I'm glad she managed to finish her studies."

"Oui." Leo looked at him, but his face was grim.

"What's the matter?" Jean-Pierre asked.

"I guess there is no beating about the bush. She's been

kidnapped."

"What?" Jean-Pierre sat up straight.

"Seventeen days ago." Leo's voice betrayed a weariness beyond his years.

Jean-Pierre stared at him, "Why are you here? Why aren't you searching for her?"

Leo turned his eyes on Jean-Pierre, "Oh, I am here because of her. You might help me find her."

"Me?"

"Or your girlfriend to be exact."

"Kirsty?"

"Doctor Kirsten Knight, if you prefer."

Jean-Pierre scowled, "I don't know anything about her being a doctor in physics."

Leo's blond brows lifted. "She lied to you. She might be the only one who can find Camille, but she's refusing to help me."

Jean-Pierre felt his lungs constrict and his body go lame, "You? You made the CIA bring her in?"

"How much did she tell you about her past?" Leo regarded Jean-Pierre with an impassive stare.

Jean-Pierre looked down, fingering his phone in his pocket, he'd taken it off silent before he arrived at the party and read her text that came through earlier.

Leo's gravelly voice surprised him when he suddenly said, "Do you know that she went crazy? That she was in a psychiatric unit for six months?"

Jean-Pierre's hand started shaking as he took a big gulp of wine, feeling it burn down his throat.

"She used pills and psychiatric help to get her back on track." Leo clenched his fist and leaned towards Jean-Pierre, "She is refusing to help me find Camille because she fears going crazy again, but I need to find Camille! Help me convince her, Jean-Pierre!"

Jean-Pierre felt numb, "I don't feel like I know her anymore, Leo."

"But she'll listen to you. She loves you."

"Does she? How do you know? What if everything about her is a lie?"

Leo's face was clouded as he regarded Jean-Pierre. "I want you to go back with me, tomorrow. She might listen to you and it's a chance I need to take."

Jean-Pierre stood up trying to hide his trembling, "I'll think about it." He turned around and made his way to his room, his head swimming with the knowledge that Kirsty had been in a psychiatric hospital. *It can't be true. How could she lie to me, hide her past?* He needed another few bottles of wine.

7:00 pm, GMT. Dublin, Ireland.

They picked up take-away chicken wraps on their way to the Bed and Breakfast where they'd booked two rooms earlier that day. Thomas walked into the cosy, old-fashioned room with Anna, carrying in her luggage for her. She hopped in behind him, went over to the wooden canopy double bed and carefully let herself down, leaning the crutches against the bed. Absentmindedly, she rubbed her hand where it had gone red. A blister was starting to form from using the crutches, she hurt all over. Thomas stood in the middle of the room, looking around as if lost. Anna shut her eyes as her body started shaking, her breathing short and swallow.

"Anna?" Thomas took a step towards her.

"Go away, please. I need to be alone."

"I can help."

"You wouldn't understand."

"What, because I was just a sperm donor, is that it?" Thomas' words were flung across the room.

"You don't know her like I do. How can you understand what I'm going through?"

"Maybe I don't, but do you know what I'm feeling? The daughter I've always wanted, snatched away before I can even meet her?"

Anna moaned and curled up into a ball on the bed as sobs started racking through her. Thomas's fists unclenched, and he exhaled before walking to the bed.

"Anna?" He reached out and touched her shoulder, but she pulled it away. He pushed his fingers through his hair, shutting his eyes in an unspoken prayer for help. He lay down next to her, pulling her into his arms. She had gone rigid, but he held her anyway.

"You're not alone." He whispered above her head.

She turned towards him then, pressing her head against his chest, clutching his shirt in her hands, "Why, Thomas? Is it punishment for what we did? For what I did, by not telling you?"

He stroked across her hair, "No, of course not. We didn't plan her birth, but God did."

Anna pulled back, her tear streaked face looking at him, "Why is He doing this to us?"

"He isn't. There is evil in this world, end of story."

The sobs welled up in Anna again and she buried her head against him anew. He let her cry, stroking her back. Something broke loose inside him, and he whispered, "I forgive you."

Her crying quieted down, and they lay together in the darkening room.

"Do you really think your grandfather's ghost knows where Ellie is? Is that even possible?"

"I don't know. Kirsty…"

"Kirsty?"

"She had a weird experience on the ranch. She saw the Lady in Blue, a saint from four hundred years ago. I thought how jealous I was because I don't have that type of supernatural experiences, but it is hard to believe it even when you experience it yourself."

She stirred in his arms, "You cold?" he asked and lifted himself up to pull the comforter on the end of the bed over them. He settled his arms around her again, and she sighed a small sigh of contentment. His awareness of her soft form against him increased and with a jolt of recognition the floral perfume she wore assaulted his nostrils. It was the same one she used years ago. Memories of that night came back to him and he stirred, "I need to go."

Anna moved her arm around his middle, "Please, stay."

She looked up at him, the tears glistening on her eyelashes, her lips so near that without thinking he kissed them. She returned his kiss with a hunger that matched his own. He broke it off, his breathing hard, "Anna, no."

"Why?" Anna's hand lifted, and she cupped his bearded cheek.

He lifted his own hand, placing it over hers, "I'm going to do things right this time with a ring on this hand before we become one."

"Again." She licked her lips, "One, again."

"Yes," he said his voice low and husky, "One, again, but this time I'm not going to run away. Forgive me, Anna. I was a coward."

She placed another soft kiss on his lips, "You're not a coward and I forgive you. The past is in the past."

He traced her face with his finger, "You think our pain helped us grow into better people?"

She swallowed before giving a nod.

Thomas kissed her again, "And do you believe in first love?"

She blushed, "Yes."

"Not many people get a second chance. I intend to take mine with you, and not mess it up this time." He interlaced his hand with hers, and she rested her head against his chest.

"You have my permission," Anna murmured before she drifted off to sleep. Thomas lay still, listening to her regular breathing not wanting to wake her, not wanting to stay either, but in the end, sleep overtook him, and he slept with her in his arms, his last thought being that he must be dreaming that the love of his life lay in his arms. It felt even better than he'd ever imagined it.

5:00 pm, GMT-5. Secret ESP Facility, Langley, Virginia.

As the day went on, Kirsty's dream felt less and less real. *How can any of it be proved scientifically? Spiritual realms that are as real as this physical realm? It can't be. I can't be a spirit being of light.* She tried to read the Bible that John had brought her, but her head kept telling her how impossible it was until she gave up and sat staring at the ceiling. She even tried to imagine going there, but it didn't work.

The depressing darkness of the previous day descended on her, more strongly than ever.

You're worthless. You were a mistake. God doesn't love you. You're stupid. Weird, crazy freak. The taunts kept on relentlessly, sometimes so loud that she put her hands over her ears. There were creatures moving about in the place but thankfully they didn't physically attack her like they used to when she'd been in the facility.

John never reappeared to hear her story as if he'd vanished. The scientists started filing out, until she was left alone. The door opened, and she saw someone come back in, striding over to her cage. It was Doctor Black. *What does he want?*

He stared at her through the mesh, and said, "You think you're so clever, but I'll figure out a way to study you."

She looked at him but shut her eyes at the hideous face of a creature curled around his neck. He smirked at her, "I'm free to go, and you are not. What would you give to be allowed to go? If you tell me everything and let me do tests on you, I'll let you escape."

Kirsty felt tempted to make a run for it, but logic prevailed, she wouldn't get far. There was no escape from her own demons. Her head shook, "No."

He threw his hands in the air, "You are a fool. How can you deny science this knowledge?" He turned on his heel and marched out of the room, but as Kirsty watched she saw a long, scaly creature loosen himself off Dr Black and slide down to the floor. The door shut behind Dr Black and she was left alone with this creature on the floor.

With frightened eyes, she watched as it coiled itself into a ball and then twisted around towards her, sailing ever nearer, until it was hovering outside her cage.

"Hello, Kirsten..." it hissed, its small eyes regarding her menacingly.

Kirsty had no desire to say hello or interact with this thing and pulled her handbag closer to her. Slowly she lowered her hand into it, feeling around for the silver cross she'd gotten from her grandmother. When her hand gripped around it, she pulled it out and held it in front of her.

The snake-like creature gave a low laugh, "You think an old silver cross can protect you from me?"

"You're not real." Kirsty said, in a quavering voice.

"Oh, I'm not, am I?" The creature slid through the Faraday cage and stopped in front of Kirsty, its tongue flicking out and in.

Kirsty gripped the cross tighter in her hand.

"What are you?"

"I'm an evil spirit or demon as you like to call us."

"What do you want from me?"

He moved closer to her, "I want you as a host. I want to join my friends inside you."

Kirsty felt herself tremble in fear, "What are you called?"

"My name is Doubt and Unbelief." He posed as if to strike her and she cried out to Yahshua within her spirit, "Help!"

A flash of light appeared next to her and a shiny being with a sword stood next to Kirsty.

"Leave her alone." The light being moved his sword down between Kirsty and the snake and the creature fled with a cry, disappearing through the door.

Kirsty slumped back with relief, wiping the sweat of her forehead, aware that the shiny being was still next to her.

"Who are you?"

"Your guardian angel." Calmly, he put his sword back into place.

I have a guardian angel? "Do you have a name?" Kirsty lay down, pulling the duvet over her.

"Mikael."

"Thank you, Mikael."

"My pleasure, daughter of light." He faded away, and she drifted off to sleep feeling drained.

11:00 pm, GMT. Undisclosed Location.

"I have it figured out."

"What?"

"You have to kill me. One night before bedtime so they don't notice till the next morning."

"What?"

"Well, that is the only way to stop them from harvesting my seed and creating offspring."

"But won't they just create another Subject 108 out of our DNA?"

"Yes, but by the time they do that, you might have figured out a way to stop them. It took them two years to develop me."

"You're two years old?"

"Technically, they used growth hormones combined with my unique DNA and voila."

"There must be another way."

"Well, I can always kill them all, elope with you to a remote island where we can procreate and replenish the earth with my kind?"

Camille's tongue lodged in her throat, "Trojan...I don't want to kill you."

"The second option then?

"Trojan..."

"Hmmm..."

"Insomnia is a symptom of aplastic anaemia."

"Yes, I know."

"What would you like to do?"

"Do?"

"Yeah, you know, if you could do anything..."

"Procreate with you on a remote Island?"

"Trojan..."

"Stand on a beach, swim in the sea, listen to music, forget who I am..."

"Do you think my dad will find us?"

"Maybe…but he won't approve of me."

She laughed then, a laugh half mixed with hopelessness and hysterics.

"Sleep well, Princess."

"Sleep well, Beast."

11:30 pm, GMT-5. Secret ESP Facility, Langley, Virginia.

Kirsty woke up with a start. The first thing she became aware of was the sweet familiar smell of the garden. Relief flooded her as she saw the river flowing in the distance with the bridge. *It's the same place. Maybe it is real.*

She started walking in the river's direction but came to a halt when a field of bluebonnets came into her view. They swayed lightly in the air; their colour luminescent. Without thinking, she bent down and picked one, breaking the stem. In front of her amazed eyes, a new one instantly grew in the place of the one she'd picked.

This was so exhilarating, that she plucked another one and another one; every time watching in wonder as a new flower replaced the one she'd just picked. It felt like the flowers were loving her, laughing with her, enjoying her delight. Pressing her face into them, their heady fragrance filled her lungs.

She looked around and it struck her that everything here felt alive, different from the earth. She had gathered a whole bushel of bluebonnets which she carried in her arms resuming her walk towards the river. Her heart asked, *Yahshua?*

Here I Am.

She faltered when she saw that the answer had come from a massive Ox, grazing in the field next to the bluebonnets.

You're an Ox? She puckered her brows together, finding it the most natural thing in the world to communicate with her thoughts.

An ox represents a servant, submission, surrender... He snorted through his large, wet nose, and she felt goosebumps all over her skin. She sat down a few feet away from him, holding the flowers on her lap. *Yahshua, today...*

I know, little one. Through your own choices and those of your ancestors, doubt and unbelief has a legal right to be in your life. That's why such a spirit could attack you. His placid brown eyes stared into hers.

Kirsty shivered involuntarily. *Can those things come here?*

No, they are limited to the Kingdom of Earth, which is also where the mobile court is. You can go there to revoke their right to you.

A court? Kirsty frowned, not liking the idea.

The Ox lumbered a few steps closer to her, his massive head in front of her, *Yahweh's judgements are the only thing that can set you free. His judgement is always to forgive you and restore you. Don't you want that, Kirsty?*

Her cheeks started getting wet as she nodded, *I do. Can we go there?*

Before she had finished the sentence, the scenery changed, and they were in a room resembling a court. Seven brightly coloured spirit beings were seated on a testimony bench. Yahweh was the judge, and Yahshua, who had changed into the form of a man, was standing next to Kirsty as her advocate. A loud voice said, "Bring in the accuser."

Before Kirsty's wide eyes the snake creature, who had attacked her only a few hours earlier, was brought in by angelic beings. He hissed her way, and she recoiled.

"I have a legal right to her!"

She turned her eyes to Yahweh and felt words come up from her spirit which she spoke aloud. "I'm guilty, Yahweh, and repent. Please judge my ancestors and me for allowing doubt and unbelief and giving it legal right in our lives and revoke it."

Yahshua spoke up, "By her confession, I ask that you forgive Kirsten and her ancestors based on my sacrifice for them. Redeem them by my blood."

Yahweh's deep voice sounded, "Doubt and unbelief, you are judged and the legal right you've had in Kirsten and her bloodline is revoked. The blood is against you, she's forgiven."

Out of the corner of her eye she saw the angels remove the

screeching demon from the court. The power of Yahweh's words of forgiveness vibrated through her being.

Yahshua went to Yahweh and got something from Him. He gave it to Kirsty saying, "These are the divorce papers. If it tries to attack you again you can show this as proof of your acquittal."

Yahshua looked into her eyes and whispered, "Now go into your DNA and find the link that contains doubt and unbelief."

Kirsty blinked and saw herself inside a strand of DNA, amplified many times over. It looked like a ladder. Moving up in it, she saw a part that looked grey and different from the rest. She took it, turned around and found herself in front of a large shimmering lake that looked like glass.

Yahshua was standing behind her, "This is the sea of glass, you can trade your faulty DNA for mine."

Kirsty looked at the lake and dipped the grey DNA into it, saying as she did it, "I trade this for Yahushua's DNA of faith."

As the DNA came out, it had changed colour and looked healthy and vibrant, she felt a laugh escape her lips as excitement welled up in her. She thought of the DNA strand and found herself back there where she replaced the DNA back into it.

She blinked and found herself on top of a mountain. It was wild and gorgeous, the views stretching out forever over more mountains and hills until they became grey and blue in the distance. She looked down at herself and gasped at the attire she had on. She was dressed like an old-fashioned warrior, with a sword in a sheath hanging from her belt.

Soft, knee length, leather boots made the mountain-climbing easy, it felt like she'd always worn them. She followed the path she was on until she came out in a clearing at the very plateau of the mountain. There was a quiet in the air, the absence of birdsong struck Kirsty and an uneasiness rolled through her stomach.

"Yahshua?" she whispered into the stillness. His presence filled her, but she didn't see Him. A still voice within her said: *This is your mountain. It represents the government of your life. Up to now you've not taken up the government so other things have been governing you. It is time to take your authority back so that you can sit in your seat of rest from where you can rule.*

Kirsty shook her head, finding the concept of ruling foreign, *I don't think I know how to rule.*

That is why you have teachers.

Teachers? Kirsty peered at the bushes, where there was a rustling.

Ruach HaKodesh is constantly with you to comfort, lead and teach you. The seven Spirits of Yahweh are also there to help you become mature. Everything in the realms works through relationship. Everything reveals Yahweh to you, for the kingdom is within Him, but the kingdom is also within you.

Within me? Kirsty felt her head swim; this was tougher than any exam she had ever written in physics. It felt like all the knowledge she previously had didn't amount to much at all.

You're a door, a gateway if you want, from Yahweh's realms to Earth. Part of your mission on earth is to replenish and restore it, allowing His glory to flow through you from here to there.

Kirsty gulped, she had a hard time imagining herself capable of all that He was saying, but she chose to believe it, for within her there was a sudden willingness to believe even if she didn't understand it yet.

The rustling in the bushes increased and Kirsty felt sweat break out on her forehead as a dragon, complete with scales and a monstrous head, came charging into the clearing. Instinctively, she grabbed the sword by her side and pointed it at him, he snarled and came for her. A boldness she'd never felt before started within her, combining with a fierce anger at this thing that didn't belong in her life.

She charged at it, screaming at the top of her lungs, plunging her sword straight up into its belly. The dragon tried to get to her where she stood underneath him, but she pushed her sword in even deeper, cutting away to the side.

A scream of pain tore out of his throat, and he thrashed to the ground, clawing at the sword stuck in his white belly. Kirsty kept out of his reach, wishing she had another weapon to attack him with. After a while his movements started to slow and green slimy goo leaked out of his stomach onto the ground.

Kirsty crept closer to him, grabbed the hilt of her sword and cut his stomach open further. As the hole widened, things started rolling out of him; crowns and jewels, scrolls and swords. It looked like he had swallowed a treasure chest. *What is this stuff?* Kirsty wondered as she picked up a crown of gold, with green stones embedded in it.

She heard the cry of a huge eagle overhead, and it landed on the side of the dragon, observing her with wise eyes. *Well, done, Kirsten. These things are your inheritance that the beast had stolen. Things you lost because you weren't governing your mountain. Come see your seat of rest.*

She climbed on his back keeping the crown with her, the sword back in its sheath. He flew up, and his feathers tickled her nose. She laughed out loud, relishing the wind in her face, and the freedom she felt in her spirit.

Look down. His still voice spoke into her heart, and she gazed down seeing many mountains and places; it felt like the world had no end.

They landed next to a carved seat in the shape of a throne. Kirsty placed the crown she had retrieved from the dragon on top of her head and after looking at the Eagle, seated herself on the seat.

Is this my seat of rest?

Yes. If you stay in it, you can govern over these lands. Whenever you lose your peace in Me, realise that something is trying to govern on your mountain that you need to overcome.

Yahshua?

Yes.

Can you help me with Leo Molineux? What should I do?

Do you want to help him?

I think so, but I don't think I can take on those...

Demonic Principalities? There was a pause and then He said: *You need the Erelim.*

The Erelim?

He gave a low laugh, his voice gentle inside her. *When you need them, ask.*

Kirsty's eyes were filled with wonder as she looked at Him. *Ask, and I'll receive.*

CHAPTER 11

8:30 am, GMT. Sunday, 17 January. Dublin, Ireland.

Anna stirred first the next morning, her awareness increased, and she felt the strong arms of someone around her. She moved her head and stared at his face so close to her own. *I feel safe.* The daylight was filtering into the room from the open windows where they hadn't closed the curtains. *Did he mean what he said, that he wants a second chance with me?* Her heart fluttered at the thought, but with a pang she remembered Ellie.

Her thoughts sprang to Thomas' grandfather who appeared to him in the alley. It was way outside of her scope of reference, but what if there was a small chance that it was real, and they could find Ellie by going to Scotland? Her gut told her that Ellie wasn't going to come back to Dublin by herself. Someone had taken her and they needed to go after them.

She touched Thomas' arm, and he murmured in his sleep, "Thomas, wake up, we need to go to Scotland!"

Anna's voice penetrated his sleepy brain, and he sat up with a start. "What?"

She sat up too. "We need to go to Scotland to find Ellie."

He rubbed his face and turned towards her, "You want to follow the ghost of my grandfather in search of Ellie?"

"Yes. I think God is helping us and we need to trust Him."

Thomas shut his eyes; his brows pinched together.

"What?" Anna studied his face with a worried frown.

He rolled his shoulders, "I asked God's forgiveness. When I was sent packing, I kind of blamed God, but," Thomas turned to her with tears glistening in his eyes, "If they hadn't forced me into a sabbatical, I would never have gone to the ranch."

Anna swallowed away the knot in her throat, "And you wouldn't have been here right now. I'd be alone." Anna looked down, before looking up, searching out his eyes, "I'm sorry for saying I don't need a man in my life. I do need you, want..."

He pulled her into his arms, pressing her against his chest, his face buried in her hair, "Anna..."

She sat back up, "We need to go." Thomas leaned forward and kissed her on the lips. Her eyes widened, and she touched her mouth, "What was that for?"

"I've got twenty-one years to make up for, I'm going to kiss you as often as I can. I have your permission if I remember correctly."

Anna's cheeks reddened, she pulled her hand out of his and cleared her throat, "I want to shower and get dressed, so you, you need to make yourself scarce."

"I'll phone the airline and make reservations. Be ready in twenty minutes." He got up, but leaned across the bed and gave her a fast kiss on the lips again. "Just for the journey."

He strode out and left Anna with butterflies in her stomach.

She got ready, finding her ankle feeling better, but still not able to put her full weight on it. Prayers for Ellie's safety rose up in her spirit and she felt a strange sense of peace come over her. Within less than two hours they were on their way through the blue skies towards Scotland.

It was only an hour and twenty-minute flight, and they were ready to start driving before lunchtime. Anna stopped in her tracks when she saw what Thomas had rented, "Really?" She rolled her eyes at him as she stared at the bright yellow BMW M4.

He shrugged, "I've kind off fallen in love with fast cars."

"I thought you were falling in love with me," Anna said as she hopped nearer and fluttered her eyelids at him.

He grinned, pulled her against him and looked down into

her twinkling green eyes, "Oh, I am, Anna Martins. You need to start practising a new signature." He smacked another kiss on her mouth and then helped her settle into the car.

The satnav said it was a bit over three hours' drive towards Kinlochbervie. The engine revved, and Thomas set off. The highlands had a scattering of snow on the highest peaks and they passed by them faster than the speed limit allowed.

Anna fidgeted with her hands in her lap.

He glanced over at her, "What?"

"How are we going to find your grandfather's ghost and what if she's being held by dangerous men? We don't even have a gun."

Thomas exhaled, "We've got to pray, Anna. This feels like one of those Old Testament stories, like when Elijah was surrounded with an army and he prayed for God to show his servant the angelic hosts surrounding them. We aren't fighting this from this earthly realm, we need to fight it from and with Heaven's help."

Anna reached over and held onto his hand, "You're right, we need to pray."

For the rest of the journey they prayed, the heaviness of intercession resting on them, increasing with every mile that passed.

9:00 am, GMT. Undisclosed location.

Camille sat on her top bunk bed, cross-legged, eating her cornflakes. She watched as the newest member of their group, Ellie, made her way across the room towards her. Her eyes were downcast and her footsteps slow.

"Can I sit with you?" she asked. Camille nodded, and the girl climbed up carefully, balancing a cup of tea. She settled down next to her, cradling the tea in her hands, her face downcast.

After a few minutes, she pushed her hair behind her ear, "I'm not sleeping well."

"Nightmares?"

She scrunched up her face, "It feels like no one will ever find us; like we are going to live in this castle forever."

"Like Tangled?"

That got a small smile out of her, "Except none of us have long enough hair to escape."

"I'm sure your parents are looking for you, as is my dad. Someone will come for us."

"I only have a mom. My dad left without knowing about me."

"I'm sorry."

She wiped at a tear on her cheek, "I used to imagine how I'd meet him and how happy he would be to discover that he had me. It's the reason I did the DNA test."

"You were hoping it would match you up?"

Ellie bit her lower lip, "It all feels so hopeless, but I know God hasn't forgotten us."

Camille turned to Ellie and studied her side profile, "Are you a Christian?"

Ellie dipped her head up and down, "Are you?"

"No, but it must be nice to believe there is a higher power looking out for you."

"He is. I know it. Ever since they took me, I've felt His presence with me."

Camille frowned, "You think He's with you even though you can't see Him?"

"I know it. It's hard to explain, but knowing God is not much different from knowing a friend. I talk to Him, and He reveals things to me and answers my prayers. It's a friendship that's as real as any human friendship."

"How did you start this 'friendship'?"

"I was invited by a friend to a prayer meeting at college. Someone was sharing about how they came to know Him. I felt so hungry inside; all my life I knew about Him, but I didn't know I could know Him personally. So right there and then I asked God if I could know Him. I thanked Him for giving me His Son. By His sacrifice on the cross my sins could be forgiven. He made a way for me to know Him."

Her eyes shone bright as the memory sprang up in her,

"As I prayed, I felt as if something changed inside me, like my soul had been made brand new. I felt His love burn through me, taking away all the rubbish. It was the most amazing moment of my life." Ellie beamed at Camille and Camille swallowed the knot in her throat.

"You make it sound so simple," Camille pressed her lips into a thin line, "You don't have the type of family I have."

Ellie reached out and touched Camille's arm, "It is simple. He loves everyone and promises that if we receive His son, He'll forgive us."

Camille tilted her head, "Do you sing?"

"Yes, I do. Why?"

"Would you like to come to see Trojan with me today? I can say I need help, maybe they'd allow you."

Ellie shivered, "You think he's safe?"

"I don't think he'd harm us. I'd like you to sing to him. He's never heard music and I think he'd like it."

Ellie's eyes closed for a moment. She opened them with a new determination in their depths, "I'll do it."

4:30 am, GMT-5. Secret ESP Facility, Langley, Virginia.

Kirsty woke up with a start. It was dark inside the facility; she switched on the lamp and saw that it was after four in the morning. She didn't feel tired but invigorated as if her encounter had infused her with strength. *I didn't just dream that. I was there.* The urge to read the Bible welled up in her, and she took it in her hands.

Please teach me, she quietly asked before she randomly opened it. This time the words flew off the page, alive and on fire. The first story she read was about a prophet and his servant on a mountaintop surrounded by a hostile army. She read about the servant's eyes being opened so he could see the heavenly army there to defend them.

Are those the Erelim? In answer to her thoughts, a soft voice inside her head said, *Yes.* She sensed that it was Ruach

HaKodesh, the One Yahshua said would be with her to teach her.

"Tell me more," Kirsty whispered in awe. She could feel His loving presence within her. For the next three hours she learned about the realms from the Bible, Ruach HaKodesh explaining it to her in detail. She didn't even notice that she read more fluently and easily than normal, her dyslexia seemingly vanished.

Her scientific mind with its practical questions got answers. Answers that astounded her in their simplicity, but also complexity. How could Peter escape out of prison? Easy, his earthly body fused with his heavenly body and moved at the speed of light which can go through physical objects.

The three young men in the burning fire who didn't burn, they just moved into the kingdom realm, bodies and all, yet remained visible to the earthly realm.

Once you understood about realms and spiritual realities, things began to make sense. Not half of the stuff in the Bible were actual physical things, but heavenly, supernatural. All the things she had always seen started making sense to her. She wasn't crazy after all, although most people would probably think she'd lost the plot completely now.

People won't believe me. Kirsty's heart squeezed tighter when she thought of Jean-Pierre. *He won't believe me. I've lied to him. He'll think I've gone crazy again.*

Have you? Ruach HaKodesh's still small voice whispered in her heart.

No. My life before was the lie. Kirsty touched the pages of the Bible. *This is the truth. You're real, not just a voice in my head.*

Who are you, Kirsty?

She closed her eyes, inhaled and said, "I am a spirit being of light who chose to come to earth to redeem my DNA through faith in Yahshua."

The path is narrow for those who believe and not many find it.

Pain pierced through her. *If I lose Jean-Pierre, our children won't be born.*

Jean-Pierre has a free will, Kirsty. Your destiny might be to be with him, but he can still choose to reject it.

A sob escaped Kirsty and she found herself praying for Jean-Pierre, that he would choose to believe. She thought of Abraham that had to offer up his only promised son, Isaac and sensed that in a way she needed to offer up Jean-Pierre and the children they'd have.

With a painful groan, she went on her knees and surrendered her desire for a family with Jean-Pierre. It felt like part of her was being torn out, but she didn't relent until she knew she'd surrendered it.

A great sense of peace descended on her and with it something soft landed on her hand. She opened her eyes and saw it was a large white feather. In amazement she picked it up, looking around as if searching for the source. She heard a giggle that echoed around in the cage as another feather appeared in mid-air, slowly descending to land at her knees. She picked it up and sat back on her bed with them.

"Hello?" Kirsty's voice sounded small in the empty place. As she peered into the dark with only her tiny lamp's light, the air itself started glowing. The glow took shape and two brilliant beings appeared, their colour continually changing between the colours of the rainbow.

"Who are you?" Kirsty asked her mouth agape at their smiling faces and beautiful large forms.

"We are Kashmelian angels. Yahweh sent us to help you."

"This place needs some sprucing up, don't you think?" The other one asked and before Kirsty's wide eyes he started twirling, a fine golden dust falling off him covering everything inside the cage.

"Come, Kirsten, pack what you need. You won't be coming back here." The first one said, his kind eyes eyeing Kirsty.

She tried to close her mouth and placed the Bible into her handbag. Flustered, she closed the bathroom door on the angels to get dressed. Next, she gathered her personal belongings and packed it into her hand luggage, remembering her toothbrush before she stopped in front of the locked gate. She looked up at the first angel and asked, "How are we going?"

"Translocation would be the fastest. You need to get to Jean-Pierre."

Kirsty's eyes bulged, "We're going to the Basque country, to Jean-Pierre?"

"Yes! At the speed of light." The second angel cheered.

"Wait!" Kirsty looked around for the paper and pen on the table and scribbled a quick note.

With trembling hands she took her luggage and said, "Okay, I'm ready, I think."

"Can I take that for you?" The first angel offered his hand for her bag.

Kirsty gave him the handle watching fascinated as her bag lifted into the air. She had her handbag over her shoulder and felt herself lift as the other angel seemed to pick her up. Out of nowhere a blue cloak appeared and settled over her covering her head.

"Up, up and away!" He announced and within seconds they were moving up through the faraday cage as if it wasn't there, through the ceiling and up into the clear, black sky.

Kirsty saw the sun's rays that were coming up on the horizon in a beautiful array of colours. The angels paused as if they were admiring the sunrise with her before they turned East and started moving faster and faster until Kirsty had to close her eyes. When she opened them again, they were hovering above the steeple of an old church.

10:00 am, GMT+1. Ugarte Villa, Spain.

Jean-Pierre woke up with a start. His head felt sluggish, compliments of the three bottles of wine he had had the night before or was it four; he couldn't remember. He heard the birds sing outside and wondered why he had a nagging feeling he'd forgotton something else. *What day was it? Sunday.*

Then he remembered. He wanted to visit the old church in the valley today. If he could recall correctly, they had a few services on a Sunday, with two in the morning. He glanced at his watch; it was just before ten. He could walk it, the road leading there was less than a mile. Some fresh air might do him some good.

Within fifteen minutes, Jean-Pierre zipped up his jacket and quietly closed the door behind him. The thought of Leo's request to go to America with him made him pause on the steps, a frown marring his forehead. Shaking his head, he started off at a brisk walk, needing to get his circulation and heart pumping. His lungs breathed in the crisp morning air.

Jean-Pierre tried to push the thoughts of Kirsty to the background, but failed. *When it comes down to it, do I love her? Yes, but I can't go through what my father had to go through. There is no way we can have children if both our genes might carry mental illness.* Tightening his face, he increased his speed.

The bells of the church were ringing, signalling eleven o'clock. He stopped at a cafe for breakfast and after that found himself sliding into a wooden pew, right on time for the twelve o'clock service. Candles were burning in the old stone church. Large paintings of Christ, the Apostles and Saints decorated the interior. With a pang, he remembered admiring the artwork, as a boy when he came with his mother. Even the carved wooden pulpit, where the Priest stood conducting the service, was a work of art.

Jean-Pierre struggled to concentrate, the only words that penetrated his churning thoughts were, "For the Son of Man came to seek and to save that which was lost."

Lost...now there was a thought. What does it mean to be lost? He felt as if he didn't know what to do, lost, so to speak. Did the Son of Man come to seek and to save him? If so, how did you let yourself be found? The thought broke through his soul. *I want You to find me.*

The service ended and as he turned, his eyes fell on a lone figure in the last row. She had a cloak on that covered her head, but as she lifted her eyes, he stared into their green depths which he would recognise anywhere. *Kirsty?*

She stood still, her eyes locked on him as if she'd been waiting for him. His feet involuntarily started moving towards her until he stood in front of her. The rest of the congregation were moving out of the church past them where they stood like two pillars.

"Kirsty?" He whispered, his voice sounding hoarse.

"Jean-Pierre." She smiled at him, her face filling with joy as she stepped up to him and hugged him tightly. His arms came around her and for one fierce moment he hugged her back before pulling away, "Where did you come from?"

"I've just arrived." Kirsty inclined her head, "Could we go somewhere quiet to talk?"

"Sure, I know of a place around the corner." Jean-Pierre turned, walking ahead of her, not sure if he should take her hand or not, deciding on not. He looked back to make sure she was still there, and she was, the dark blue cloak making her look like one of those saints of old. Jean-Pierre felt a strange trickling down his spine, something was different about her; very different.

They entered the small cafe and found a table against the wall, hidden from sight.

"Have you had lunch?" She shook her head and he ordered her a fresh pancake with blueberries and coffee for them both.

"Jean-Pierre, I've got some things to tell you. Will you hear me out before you react?" Kirsty twiddled with the red serviette on the table.

Jean-Pierre sat back, taking a big lungful of air, "I know some of it."

"You do?" Kirsty's eyes were big.

His brows furrowed together, "I know that you didn't tell me that you were a doctor in Physics and worked on the ESP unit for the CIA."

"How?"

He shrugged, "It doesn't matter."

"I'm sorry I lied to you. I want to explain. It's not an excuse, but it might help you to understand."

"I'm listening."

"When I met you, I'd been busy establishing a brand-new chapter in my life. Things went very wrong with the experiments I was doing in ESP, and I had to have treatment in a mental hospital for six months. After that, all I wanted was to forget the past and become a new person."

Kirsty sought his eyes, her own filling with tears. In a quiet voice she said, "Then you fell in love with me. For the first time there was someone in the world who loved me for who I was. I'd never had that. I couldn't face telling you about my past. I was so scared I'd lose you."

Jean-Pierre's mouth was dry and he took a sip of water, keeping his gaze on the red and white striped table cloth.

The waiter brought their order and Kirsty waited for him to leave. She took a grateful sip of the coffee before continuing. "The longer we were together, the more I thought that the right moment would come up to tell you, but after you shared about your mom, I knew that moment might never come. I kept reasoning that the past didn't matter; why should it destroy the future I could have with you?"

Her voice went softer, "I was wrong though, you can't hide from the past, or lie about it. I'm sorry, Jean-Pierre. I hope you'll be able to forgive me. I've made a promise to myself that I'm never going to lie to you again about anything."

Jean-Pierre's jaw clenched, "Okay, so tell me what you found out about your birth parents."

Kirsty took a bite of her pancake and said, "They lied. My family covered up the scandal of my birth. I was born to my sister when she was sixteen. She'd slept with their Native American gardener's son. So, my adopted parents are actually my grandparents."

Jean-Pierre's mouth hung open, "How did you find out?"

"Our maid, she was there and was sworn to secrecy, but she is retiring now and decided to confess it to me. I went to my mother's estate in Austin that morning before I met you and confronted her. She denied it, but she warned me that if I told anyone she'd tell the world I'm a fraud, and that I'd been in a mental facility. That is part of the reason I didn't want to tell you; the other part was that I was ashamed that my family had lied to me."

Jean-Pierre's hand moved across the table and he touched hers, "I'm sorry, it's horrible that they've lied to you all your life."

Kirsty's eyes filled with tears, "You know what that feels like, don't you? With your dad, lying about your mother and now me lying about my past. I'm so sorry, Jean-Pierre. If I could do it over, I wouldn't lie to you."

Jean-Pierre pulled his hand back, his face tightening, "I don't know. It's wrong, but if I think of how traumatised I would have been as a child, seeing my mother go crazier and crazier." He shook his head.

He looked at her and then away, "What was wrong with you? Why did you need treatment?"

"It started with the remote viewing experiments. When I tried to find people who were kidnapped, I started seeing things, monsters or demons, call it what you like, but since I didn't believe in any spiritual stuff, I thought it was all make-belief.

When I was a child, I used to see things, and I was sent to a psychiatrist who told me it was only my imagination, my mind playing tricks on me. With the remote viewing, suddenly these things started following me around, attacking me, making me scared and paranoid. I couldn't get it to stop, so I needed help."

"So, your mind was playing tricks on you?" Jean-Pierre asked.

"You see, that's just it. I was wrong. It wasn't make-belief or imaginary, it was real! Demons or evil spirits exist. I was opening the wrong doors, so they attacked me, but I know better now."

Kirsty's eyes shined as she looked at Jean-Pierre, "I met Him, Jean-Pierre. Yahshua or Jesus, He's more real than you or me. And Yahweh, what can I say about Him, He's out of this world. He showed me who I am, who I'm meant to be. I've never felt so loved."

Jean-Pierre's eyes were wide as he stared at her, "What are you talking about? The Kirsty I know believes that nothing can be known of the existence or nature of God!"

Her eyes almost glowed as she beamed at him, "I was wrong. Oh, Jean-Pierre, I was so wrong. You can know Him; His kingdom is more real than you can imagine! I've seen it."

She's gone off the deep end. Jean-Pierre's stomach felt like a stone, he noticed that she was finished with her pancakes. "Shall we go?"

8:30 am, GMT-5. Secret ESP facility.

The caretaker swiped his key card at the facility and walked in, carrying the takeaway breakfast he'd picked up. He was under orders to feed some scientist who was doing extra studying in the Faraday cage. He shook his head to himself. *Scientists are weird.* He noticed the security guard posted outside as usual; these CIA guys didn't take their business lightly.

"Breakfast is served." He called out as he approached the cage, wondering if the man or woman were still asleep. He didn't have a key to the cage, but there was a small opening, like at a bank, where you could put something into the cage.

His eyes took in the interior of the cage; he squinted, rubbed his eyes and took another look. Slowly, his hand went down to his phone and he texted Dr Lemming. A few minutes later Director Smith received a text which read: *The bird has flown the nest and left behind two feathers and gold dust.* He reread it just to make sure and then ordered his security detail to take him to the ESP facility, downtown.

Striding in, he found the caretaker, security guard and Dr Lemming all standing around the cage, each one avoiding his gaze.

"What in heaven's name is going on here?" He demanded.

Dr Lemming cleared his throat, "The caretaker brought her breakfast this morning and this is what he found."

The Director took in the gold dust-covered room with the two white feathers lying on the bed and felt a chill go down his spine. "Have you checked the footage?" He growled.

"I waited until you got here." Dr Lemming led the way to the nearest computer and logged onto the security feed. He went back a few hours until they saw movement and watched as Kirsty Knight started to read her Bible by the lamplight.

They fast forwarded a while, until the Director said, "Wait! What's that?" They stared in disbelief as two bright, colourful lights appeared inside the cage. They saw her pack her bag and then they clearly floated upwards with Dr Knight in tow through the ceiling and away. Between clenched teeth, he gritted out, "Do you have any explanation for what we just saw?"

Dr Lemming wiped the sweat off his brow and shook his head, "It appears to be supernatural, Sir, Director Sir."

"Hey, I see a note on the table!" The caretaker announced from where he stood near the cage. He had tried without anyone noticing, to collect some gold dust through the hole.

Director Smith opened the cage and walked over the gold-covered floor. With his heartbeat loud in his ears, he read the note and frowned before taking out his phone. Remembering that he was in a Faraday cage, he walked out and texted a message. Hopefully that would have the man off his back.

"Clean up this mess and delete all the footage we have of Dr Knight ever being here. Nobody, and I mean no-one, is to speak of this to anyone." He glared at each person, noting the caretaker's jubilant face before he marched out the door. When he got back to his office, he shredded the paperwork concerning Dr Knight and then deleted every single file and newspaper article that contained her name and connected her to the CIA.

When he was done, Dr Kirsten Knight ceased to exist. He left the identity of Kirsty Knight, the web designer, in place and replaced her years studying at the elite, fast-track physics university with a grant from themselves and her time working for the ESP unit, with an average high school diploma and work references in various places. Her time in the psychiatric unit he also erased, since they'd booked her in hoping they could fix her and use her again.

The Director of the CIA sat back, his taut face relaxing a fraction. He'd done all he could to cover his back. If anyone were to ask, he'd never heard of Doctor Kirsten Knight, and he would make sure the rest of his department said the same.

2:00 pm, GMT+1. Ugarte Villa, Spain.

They started walking back to Jean-Pierre's father's villa. Kirsty was babbling about mountains and dragons and Jean-Pierre wondered if he should phone the same psychiatric unit his mother was held in. He observed her sideways, where she was almost skipping like a little girl beside him. *I can't believe this is my Kirsty, she's never acted so carefree and happy. This might be an alternate personality.* His heart felt like breaking into a thousand pieces.

As they neared the villa he remembered Leo. He didn't know if he was staying at the villa or in the village, but just to be on the safe side, he took her around to the studio. He fetched the key under the stone and opened it up, switching on the lights and closing the door behind them. Kirsty had walked into the middle of the room where she stood stock-still gazing at the seven portraits Jean-Pierre had drawn.

Standing by the door, Jean-Pierre rubbed the back of his neck. "It's just some children."

Kirsty turned around, "You've seen them too? Oh, Jean-Pierre, you've drawn them marvellously!"

She walked over to the one picture depicting a girl, "This is Mia; she's so chatty. She told me all about how they're cheering us on. I spent the most wonderful time with them!"

Jean-Pierre felt his throat burn, "What are you talking about, Kirsty? They aren't real, I only dream about them."

"They're real, Jean-Pierre! As real as you and me. These four," she pointed to four of them, "are the four children we've lost. And these three," she pointed to the other three, "are the ones we're still going to have; Caleb, Sebastian and Maria. Yahshua told me that Caleb is already inside me."

She held her hand to her stomach, wonder on her face.

Jean-Pierre felt his legs go lame and he took a step closer to her, "Kirsty, you sound deluded. You can't meet with our deceased children and see our future ones. It's not possible! I don't want children with you anymore. We have too many mental illness genes between us now." He tried to gentle his tone, but it still sounded harsh in his ears.

Kirsty looked at him, her eyes turning sad, "I guess it's too much for you to take in." Kirsty walked over the pictures of Sebastian and Maria, "Do they feel real to you in your dreams?"

Jean-Pierre refused to answer her, staring down at the floor. *This is crazy. She sounds so convinced, but it's impossible.*

"I love you, Jean-Pierre and I'm sorry for everything." Kirsty touched the picture of Sebastian's face, gently tracing his features.

There was a sound at the door and they both turned towards it, Kirsty giving a gasp as she recognised Leo's face.

"What are you doing here?"

"I could ask you the same thing." Leo retorted as he stepped inside the studio, closing the door behind him.

Jean-Pierre looked at Leo and then at Kirsty, "Leo is an old family friend. His daughter, Camille, was my first girlfriend."

Kirsty sputtered, "Family friends? First girlfriend?"

Leo smirked at her, "I told you, I know someone you know, that no one would miss. Imagine the headlines: 'Crazy girlfriend shoots artist partner for deserting her'." He moved his hand inside his jacket and it came out holding a slender handgun with a silencer.

Jean-Pierre took a step back, stepping in front of Kirsty, "What are you doing?" he asked Leo, his face filled with bewilderment.

"I need to give Doctor Knight some extra motivation to help me find Camille."

Kirsty moved so she was standing next to Jean-Pierre, she took his hand and looked at Leo. "I want to help you, and I've found a way."

"You have?" Leo's brows rose in incredibility.

"Yes, we can't fight those evil entities that are guarding the place she's held in on our own. We need help. God's help."

Leo scoffed, "I told you if He exists, He isn't bothered by our little problems."

"You're wrong, He's very much involved. He loves us and

He'll help you if you ask for it."

Leo gritted out between clenched teeth, "I'm not going to ask some high and lofty God who lets us go through pain and suffering for help."

Kirsty licked her lips, "But there's no other way. He said the Erelim could help us, they're warring angels."

Leo let out a cry, lifted his gun and shot Jean-Pierre in the shoulder. Kirsty screamed as Jean-Pierre crumpled to the floor.

"No, no, Jean-Pierre!" There was blood gushing out of the wound, she tore a piece of her shirt off and tied it around his shoulder, as tightly as she could, to stop the blood-flow. The cold metal of the silencer pressed against her temple, "If you don't help me, right now, I'm going to kill him."

Tears streaming down her face, she lifted it up and prayed aloud, "Yahweh, I need your help. Yahshua, send your angels, please help!"

There was a flash of light and all three of them started swirling into the air, Leo screamed in terror and Kirsty held onto Jean-Pierre, cradling his head on her lap. The wind whipped around them like a whirlwind.

Within seconds, they landed in the middle of a narrow, long, winding road between mountains. Leo fell to the ground holding onto his head as if in agony, still gripping the gun tightly in his other hand. Jean-Pierre's eyelids fluttered open and closed. When they opened again, he seemed to focus on their surroundings, "Where are we?"

"I don't know. I think we translocated." Kirsty tenderly moved his fringe out of his eyes, "I'm sorry he shot you. It's my fault."

Jean-Pierre stared into her eyes, the pain making him dizzy, "Kirsty, is this real?"

She nodded but looked up as an engine's noise reached their ears. From far away they spotted a bright yellow BMW M4 racing their way. The car braked and stopped a few feet away from them and out climbed Thomas and Anna. Thomas stared at them in surprise, his eyes taking in Leo who had recovered enough to sit upright with the gun now half concealed under his jacket.

"Kirsty?" He ventured, his voice travelling through the stillness.

"Thomas, what are you guys doing here?" Kirsty asked.

Thomas cleared his throat, "Ellie, our daughter has been kidnapped. We came here to look for her."

Kirsty's eyes widened, "You have a daughter?"

Thomas looked over at Anna where she was leaning on the car door, a blush starting on her face, "Yes. I never told him."

Leo spoke, "That's quite a coincidence. My daughter, Camille has also been kidnapped. So this is what we're going to do; you're going to give us a lift and help us find them."

He took the gun out of his jacket and pointed it at Thomas and Anna, "Do I have your cooperation?"

Anna had gone pale and Thomas clenched his fists. "Yes." He walked over to Jean-Pierre and Kirsty, "Is he badly hurt?"

"I don't know, it's only his shoulder and the bleeding seems to have stopped for now." Kirsty looked around, "Where are we?"

"We are on our way to Kinlochbervie in Scotland. I don't think there is a hospital or doctor anywhere nearby."

"My daughter is a doctor. When we find them, she can help." Leo said, his voice impatient, "Get into the car!"

Anna, Jean-Pierre and Kirsty squashed into the small backseat of the car with Leo taking the passenger seat next to Thomas in the front.

They started driving and Leo drilled Thomas with his eyes, "Do you know where they're keeping them?"

Thomas's cheeks coloured, "Not exactly. My grandfather told me he knows where she's being kept and that we need to come here, then he'd show us."

The silence felt heavy in the car, "How does your grandfather know?" Leo asked in a low voice.

"I don't know, but he isn't exactly alive in the physical sense, so maybe you know more when you are in the hereafter."

Leo almost choked, "You are following your grandfather's ghost! You're crazy!"

They rounded a corner and in front of them, there appeared what looked like an orb of light. Thomas slowed down the car until they were crawling, the orb hovering in front of them. The next moment, the orb started moving forward at speed. Thomas put his foot down on the accelerator and followed suit. The orb kept up the pace leading them higher and higher into the mountains.

CHAPTER 12

3:30 pm, GMT. Undisclosed Location.

Ellie followed Camille into the giant's cage trying to not stare at him. There was so much of him, it was hard not to. He sat up and allowed Camille to take the usual blood sample and pressure.

Inside her thoughts Camille said: *This is Ellie. She's a music student. I thought you might like a surprise.*

He lifted his eyebrows. *A surprise?* Floated into her head, his lips not moving.

Camille nodded and thought: *She's going to sing for you. You said you would like to hear music? I couldn't get the whole orchestra, but I have the lead vocalist.*

The left side of Trojan's mouth lifted as he hid a grin. *Let's hear it then.*

He was sitting on the trolley with Ellie standing close to the gate, her back to the rest of the room. Camille remained next to him, she looked at Ellie and gave her a thumbs up.

Ellie cleared her throat and then in a crystal-clear voice started singing, "Amazing Grace, how sweet the sound, that saved a wretch like me. I once was lost, but now I'm found. Was blind, but now I see."

She started softly but increased in volume until her voice rang out and filled the whole place. Closing her eyes, she continued the next verse until the entire song was finished. There was a hush in the room, even the scientists stopped their work and sat staring at them. Trojan wiped at his cheeks, finding them wet. Nothing had ever moved him like that.

Thank you, Ellie. She jolted as she heard his gruff voice inside her head, and her wide blue eyes stared at him in wonder.

"My pleasure," she stuttered.

The door to the room banged open and the footsteps of a few men could be heard. Camille's eyes widened, she paled and hissed, "Ellie, go hide behind the furthest pillar now!"

Ellie didn't turn to look at what had frightened Camille but ran and made herself flat behind the furthest pillar out of view of most of the room.

Trojan observed the group of twelve men and asked Camille, in her head: *Who are they?*

It's... Camille struggled to form her thoughts. *It's my Uncle Fiacre.*

He must be the mastermind. It filtered into her thoughts, and she recoiled at the thought of her own flesh and blood being behind her kidnapping. But then she righted herself; she knew her uncle and it didn't surprise her.

The man of their thoughts walked up to the bars, rubbing his hands together, "Well, well, how lovely it is to finally see Subject 107 in the flesh. When I heard how well he was being handled by my very own kin, I had to come and see for myself."

He focused his piercing blue eyes on Camille, "Of course, what else would you expect of Elise's daughter? You take after your mother; too soft and compassionate. No wonder she killed herself when she had to comply with the brotherhood."

Camille's eyes sparked and she retorted, "You leave my mother out of this!"

He laughed, "Now, that spark you got from my brother; Leo always struggled to keep a lid on his temper." His face scowled, "How he managed to protect you is beyond me. He betrayed the brotherhood, the Master, by shielding you, but all that ends now."

He leaned closer to the bars, "When I'm done with you, your father will wish he hadn't shielded you."

Camille could feel Trojan tense up next to her, she moved

her hand over his and in her head said: *Don't give yourself away. He likes to play mind games.*

Aloud, she said, "You've outdone yourself this time, Uncle. Even I am impressed with the genius of this invention."

Fiacre rubbed his chin, "Well, yes, so far it hasn't yielded the results I'd hoped for, but they tell me patience is needed. I've come to supervise the harvesting of this subject's seed. It should supply us with what we need to procreate enough of his kind to eventually have a functioning, suitable subject."

He gestured at Professor Demid Petrov, "Open the gate and let her out."

In his haste, the Professor forgot about Ellie who was hiding out of sight. Camille left Trojan, who studied her broodingly, his instinct screaming to act, for he could smell the danger, her fear making him see red.

One of the guards grabbed her by the arm and brought her over to Fiacre. He leered at her like a Cheshire cat, his stocky body shorter than her own, but his blond hair the same colour as hers confirming their family genetics.

"Camille, I hadn't realised you'd grown into an even prettier version of your mother. He touched a strand of her hair, "Keep hold of her, will you?" He asked the guard, who kept Camille's arm securely in his grip.

Fiacre turned towards Trojan, "I have a feeling that you've been holding out on us, Subject 107. So, I'm going to do a little test on my theory. If you give me any trouble at all with harvesting your seed, I'll cut off some part of your pretty doctor. Do we understand each other?"

To accentuate his point, he brought out a slender, silver knife, that glinted in the fluorescent light. He brought it close to Camille's face, touching her cheek with the cold side of the blade.

"Do it." He barked at the guards and Prof. Petrov, who stood ready with a special test tube for catching the seed. The gate opened, and three of the guards entered with the Professor and another scientist; each guard had an automatic gun in their hands ready for anything. The other eight guards stood in a semi-circle their weapons trained on the giant. Camille had frozen when the knife touched her cheek, her heart hammering in her ears.

Camille, when I say 'now', fall flat. Trojan's urgent command echoed inside her head and before she could reply, she heard, *NOW!*

She threw herself down, wrenching her arm out of the guard's grip. A loud explosion of gunfire sounded above her head and she screamed. It felt like an eternity before it ended although it lasted only a minute.

Camille slowly lifted her head, observing the dull, staring eyes of the guard next to her first, the silence petrifying. Camille frantically sat up looking for Trojan. He was still sitting on the trolley where he had been. Blood was gushing from a few places on him. The three guards who were near him were all dead, one thrown eighteen feet away against the wall. No one seemed alive besides the two of them.

"Trojan, are you okay?" Camille asked, her voice hoarse.

"I think so." He said, still holding the gun upright in his hand, his eyes ablaze with hatred as he stared at the bodies of the dead on the floor.

"It's okay, you've killed them. They can't hurt us anymore." Camille said in a soothing voice, as she took a few steps closer to him.

3:30 pm, GMT. Scottish Highlands.

They followed the orb, the road leading higher and higher. Thomas cranked the heating up in the car for the air was getting cooler. Kirsty held Jean-Pierre, whose forehead was breaking out in sweat due to the pain. In her heart she found herself praying. *Yahshua, please help!*

What would you like Me to do? She heard his gentle voice within her clearly as if He was next to her.

Heal Jean-Pierre? Kirsty ventured, half-unbelieving that she could ask for this.

Jean-Pierre gave a small moan and Kirsty slipped her hand over the wound. Closing her eyes, she imagined that she was in the garden next to the river. The water was gurgling, flowing, teeming with life, with leaves floating downstream on it. Kirsty bent over and picked up a leaf out of the river, its golden colour glistening in her hand. She imagined placing it on Jean-Pierre's wounded shoulder wanting to transfer the life pulsing in the leaf to him.

She felt him shudder beneath her hand and when she opened her eyes, he had lifted his head and was staring at her, his eyes wide with something like fear in their depths. He raised his hand and felt his shoulder, pushing the strip covering his wound aside. Kirsty moved her hand away and saw a hole in his shirt, but instead of a wound there was a round scar on smooth skin. Lifting wide eyes to him, her face beamed, "He healed you!"

Jean-Pierre was exploring his shoulder, moving it around in the limited space, speechless. Thomas looked back in the mirror, "He's healed?"

Kirsty grinned, "Yes! Yahshua healed him!"

Thomas' eyes locked with hers, "You believe?"

"I do. Thank you for praying for me."

Anna peered around Kirsty at Jean-Pierre, her mouth open, "How did you heal him?"

"I went into the kingdom, took a leaf from the river and placed it on him." Kirsty happily said, her eyes sparkling. "He's so good!"

Anna looked down at her bandaged ankle, "Do you think you could do that for my ankle?"

"Be quiet!" Leo growled. He didn't dare take his eyes of the orb. Although he didn't know what it was, he knew it was leading them to the place where they held the girls. It barely registered that Jean-Pierre had been healed, his mind not making sense of any of this.

Quietly, Kirsty placed her hand on Anna's ankle. Anna felt a warmth go through it and when she carefully tried to move it, the pain was gone. Her face broke out in a grin and she said, "Thank you, Kirsty. Can you forgive me? I judged you at the ranch. I was jealous after seeing you leave Thomas' bungalow."

Kirsty blushed, "Nothing to be jealous about. I'm sorry too. It wasn't the best behaviour."

Jean-Pierre looked between the woman, "What happened?" he whispered.

Kirsty bit her lower lip, "I kind of drank half a bottle of whiskey with Thomas the night after you left. Nothing happened, we talked and passed out."

Anna's face softened, "I can't believe we're together again, Thomas and I."

Jean-Pierre moved his hand and took Kirsty's, "Kirsty…" but before he could complete his sentence, Leo gave a shout.

The orb had been leading them up a narrow, gravel road and as they rounded a curve, a large, stone castle appeared in front of them. The orb changed form and for a few seconds a young man could be seen, who waved at them before disappearing. Leo turned to Thomas, his eyes round, "Was that your grandfather?"

Thomas slowly nodded his head, swallowing the knot in his throat, "He said he's part of the cloud of witnesses and that they're helping us."

Leo opened the door, forgetting to keep the gun on the rest of the group. He started running towards the entrance of the castle, his only thought to get to Camille.

Before he neared the entrance, he ran into an invisible wall which stopped him in his tracks. Behind him everyone else had climbed out of the car and stood looking at the formidable castle.

Kirsty spoke up, "Something isn't right."

Leo was knocking against the invisible wall, trying to break through it. Before his astonished eyes, the wall began to take shape in the form of scales, the massive back of a dragon appearing with its head in the clouds. It lowered its head hissing at Leo who ran back to hide behind the group by the car.

"What is that thing?" Anna stuttered.

"That is the main principality governing whatever is happening here," Kirsty said, a tremble racking through her frame, instinctively she took a step back.

There appeared smaller, gargoyle-like creatures fluttering around the dragon, all of them screeching. They were clearly agitated. The dragon fixed his gaze on the group of people, "Why do you disturb me? You shouldn't be here."

With weak knees Kirsty tried to speak, her tongue sticking

to the roof of her mouth. Closing her eyes, she imagined herself stepping into the kingdom. In front of her, a throne appeared which she instinctively knew was the throne of mercy and grace. Hope rushed through her and she found her voice, aloud she said, "Yahweh, I ask you for the Erelim. We need Your help."

There was a piercing cry above her and her eyes sprang open. The dragon's bloodshot eyes were fixed on her. With menace he said, "How dare you call the Erelim?" His face turned incredulous, "I know you. You've meddled in our business before, but we stopped you. I'm surprised you've dared to face us again, insignificant little human!"

Her insides seemed to freeze, as the memories came flooding in. Immobility had taken hold of her whole being. She felt someone take her hand, it was Thomas who was staring at the dragon with anger in his face. He spoke up, "Be quiet. You don't know who you're speaking to. She belongs to Yahweh now. He will send His Erelim to defend and protect us."

The dragon pulled back his mouth to reveal cruel, sharp teeth, "You're bold for a human, but foolish. He's not going to listen to her or you. We haven't seen the Erelim in hundreds of years. I'm in charge here and I have other things to attend to." He turned his back on them and lowered over the castle, settling down until his form and the castle seemed to merge.

"No! No! No! We've got to get in there!" Leo was beside himself, his hands in his hair, the gun dangling uselessly.

Anna gripped Thomas' other hand tightly, tears rolling over her cheeks. They shared an agonised look; their daughter was in there too.

Jean-Pierre tucked Kirsty's hand, pulling her to face him, "Kirsty?"

She sucked in a desperate breath, the fear that had gripped her still there.

"Breathe, Kirsty, It's all right. You're not alone. I'm here."

He stroked over her hair, moving it behind her ear. "Do you believe that God said He will send the Erelim?"

She nodded.

"They're the warring angels, right?"

She nodded, a frown on her forehead. "I thought they would

just come, but maybe something's wrong.

Jean-Pierre looked around at everyone, his eyes falling on Thomas, "Thomas, when God sent angels to fight a battle in the Bible, was there something specific the people used to do?"

Thomas rubbed his beard, "Well, they often shouted, praising God when they went into battle."

"Then that is what we need to do."

Kirsty's eyes widened, "You mean, we need to praise Yahweh with joy in the face of the impossible?"

"Yes."

She reached out her hand and gripped his. "Together?"

He smiled and squeezed her hand. "Together."

Kirsty looked at the others, "Come everyone, we need to praise Yahweh for sending the Erelim."

Leo looked at them in bewilderment, "But they aren't here."

"They are, but they need our voices."

Softly at first, but then ever increasing in volume, the small group of people started raising their voices in shouts of praise to God. Leo didn't join in, but kept a wary eye on the dragon, who seemed almost invisible again. The smaller ones began screeching as the volume of the people increased. They didn't like the sound at all.

A low growl emanated from the principal dragon and his head lifted, "You are trespassing, leave me be!"

At the top of her voice, Kirsty shouted, "Yahweh, thank you for the Erelim. Thank you for helping us overcome!" She forgot her fear as supernatural boldness surged through her.

With a screech of outrage, the dragon, along with the smaller ones, moved towards the group of people to attack them. Instantly, the air lit up with piercing lights like spotlights at a sports stadium.

Jean-Pierre and the others gasped as they observed hundreds of fifteen-foot angels dressed in shining armour surrounding them on all sides. The ground trembled as they unleashed a great war cry, the vibration of the sound throwing the dragon and its minions back. The humans watched as a fierce battle broke out, all the time keeping up their shouts of praise. After an intense battle, the dragon fled, his minions in tow, leaving the castle unguarded.

Kirsty had fallen down on her knees, "Thank you, thank you Erelim. Thank you for sending them, Yahweh, Yahshua."

The lead angel who had led the attack turned towards Kirsty, his fierce face burning into hers. He gave a small nod and they disappeared.

The running of footsteps sounded outside the door, and Camille's father burst into the room, "Camille!" He took a few steps closer and then pulled out his gun pointing it at Trojan. Camille moved

in front of the gun, "Non papa, he saved me, don't shoot him."

Her father's face conveyed his unbelief, but he slowly lowered his gun, "I'll put my gun away if he puts his down."

"Please do it, Trojan."

There was a grunt behind her, and Trojan dropped the gun on the floor, it clattered on the stones. "It's empty anyway," he said.

Leo lifted his eyebrows at the giant's immaculate speech. "I guess I need to thank you," he said reluctantly before he embraced Camille, holding her tightly against himself. "Ma fille, I was so worried. Are you okay?" He kept his hands on her shoulders and pulled back, his eyes searching her face.

"Je vais bien papa, I knew you'd find me." Her eyes filled with tears and they hugged again.

There was a movement from the back of Trojan's cage and Ellie came out, her body shaking. "Ellie, are you okay?" Camille asked turning towards her.

"Are you, Ellie?" Leo asked. Ellie nodded and he replied, "Your parents are outside. You should go to them."

Her eyes grew large and she ran out the open gate, past the dead men and out the door as if a pack of wolves were on her heels.

Leo drank in every detail of Camille's face, "I didn't think I'd find you, but, and I don't believe I'm saying this, God helped me."

"God, Father?"

He nodded, his eyes filling, "Can you believe it? Of all people, He helped me."

Camille swallowed, her throat thick, "Ellie told me that He loves everyone and that whoever chooses to believe in what His Son did for us will be saved."

"Saved, hey?" Leo gave a little chuckle.

Camille gave a yelp as she was yanked back away from her father. Before she could utter another sound, an arm went around her neck pressing against her windpipe. Her uncle, Fiacre, had been shot through his calf. Not seriously injured, he had pretended to be dead waiting for the right moment.

He pulled her further away from Leo, "Hello, brother, how good of you to join us."

"Let her go, Fiacre!"

"I can't believe you would betray the Master so much as to actually talk about God, His sworn enemy."

"The Master is no friend of ours, Fiacre."

"Silence or I slit her throat!"

Fiacre lifted the silver knife in his hand, holding its sharp edge against her throat. "You've always been soft about her. She made you weak, brother."

He scuffled back another step or two, and then bent down with Camille and picked up one of the guns on the floor.

"Please, Fiacre, kill me but let her go. She has nothing to do with this."

"You're wrong, brother. Who would have thought that matching your DNA with that weakling Elise would bring about the perfect combination to help make one of the men of renown?"

The tears were running down Leo's face, "Let her go." He pleaded and took a step closer to them his hand reaching into his jacket.

"No, you don't." Fiacre fired off a shot, and Leo fell to the ground blood seeping from the hole in his forehead. Camille screamed and at that moment Trojan bent down and walked out of the open gate of the cage. He grabbed Fiacre from behind and lifting him clear of the floor, tore Camille out of his grasp and gently placed her on the ground.

Holding Fiacre in front of his face, with measured words he said, "You think you're so clever, little man, but your cleverness is foolishness, even my kind had more decency than to kill our own kin."

With that he increased the pressure and Fiacre's screams became gurgled as his breaking ribs pierced his lungs. Trojan threw him down on the floor and stepped on him, crushing his body underneath his foot.

Kirsty looked around; everyone was there except Leo.

"Where has he gone?" She asked.

They heard someone running and a girl with flying, long, reddish-brown hair came running out of the castle.

Anna gave a scream and ran towards the girl, embracing her.

"Ellie! Oh, Ellie!" Mother and daughter embraced.

Thomas drew nearer to them. Anna looked up and then back at Ellie, "Ellie, there is someone I'd like you to meet."

"Dad?" Ellie looked at Thomas, the hopefulness in her face piercing his heart.

"Ellie." He opened his arms and she ran into them. It felt like coming home, like they'd always known each other.

"Oh, my beautiful daughter, I'm so happy to meet you."

She laughed, "That is exactly what I've always imagined you'd say."

"I love you, Daddy. I always have."

Thomas drew Anna closer and Ellie's eyes widened, "You two? Together?"

She jumped up and down, squealing in delight, "This is better than I imagined!"

Thomas introduced Kirsty and Jean-Pierre, then Ellie filled them in on what had happened inside. They approached the castle, Ellie leading them to the room where the girls were held. They found the guard with the keys quite dead; it appeared that he had met Leo in the hallway who'd shot him.

Taking the keys, they unlocked the girls and helped them

get out of the castle, giving them directions to the nearest town which wasn't more than two miles down the mountain. The girls thanked them and like calves let out of a stall they ran away, overjoyed to be free.

They walked back to the main hall where they heard a gunshot and then an unearthly shout. They started running, Thomas, Anna, Ellie, Jean-Pierre and Kirsty, straight for the main hall.

Camille had run to her father's prone body and sat sobbing next to him, her hands covering her face. She felt a soft touch on her hair and Trojan's voice in her head said, *I'm sorry Camille. Camille...*

She opened her eyes, taking her hands from her face and looked up and up and up in search of Trojan's face. When she found it, she saw him grimace as if in pain. He was swaying slightly.

"Trojan, you need to sit down!" Camille sprang up and watched with concern as Trojan sat and then lay down flat on his back, his breathing irregular. She touched his forehead finding it full of sweat and her face crumpled in a frown, "You were supposed to have a blood transfusion today, weren't you?"

Looking around she saw the blood storage unit in a dark corner of the room. She couldn't do this on her own, though she needed help. Trojan's breathing was shallow as she inspected the places where he'd been shot, finding to her relief mostly flesh wounds. *Don't you dare, die on me, Beast!* she thought, and she could hear his faint chuckle in her head.

I deserve to die, Camille. Look around you, I'm a murderer, he whispered into her thoughts.

A shudder ran through her, but she kept her eyes on his face. *We've all done things that are wrong. My dad said God helped him find me. That means that maybe, maybe there is a chance that we could find His forgiveness.*

The door opened and she looked up in alarm, but her face changed when she saw Ellie hand in hand with a woman and a man on her other side. She searched the rest of the group her eyes stilling on someone she knew, "Jean-Pierre!"

He ran towards her and crouched next to her, "Camille, are you alright? We heard the gunshot!"

She grabbed his arm, "I'm fine, but Trojan isn't. You need to help me give him a blood transfusion." She paused and stuttered, "The gunshot was Dad, he's dead." Jean-Pierre placed his hand over hers and pressed it, "I'm sorry."

Jean-Pierre took in the giant's full twelve feet and turned his eyes on Camille, his eyebrows furrowed, "What or who is he?"

"I don't have time to explain. He's sick and in need of fresh blood."

Camille felt someone stand behind her and she turned, her eyes locking with a woman whose green eyes seemed to shine.

"Hi, I'm Kirsty." She crouched on her other side and studied Trojan, "I don't think the blood transfusion is going to save him." She said in a calm voice.

"Are you a doctor?" Camille asked, her voice sharp.

"No, but I sense that Yahweh wants to do something different for Him, but it's going to need the combined faith of all of us."

"Yahweh?" Camille's voice wavered. "You mean God?"

Kirsty nodded, her eyes not leaving Trojan's face. Jean-Pierre covered Camille's hand, "Listen to her, Camille, she prayed for me and my gunshot wound got healed barely an hour ago."

Camille turned wide eyes to Jean-Pierre, noticing the hole in his shirt where a small round scar showed in his shoulder. "You're kidding."

Jean-Pierre shook his head, cleared his throat and said, "A few hours ago I would have said the same, but you won't believe what has happened since. We were in the Basque country barely an hour ago where your father was trying to convince Kirsty to help find you. He shot me in the shoulder and then Kirsty prayed, and we all translocated to Scotland in the blink of an eye."

Jean-Pierre turned towards Kirsty, tears glistening in his eyes, "I thought she was crazy, but I was wrong. God and His Kingdom's real."

Camille took a deep breath and turned to Kirsty, "What do

you propose we do?"

Kirsty shook herself from where she seemed to have been in deep thought and she looked around the group, "Is everyone here a believer?"

Thomas, Anna and Ellie nodded.

Jean-Pierre said, "I might've only been one for the past hour, but I believe."

Camille felt warm tears run down her cheeks, "I want to believe, but I don't know how."

Kirsty smiled at her, "It's easy. Accept that what Yahshua did on the cross He did for you. Turn away from your sin and receive His forgiveness. Then ask Him to show you His kingdom!"

Camille did just that. When she was done, she opened her wet eyes and said, "I guess I'm a believer now."

Kirsty motioned everyone closer, "I want you to place your hands on him."

Everyone formed a semi-circle around his head, placing their hands on him. He stirred and Anna gasped as his arm muscles bunched beneath her hand. Thomas took her other hand and held it tightly.

Kirsty fixed her eyes intently on Trojan, "Trojan, do you want the forgiveness of your Creator? Do you accept that his Son's sacrifice was enough to redeem your sin?"

Trojan's eyes fluttered open, and he fixed it on Kirsty's, "I do." He said aloud, his voice weak but clear.

She gave him an encouraging nod and then said, "Everyone, close your eyes. Imagine we're going into the Kingdom of God. His kingdom isn't up in the sky somewhere, but inside us, a different dimension. Yahshua is the door and we're going in through Him.

There is a sea of glass in front of Yahweh's throne. It is the sea of glass from the book of Revelations. There was a moment of silence before Kirsty said, "Can you see it?"

Everyone murmured positively.

"Do you see Trojan there with us? We've taken him in and we need to dip him into the sea of glass so that his DNA can be healed."

Aloud, she prayed, "Yahweh, thank you for giving us

Yahshua to make the way for us to know You and enter your kingdom. We ask that you heal Trojan's DNA. Please fix it, Father."

Thick cloud filled the air, His loving presence enveloping them. They could see the brightness of His light shine from the throne as they lowered Trojan into the sea of glass.

Ellie and Anna gasped, they felt Trojan's arm under their hands start to shrink. Everyone opened their eyes to stare with wide-eyed wonder as Trojan's body shrunk down to the size of a tall but regular man. His sixth fingers and toes disappeared. The hospital gown covered him like a long dress, lying in folds on the ground. All his wounds healed up instantly.

They all burst out in shouts of praise, the glorious truth of God's redeeming love and healing right before their eyes.

Trojan sat up and looked around as if he'd just been born. Camille took his hand which, although large, could fit around hers in a comfortable grasp.

"Trojan?"

He looked at her, down at himself and at her again, "He forgave us?" He spoke softly, full of awe.

She nodded, her tears dripping on their hands. Trojan's eyes filled too and they wept together for joy.

After a while, Kirsty spoke up, "We need to leave. I sense that other people are coming and we shouldn't be found here."

Camille gave a sharp intake of breath, "The other girls, we forgot about the other girls!"

Jean Pierre gave her a reassuring smile. "It's okay, Camille, we've let them out. They went down the mountain road and should have reached the main road. There is a town about two miles from here."

"How are we going to leave? I don't think the BMW is going to fit all of us." Anna said. She grinned at Thomas. "You should have rented a minibus."

He shook his head, his smile sheepish, "Maybe."

Kirsty looked around the room, a sudden joyous look on her face, "I think I can arrange a ride for us, but first we need to destroy all the research they have on the corrupted DNA."

They set to work creating a small bonfire out of all the

paperwork they could find and smashing the computers' hard drives.

Camille covered her father's body, her face a mask of grief. Trojan took her hand, "I think he might have chosen forgiveness before he died."

Camille buried her head into Trojan's shoulder, "I hope so."

"Okay, people, gather round, our lift has arrived!" Kirsty called them from the centre of the room. They all gathered together, and bright, colourful lights appeared all around them. Ellie rubbed her eyes, barely believing what she was seeing.

"Thank you, Kashmelian angels. We appreciate your help." Kirsty spoke, looking at them with love.

One turned to her and beamed, "Our pleasure, daughter of light. Where do you want to go?"

"Trojan? Camille?" Kirsty looked at them.

Trojan spoke up, "Could Camille and I go to a deserted Island?"

Camille's head jerked back, "Trojan! I'm not going to a deserted island with you!"

He grinned at her, "Why not, Dr Camille?"

She spluttered, "Because I'm not married to you!"

Trojan lifted his hands, "How do we get married?"

Thomas cleared his throat, "Well, I'm an ordained minister, although I'm on a sabbatical. I could legally marry you." He looked at Camille, his face apologetic, "That is, if you want to get married in five minutes, now, here."

Camille felt her blush spread to the roots of her hair. "I…"

She sought out Trojan's eyes which mirrored love back at her, the type she'd always dreamed of, but never found. Mesmerised by his gaze, it solidified inside her, the knowing that he was the one. She looked around the group, "I don't have anyone I want at my wedding, so yes, please marry us."

One of the angels moved towards them and said, "I think we need to spruce you up a little for a wedding, don't you?"

With that he started twirling and sparkling things fell off him. When everyone looked again, Camille was standing in a shower of gold, her own clothes changed into a white dress complete with shoes. Trojan had on white linen trousers and an open-necked top. There was a gold crown in Camille's hair and when Trojan opened his hand, two rings lay nestled there, the one round with an intricate pattern on and the other with a large pearl that changed colour. The angel bowed and said, "With compliments from your Father."

They stood hand in hand as Thomas led them through the short phrases of lifetime commitment. He paused and asked, "What's Trojan's surname?"

Camille's eyes shone as she said, "Molineux. It is high time our family name gets redeemed."

Thomas said, "Do you Trojan Molineux take Camille Molineux as your lawful and wedded wife?"

Trojan gazed deep into her eyes and said, "I do." He pushed the ring onto her finger which fit perfectly.

Thomas repeated the vows for Camille, she looked into Trojan's eyes, "I do," she said, and her heart fluttered with joy.

"I now pronounce you husband and wife."

The angels quietly watched the proceedings their joy palpable, but at Thomas's pronouncement, two of them drew near to Trojan and Camille and surrounded them. All four of them started to disappear, "Time for the honeymoon!" One of the angels said as a joyful laugh echoed through the room before they vanished into thin air.

Kirsty looked around at the group, "Do you want to go to Ireland, Thomas, Anna and Ellie?"

«Wait!» Jean-Pierre spoke up. Kirsty turned to him and inclined her head, "What?"

He moved to stand in front of her, where he went down on his knees, "Kirsten Knight, I know that I haven't been the man you needed me to be in the past, but I want to do things right from now on. Would you…" He choked up, struggling to form the words, "Would you be my wife and have my children?"

Kirsty's eyes filled and she reached out to him. He took her hand, "I'm sorry, Kirsty, I'm sorry I didn't believe you. Can you forgive me?"

She nodded; her throat thick.

He looked at her, his dark eyes searching her green ones, "Is that nod saying you can forgive me or that you'd be my wife? Or both?"

One of the angels giggled and Kirsty smiled through her tears, "I forgive you and I want to be your wife, Jean-Pierre Ugarte Garcia."

"Now? I want you to be Kirsty Ugarte Knight from now on and forever." Jean-Pierre stood up, pulling her under his arm. She laughed and said, "Yes, but hurry. We're running out of time!"

The angel who giggled gave a great whoop and started swirling around them, showering them with gold dust. Kirsty's clothes changed into a gorgeous shimmering green dress and Jean-Pierre had on a green matching shirt with dark trousers.

Jean-Pierre gasped as he looked at the rings in his hand, for it was his mother's ring that he'd kept hidden in the Basque country at the villa, thinking that he'd use it one day for his wife. It had green stones set around a pure white diamond. His own band had lettering on that seemed to glow. "What does it say?" he asked looking up at the angel.

The angel inclined his head, "It says 'Beloved', for the Father loves you, son of the Kingdom."

Thomas married them and Jean-Pierre kissed Kirsty tenderly after they said I do.

"Kirsty Knight, what have I done to deserve you?" She cupped his cheek with her hand, "Beloved, we don't deserve anything, but He's given us this gift, each other and the children we're going to have."

One of the angels spoke up, "We need to leave."

Thomas cleared his throat and said, "Could we go to Londonderry?" Anna looked at him and took Ellie's hand in the one hand and his in the other.

Two of the angels moved until their light surrounded the three and they disappeared out of view.

"Where do you want to go?" Jean-Pierre asked Kirsty.

"Can we go to the Basque country to your home?"

The two remaining angels swirled around them and they vanished, leaving the castle empty for the men dressed in black who pounced on it, to scratch their heads at the bright yellow BMW standing in the road, all the dead inside and the destroyed equipment. A few of them cursed; no one knew what to do, so they covered it up as if it had never happened.

Somewhere in Kazakhstan, the hacker turned his head at a sound at his door. So, they'd found him just as planned. He pressed the key to destroy his systems; the photo already shredded. It was the dawn of a new era. Their plans would shock the world and bring them to their knees. When it happened, they would turn to the greatest hacker they knew, him. A smile lifted his features, before he lifted his hands in surrender. Finally, there would be order in this world. Besides, like his favourite film hacker used to say: "I'm invincible!"

EPILOGUE

11:00 pm, GMT+1. Sunday, 24 January. Agreda, Spain.

Kirsty stared at the remains of the Lady in Blue, displayed in the Monastery of the Immaculate Conception in Agreda. It was only a two-hour drive from Vitoria-Gasteiz, and they'd driven down for the day. She marvelled at seeing the nun's incorruptible body looking so beautiful after four hundred years. Her portraits looked exactly like the nun she met in her dream on the ranch.

Someone sat down next to her where she sat in the front wooden pew, "Peaceful, isn't it?"

Kirsty's head swivelled towards the voice for it had a familiar sound to it. She gasped as Maria de Jesus de Agreda sat next to her looking at her own body in the casket. *She looks older than in my dream. But it can't be her!*

Kirsty struggled to find the words she wanted to say. Maria turned her head towards Kirsty and gave a little start, "It's you!"

"Me?"

"The woman from the year 2016 who visited me in the Americas while I was there. Kirsty, isn't it?"

Kirsty nodded and found her voice, "It happened only fourteen days ago in my time." *It really happened! I was there, not just dreaming about it.*

Maria beamed, "I've often wondered what happened to you. How marvellous to find out!"

Kirsty inhaled and said, "I came here to thank you and

honour you for encouraging me to seek my destiny. You helped me to find Him, to find the Kingdom and help the people who needed me."

Maria gave a deep, happy sigh, "Thank you, Kirsty. His ways are so much higher than our ways. I often come here to encourage others and here He blesses me with you!"

Kirsty looked at Maria next to her and to the casket and back at her, "I want to walk with Him like you did."

Maria inclined her head, "You just walk with him the way Kirsty was meant to walk with him. We all have our own race to run."

"Our own scroll to fulfil?" Kirsty's eyes sparkled.

Maria laughed, "You've said it. Knowing who you are in Him is only the beginning!"

Kirsty turned towards Maria again, but she was gone. She heard footsteps coming down the aisle and Jean-Pierre, who had been admiring some of the art in parts of the building, came towards her. He sat down next to her, "Where's the nun you were talking to?"

Kirsty turned wide eyes to Jean-Pierre, "You saw her too? It was her, the Lady in Blue. She remembered me! I really did translocate back in time 400 years."

Jean-Pierre looked at Kirsty, his eyes wide, "Wow." He looked at the remains in the coffin and goose bumps raised on his skin.

"I know, right? She says she used to wonder what happened to me, and she was delighted to find out, saying God was surprising her."

Jean-Pierre pressed her hand, "And to think you thought you were only dreaming."

"That red stain on my T-shirt was the thing that got me questioning God's existence. Convinced by a chilli stain from 400 years ago!"

Jean-Pierre laughed, "I had it easy, I just had to translocate from Spain to Scotland and be healed of a gunshot wound to get me to believe."

He turned dark, serious eyes on Kirsty, "Thank you for not giving up on this hard-headed Basque man."

Kirsty blushed, "Thanks for bringing me here today. It was special."

Jean-Pierre pulled her under his arm, pressing her against him, "My pleasure, my wife."

"I like it when you say that." Kirsty said, her eyes twinkling before they widened, "Do you realise what this means?"

Jean-Pierre shook his head, "What?"

"This means I have a Mi'kmaq grandmother!"

"The one you met when you were in the Faraday cage?"

A smile broke out on her face, "Yes! We need to go find her. She seemed lonely."

"Whatever you wish, my wife." Jean-Pierre wiggled his eyebrows at her and she laughingly chased him to the car.

Six months later.

10:00 am, GMT+1. Sunday, 17 July. Londonderry, Ireland.

Thomas felt a faint sweat break out on his forehead where he stood in the front of the church. He'd been in the front of a church too many times to count, but never as a bridegroom waiting for his bride. He marvelled at all the times he'd married other couples without realising the amount of stress the bridegroom was going through right in front of him.

I should've encouraged them more. As it was, the pastor about to marry him and Anna, was studying his notes, not giving him any notice. He turned his gaze down the aisle thinking of Anna on the other side of the door. *I wonder if she's feeling as nervous as I am.*

He fiddled with the lily fastened to his lapel and when he looked up, his eye caught Luke's eyes in the second row. Luke gave him a slow grin as if he understood what he was feeling and a sheepish grin bloomed on Thomas's own face. He'd married Luke a few years ago and it seemed Luke was saying, 'you deserve to sweat'. Luke and Emily were there with the twins, and their tiny, beautiful baby boy called Zander. His eyes wandered down the row of people pausing at the tallest man at the end who sat next to a tall blond. They were talking to each other, their faces animated.

It felt like years ago although it had only been six months since their ordeal at the castle. Thomas still marvelled at it all and found that his relationship with His Creator had gathered a depth it had never had before. Discovering how accessible his Father's Kingdom was to him, to see and not only to hear Him, had transformed his life. The love he felt for creation flowing out of Yaweh's love for him and everyone took his breath away. His Bible had come alive with new revelations and hidden meanings.

The organist started the first note of the wedding march and Thomas's breath hitched as through the wooden doors walked his bride in full glorious white on the arm of her father. She wanted to go for rainbow colours, but he'd convinced her to marry him in pearl white to signify how God had restored her purity; restored them.

The way God had smoothed over their Protestant and Catholic families was a miracle. They weren't sitting on the same side of the church, but they were both in the church. Ellie was walking ahead of Anna in a rainbow-coloured dress, Anna did get her creativity in there. His eyes locked with his daughter's and they shared a happy smile. This was a dream come true for them both. Then his eyes locked with Anna's and the world faded away.

Afterwards they spent time with their guests around an afternoon feast outside in the church gardens. The sun was shining in full glory, the sky as clear and blue as you could wish for. Thomas joined Jean-Pierre and Kirsty where they stood chatting to Luke and Emily. Jean-Pierre was holding baby Zander. He hadn't seen them since the castle although they'd been in contact via WhatsApp.

"I forgot to ask you, how did you get hold of Camille and Trojan to invite them to the wedding for us?" Thomas asked Kirsty.

She laughed and said, "I didn't."

Thomas's eyes widened, "But how?"

Kirsty shrugged, "I tried to search for them online, but there wasn't any information. So, I went into the Kingdom and asked Yahweh for help. The next minute I saw them both at some sort of estate. They were having tea on the lawn. I chatted to them, had tea, invited them to the wedding and here they are."

Thomas shook his head, "If I didn't know you, I'd think you're crazy."

Kirsty laughed, her laughter happy and free, "You and me both."

Jean-Pierre had handed the baby back to Emily and put his arm around Kirsty, caressing her face with his eyes, "There is nothing crazy about you, Laztana, except maybe the amount of money you're spending on this baby's room."

She touched her pregnant bump tenderly and shyly looked at Jean-Pierre, "We're so blessed. I can barely contain the joy sometimes."

Thomas swallowed the knot in his throat, "Us too. God's ways sure are mysterious and good."

A little hand pulled at Kirsty's hand. "I told you He would help you." Grace smiled up at Kirsty.

Kirsty took Grace's hand and looked into her eyes. "You were right, Grace. He did."

Emily smiled at them. "I'm so happy for you. Your testimony is amazing."

Luke stifled a yawn, "Now our children can grow up together. Y'all need to come visit us often.

"Maybe Ellie will have a little brother soon." Kirsty said to Thomas with a sly look in her eyes.

Thomas's mouth opened and closed, "Don't tell me you've seen him?"

Kirsty laughed, "My lips are sealed. You'll have to go look for yourself."

"Look for what?" Anna joined them, beaming up at Thomas.

Thomas felt his cheeks go red. Anna looked around the group and Kirsty said, "I was telling him to go look whether there is a little brother for Ellie."

Anna's laughter rang out, "Yes, he'd better have a look, for I'm not telling him what I've seen until he has."

Thomas turned big eyes towards Anna, "You've seen

something?"

She pouted her mouth, "Maybe, maybe more than one."

"Twins?" Thomas felt sweat break out on his forehead.

Emily stifled a giggle, "Anna, that'd be brilliant. My girls would love to mother them."

A large hand slapped Thomas on the back and he righted himself, turning towards the tall man behind him. "Trojan, you've got to help me. They're conspiring about seeing lots of babies in my future."

Trojan gave him a wide grin, "That sounds biblical, Minister. Be fruitful and multiply you know."

Thomas gave him a scowl, "I don't see you doing it yet."

Trojan pulled Camille under his shoulder, "We will. Watch this space, we first had to get a few things into place."

The group looked at each other, the journey Yahweh was walking with them, a wonder and joy to each of them.

There was a giggling somewhere in the crowd and their heads swivelled in search of it, Ellie came towards them her eyes bright, "I think they're here celebrating with us."

Grace looked at her with large eyes, "The angels?"

Ellie nodded and the twins searched between the people for the colourful angels they'd heard so much about.

The adults smiled at each other, excitement for what lay ahead stirring in their spirits. This was just the beginning.

FROM THE AUTHOR

Dear Readers

Thank you for reading the Seer. I hope you've enjoyed it and that it stirred in you a hunger for the more that Yahweh has for you. Jesus tells the story of the seeds that fell on the ground in Mark 4. At the end, he says in verse 8: Other seeds fell into the good soil, and as they grew up and increased, they yielded a crop and produced thirty, sixty, and a hundredfold.

Someone told us in a message once that this crop resembles the different depths of our walk with Christ. There is nothing wrong with thirty- or sixtyfold, but there is a hundredfold that the Father longs for his sons to press into – where what Yahshua prayed for us is fully revealed – John 17:24 – "Father, I desire that they also, whom You have given Me, be with Me where I am, so that they may see My glory which You have given Me, for You loved Me before the foundation of the world."

Yahshua spoke about His kingdom, not as a place to only go to after we died, but as a place He longed to share with us, in the here and now.

May he who has ears to hear, hear and he who has eyes to see, see.

Shalom from my home to yours.

P.S. You can read Luke and Emily's story in The Protector – available on Amazon.

ABOUT THE AUTHOR

Clara Berge is a South African born author who lives in England. Besides being a dreamer she is the wife of an amazing man, mother of five wonderful children, and the keeper of her home. Disclaimer - Her stories are sometimes born between piles of laundry. Contact her at CBwritingwithheaven@gmail.com

SeraphCreative

Heaven's Heart for Earth

Seraph Creative is a collective of artists, writers, theologians & illustrators who desire to see the body of Christ grow into full maturity, walking in their inheritance as Sons Of God on the Earth.

Sign up to our newsletter to know about the release of the next book in the series, as well as other exciting releases.

Visit our website :
www.seraphcreative.org

BV - #0039 - 111220 - C0 - 203/127/14 - PB - 9780648584742